D0850066

THE
ENGAGEMENT
PARTY

THE ENGAGEMENT PARTY

A NOVEL

FINLEY TURNER

CROOKED
LANE

NEW YORK

Copyright © 2023 by Finley Turner

Published in the United States by Crooked Lane Books, an imprint of The Quick Brown Fox & Company LLC.

Crooked Lane Books and its logo are trademarks of The Quick Brown Fox & Company LLC.

Library of Congress Catalog-in-Publication data available upon request.

ISBN (hardcover): 978-1-63910-597-7
ISBN (ebook): 978-1-63910-598-4

Cover design by Heather VenHuizen

Printed in the United States.

www.crookedlanebooks.com

Crooked Lane Books
34 West 27th St., 10th Floor
New York, NY 10001

First Edition: November 2023

10 9 8 7 6 5 4 3 2 1

To Mom. I miss you.

PROLOGUE

SOME DAYS, WHEN my mind is restless, I revisit the subway platform. Like an animal who leaves home, I always wander back, hungry and with filth clinging to me, searching for comfort. But I find no comfort there. All I find is guilt.

Sometimes I pretend it was all part of a movie and that all it would take is to yell, "Cut!" and turn the camera off. In my head I change the script and wardrobe. I modify the set, just like I do every day for work. But no matter how many times I alter the camera angle or how many times I gut and rewrite, the ending is always the same. My mind won't allow anything else to happen.

The pulse of chemicals preserves the memories, making them sharper. Making them sting more. In a way, the memories are addicting too.

I know this doesn't make me special. Everyone has had the dream at least once in their life—the dream where your mind disobeys all logic. Whether you're trying to run and your legs just aren't moving, or you're punching through air like molasses, you're being betrayed by your mind.

At least some people can conceal that betrayal to those dark hours of sleep while they lie in the safety of their bed.

I, on the other hand, am betrayed ever hour of every day. Asleep or awake. There's no pattern in the timing.

I simply blink, and there I am.

Screaming on that same subway platform that will never let me leave.

1

Two nights ago, it finally happened—the moment that I'd been imagining since the day I met him. As I lay in bed, the sheets tangled around my legs and the morning sun cutting through drifting dust like snow, I twisted the ring around my finger.

It still felt foreign on my hand as I caressed the silver band and the sharp cut of the single center stone. I pulled my hand from under the cover and extended it toward the sunlight, watching it spark colors along the white bedding.

"Kass?" Murray's voice startled me despite the comforting gruff of his sleepy voice. "Do you still like it?

I turned my head to him, taking in the golden-brown glint in his eyes that bled seamlessly into the green. Freckles of the same golden-brown dotted along his prominent nose. It was a bit crooked at the bridge, but I loved that. I suddenly wanted to ask how that happened—there were so many things we didn't know about each other yet, and the thought of the years to come sent a thrill through me. Would our children have his nose? Would they have his lanky height? We'd decided we wanted two kids, one boy and one girl—as if those were things we could plan.

"I love it," I said as I reached out to brush aside a piece of his hair. Like his eyes, the sun streaming in laced his hair with gold. Self-conscious of the sleep on my breath, I planted a kiss on his forehead instead of his lips. Although it was now Sunday morning and he'd proposed Friday night, the time in between had been a blur of one continuous celebration. We'd overindulged in champagne and chocolates last night, and while the sugar was wreaking havoc on my temples, I'd never been so happy in my twenty-three years of existence. I'd never been so weightless.

Gone were the worries of deadlines at work—namely, the set design I'd been asked to scrap and rework. No more annoyances with friends or family. This was simply *our* moment. Our golden hour.

"You look beautiful," he said, caressing my cheek with his thumb. "Come here," he murmured as he nuzzled into my neck before pulling me in for a real kiss. The warmth of his lips brought me back to the first kiss we'd had as an engaged couple, after I pulled him up from one knee and responded with one long, high-pitched squeal. He'd had to confirm later that that noise did, in fact, mean yes.

Heat was building in my body, and I threw off the comforter, wrapping my legs around his waist. Murray lay below me, the deep divots above his hip bones leading my eyes downward to his pale, smooth skin that was dotted with freckles and scars, a cipher to the story of his life—so much of which I hadn't learned yet. He reached for my hips, veins pulsing beneath warm skin.

A series of loud knocks erupted from the door, and my thighs reflexively constricted around him, both of us startled by the noise. A moment of silence passed before a man spoke, his accent unidentifiable. "Courier delivery for Mr. Sedgemont."

"Oh wow, a *courier*." I giggled, unfurling myself from him. "It must be from the Queen herself."

Murray slid out of bed and pulled a pair of dark gray sweatpants over his boxers before trotting to the door in bare feet.

For Murray's long legs, it was only four steps, as our Brooklyn studio apartment was just one open room, with a microscopic bathroom the size of a linen closet. Although the apartment was cramped, it was fantastic for nosy people such as myself. I could shamelessly observe everything—no room for secrets.

Which made it even more impressive that Murray hid the ring and his plan from me, I thought with a smile. I shouldn't be surprised, though. Murray was meticulous in everything he did. He was always the one to plan everything, from our grocery shopping to our date-night dinner plans. It helped settle my anxiety, knowing he had everything under control.

He pulled open the door to reveal a man standing there with a large envelope, both his hands gripping the sides, like a nervous host of an award show. His posture was rod straight and unnaturally stiff, and his maroon polo had a white crest embroidered over his left breast, but no company name.

Murray took the envelope from the man, with a thank-you, before shutting the door. He brought the envelope to the bed and plopped down next to me, both of us like children on Christmas at the sight of an unfamiliar delivery.

"Don't you think that was a little weird?" I asked, slightly amused. "He didn't have a badge or anything."

"Outsourcing deliveries, I guess?" he said. "You want to open it?"

"How do you know me so well?" I smiled, taking the envelope from him. Our fingers brushed as I took it from him, sending a jolt of happiness through me. This was my fiancé, I reminded myself, reveling in the thrill of his new title.

I studied the envelope, excited to see what was inside. Murray knew one of my small joys in life was opening mail—there was something about the nostalgia of it. Most of the time the only mail we got was crumpled to-go menus shoved into our tiny mailbox, so this felt special.

I pulled out the contents, revealing thick, expensive paper enclosed with a crimson wax stamp. I ran my finger along it—it appeared to be some sort of crest.

"Oh," Murray said at the sight of the seal. "Can I have that?"

"Sure," I said. I watched his face, trying to decipher what he was feeling.

Murray took the envelope from my hand, and instead of carefully prying the stamp away from the card stock, he snapped the wax in half. I winced at the unnecessary fierceness of it. I'd kind of wanted to keep it.

"Mur? What is it?" I asked, eager to see who could possibly still use wax stamps. It was gloriously over the top. The envelope unfolded, revealing an invitation inside, its looped text gilded with gold. He tilted the invitation toward me so we could read it together.

Mr. and Mrs. Phillip Sedgemont
Request your presence at the celebration of
Mister Murray Sedgemont and Miss Kassandra Baptiste's
engagement

Sedgemont Estate
Fourteenth of August
Six o'clock

"Your parents are throwing us a party? In a week?" I asked, my voice rising an octave. I'd never met a single member of his family. They weren't a huge part of his life, and he rarely spoke about them. I honestly hadn't even known his father's first name until now. And I still didn't know his mother's, I thought. I guessed that the old-fashioned tradition of excluding the wife's name was a hint as to his family's beliefs.

"Looks like it," Murray huffed.

I grazed my finger against the edges of a small card that fell out of the invitation. *Répondez s'il vous plait,* it said, followed with no contact information, as if everyone should already know it. I'd never seen RSVP written out before—another sign that this would be more formal than any party I'd ever been to.

"I didn't realize you'd even told your family yet," I said. Murray had made it clear from the beginning that he was no longer close to them and had no desire to be. He'd never told me why, and I'd never found the right time to ask.

"I haven't," he murmured. He tossed the invitation on the bed and put on a T-shirt. It looked like a band T-shirt but was so faded and tattered that I couldn't read the print.

We'd made one call after he proposed. My head had been shimmering with a full bottle of Veuve Clicquot—an extravagance I'd assumed was a gift from Murray's boss, who was still reveling in the success of the art gallery's last show. My parents had cheered through the speakerphone, their excitement slightly muffled by what I imagined to be my mom being squeezed tightly by my dad. His hugs were always a bit too enthusiastic—my family were big fans of affection. And being loud.

"Wait, so how could they even plan a party this fast?" My voice hitched with the beginning of a laugh, but it sputtered out.

"They've been waiting for this since the day I was born," he said with a hint of embarrassment.

"Just like me," I said as a smile spread across my face.

"You cheeseball," he said. His previous annoyance with his parents disappeared from his face, replaced now with a goofy grin.

"You need to give me a full TED Talk on your family. I won't be as nervous if I know what to expect."

"Well"—he paused, chewing on the inside of his cheek—"they're rich assholes."

"Okay, never mind. I'm more nervous now." I'd gathered that Murray's family had some money from his stories of private schools and his lack of student debt, but he'd never confirmed it until now.

"We'll have a good time," he reassured me. "Their parties are always fun."

Despite the strangeness of the invitation, a thrill bloomed in my chest. I was excited to celebrate the happiest moment of my life, and although it was nerve-wracking, soon I would be able to meet my future family-in-law. And by the sound of the invitation, we'd get to dress up and drink on someone else's dime, which was always when the drinks tasted the best.

"Well," I said, "I guess we'd better get our ducks in a row."

2

THE REST OF the week was a flurry of congratulations and frenzied attempts to wrap up projects at work. Murray was much closer to career stability than I was—his recent show at the art gallery had been a huge success, and as of today, nearly every single painting had sold. He was finalizing paperwork at a leisurely pace, but I, on the other hand, felt like I was on the verge of being fired.

The set I'd designed had been approved, but exactly one week into building it, the director wanted to scrap the design and start over with something completely different. There was no way I'd be able to finish the redesign before leaving for North Carolina, so I'd been scrambling all week to placate everyone in charge.

Despite the stress, this is what I've always wanted to do, and I knew I had to prove myself. After graduating from NYU, I'd gone straight into set design. I'd worked my way from small community-theater productions to off-Broadway shows, and I was struggling to keep up.

After a long day at work, I finally got back to our apartment at eight o'clock, worn down from being barked at all day, when there was a knock on the door. Murray rose to get it while I, exhausted, yanked my boots off, letting them fall onto the floor with a thump.

I immediately sparked back to life at the sight of my best friend, Zoey, as she burst through the door with a bottle of red wine and package of Oreos.

"For the future bride and groom!" she yelled as she set the gifts down. She yanked me up for a hug, squeezing the air out of my lungs. This was the first time I'd seen her since the proposal, and this meant more to me than all the congratulatory direct messages on social media combined. For all I cared, I could never receive another DM in my life if it meant I had Zoey's approval.

"So how did it go? I want to know every detail," Zoey begged me as she nestled into an armchair.

"You tell it," I told Murray. "I want to hear it from your perspective."

"We started with dinner. She had no idea the entire time—it was hilarious," Murray said.

"I was so clueless. And I spilled red wine all down my top. Absolutely mortifying. I was so confused when he insisted we come back to the apartment to change," I said quickly, my heart racing just thinking about it all.

"Then I took her to the gallery. All the lights were off, and there were candles everywhere."

"Fake candles, obviously," I interjected, thinking about how the soft gold light had flickered across the art.

"Of course—can't burn the place down or I'd be unemployed. And then I got down on one knee, and she immediately let out this little squeak. It was the best noise I've ever heard. So then, before I even said anything, we both start crying. Even after I asked her, she kept squeaking, and I had to ask her if she was saying yes." We all laughed, but I had to blot away tears at the memory.

"So what did you say to her? How did you phrase it?" Zoey asked.

"Well, I started by telling her how much she means to me." His voice cracked, and he struggled to continue.

I chimed in, knowing how much he hated talking while on the verge of tears. "He said that even though we've only been together for a short period of time, he's never been happier. And that he didn't want to waste another day when we both knew we would be together for the rest of our lives." Murray reached over and wiped a tear away from my cheek.

"Aw, Murray. I had no idea how cheesy you were." Zoey laughed, blotting away tears from her own eyes.

The three of us continued talking while we ripped through the wine and package of cookies. Eventually the topic veered toward our trip to North Carolina.

"So, get this. We're leaving tomorrow for North Carolina. His family is throwing us a surprise engagement party," I said as I showed her the invitation.

She took it in her hands and placed it on her palm, feeling the weight of the paper. "This is fancy as hell. Murray, you got some sort of secret family money you want to tell us about?"

Murray laughed. "Y'all are crazy," he mumbled with a smile as he took the empty wine bottle to the recycling. I wondered if he'd ignored her question on purpose. Was he keeping it a secret on purpose, or was it insignificant because he wasn't close to them?

"*Y'all!*" Zoey howled with laughter. "His Southern roots are already coming out, and you haven't even gotten there. So, are you nervous?"

"Absolutely terrified," I said. Murray came behind the couch and squeezed both my shoulders.

"It'll be fine," he said as he kneaded his thumbs into my tense muscles.

"Yeah, it's normal to be nervous, but I wouldn't worry too much about it. Once they see you two together, it'll be obvious this is a good thing. I mean, have you two ever even had a fight?"

I tilted my head back and looked at him, his smiling face distorted from the upside-down view. I looked back at Zoey. "Not really. It's just . . . easy."

"Well, cheers to you, because I sure as hell don't know what that's like."

Murray planted a kiss on the top of my head. I was telling the truth—our relationship was easy. And if his family was anything like him, we would get along just fine.

3

"WHAT DO YOU think about this one?" I said, holding up a canary-yellow, floor-length dress. It was one of my favorites—a steal from an online sale—and I'd worn it to an embarrassing number of summer weddings.

"I love that one on you," he said, glancing up from his laptop perched on the kitchen counter. "I think it's perfect." He smiled sweetly and returned his gaze to his laptop.

Although we were still buzzing from our engagement, bills had to be paid, and vacation time had to be requested and approved. Murray's parents had included an equally extravagant insert in the invitation, requesting that we arrive at their house next Thursday for dinner so they could get to know me before the party. The presumptuousness of it raised my hackles—them thinking we would be able to drop everything to come visit—but I also enjoyed knowing how much they wanted to meet me.

Murray had made a quick call to them after the initial shock of the invitation wore off, stepping outside where I could no longer see his rigid muscles nor hear the tension in his throat. I wondered what was said—there was a hesitant thickness to the air, like Murray had tried to make an excuse not to go, but was left with no choice but to go along with it.

Murray's soft smile faded as he furrowed his brow at our online rent portal. He picked up his phone with a shaky hand, likely checking his bank account to make sure he could cover his half. We'd been living in New York City for years—albeit separately until two months ago—and rent always arrived like an icy slap to the face.

Some of our friends had urged us not to move in together so quickly—only two months after we started dating—but when confronted with the fact that splitting rent and other bills meant I could afford to replace the warped and pitiful bike I used to get around for a model that could actually steer straight, their arguments quickly deflated.

My mother had described our relationship as a "whirl-wind romance," and she was right. We'd met briefly as students at New York University but didn't meet again until years later, when we'd bumped into each other at a bar, our eyes locking instantaneously as I walked inside. We'd spent the whole night talking, and now, four months later, here I was with a ring on my hand. I tried to remind them that plenty of people had long engagements these days, so it's not like we were going to be walking down the aisle next week.

I turned back to my raggedy suitcase, studying my carefully curated "future daughter-in-law" outfits—a cream-colored knit sweater with my nicest jeans; a floral Kate Spade wrap dress I'd gotten at Marshall's for seventy percent off; and a few other pieces of my nicest, most neutral clothing. I would have to leave behind my black platform Doc Martens and all my other paint-speckled and ripped clothes I wore to work. I needed to up my game for the Sedgemonts.

No matter the clothes, my jewelry always stayed the same. A hand-pressed gold pendant with a single clear stone in the middle. The gold was warped and probably fake, and the stone was due to fall out any day now, but it was a gift from an old friend that I always wore. And now my engagement ring would be the only other constant to my otherwise unbridled closet.

Nervousness bubbled in my chest at the thought of presenting myself to Murray's family. I wanted them to like me.

I *needed* them to like me.

My phone buzzed against the nightstand, the vibration scooting it closer to the ledge. I unplugged it, snatching it up, a smile already spreading across my face at the expectation of congratulatory messages. I'd posted a picture of us late last night, me smiling like a fool, with Murray on one knee, and I'd captioned it with a single red heart. My only gripe with the photo was that you couldn't see his face, but I swore you could still tell he was smiling just as big as I was. His boss had helped him hide the gallery's iPad and had set it up to record before scurrying out the back door. Since I'd posted the picture, notifications had flooded in, to the point where I'd had to put my phone on "Do Not Disturb" overnight so I could get some sleep.

Despite all the kind messages, one thing was stuck in my mind, stirring up confusion. Murray had said he hadn't told his family yet when we'd received the invitation. So how had they known and begun planning so quickly? With only a week between the engagement and the party, it seemed an impossible task.

Five new Instagram comments and one new message request stared at me expectantly on my lock screen. I flipped through the comments, shooting out quick thank-you's, then tapped "Messages." The message was from user0815, and their name was so similar to the bot messages I always received that I nearly deleted it. Curious, I clicked into the message and glanced away to throw a stick of deodorant into my toiletry bag.

I looked back at the message and heat flushed my cheeks. A single word was on the screen.

Bitch

I blocked the account and set my phone facedown on the bed. My mouth was dry, and I shuffled unsteadily to the kitchen for a glass of water. I took a sip, letting the cool water sit on my tongue for a moment before swallowing.

This one word from a cowardly stranger was not going to ruin the high I was on.

I would not let anybody ruin my happiness.

* * *

It was finally D-Day, as I'd been calling it the entire week: the day we flew to North Carolina to see Murray's family. All week I'd been the nervous one, but Murray had usurped my nerves in the blink of an eye. He fidgeted in our apartment doorway, jangling his keys. I could see him twitching out of the corner of my eye as I shoved my toiletry bag into my suitcase.

"You okay?" I asked as I scrambled to zip up my bag. Since we'd woken up, Murray had been a ball of anxiety, buzzing around the apartment, packing and repacking his bag. I was usually the anxious one, and he would be the anchor in reality, but now we were both untethered and feeding off each other's nervousness.

"I'll be fine once we get there. We just need to hurry."

"Did the airline mess up our flight?" I asked, panic creaking in my voice.

"No, it was me," he grumbled. "I was trying to pay the bills, but there was an issue with the portal. I'm sorry, I fucked up and thought the flight was later. But we have to go *now*."

I hated being late. If you were late to a party, that was one thing, but if you were late to a flight, they didn't care enough about you to wait. They would leave you stranded. My gut bubbled with anxiety. It was irrational for me to be this worked up—there were always other flights. But we were on a tight schedule, and you can only meet your in-laws for the first time once.

Murray ushered me out the door, and I tried to breathe deeply and let go of my frustration. He was incredibly organized and measured in everything he did, and I was beginning to see that this invitation from his parents had unnerved him in some deep way, making him fumble and twitch with anxiety.

"There weren't any cars available. We have to take the subway," he said, his suitcase slamming against each step as we hurried down the apartment stairs. "I'm sorry."

My muscles clenched tight, freezing me in place behind him as he continued downward.

"No," I said firmly. "No, I'm sure there are cars. Check again. Or we can get a taxi."

Murray didn't respond for a moment, and I could tell he was getting increasingly frazzled. "It's about to rain. Taxi's never gonna happen." He was right—the air in the stairway was heavy with humidity that pressed down hard on us, slicking our clothes to our skin like a paste.

My foot slipped on a stair, but I righted myself quickly. My legs wobbled and my heartbeat thrummed behind my eyes, distorting my vision. Murray was the only one who understood why I rode my bike everywhere—why I avoided the subway at all costs. But I was the only one who knew the full story.

We stepped out of our building, and I blinked hard against the sun that peeked through a curtain of clouds as we rushed along the sidewalk toward Utica Avenue, our luggage wheels chattering against the sidewalk with obnoxious clicks at each crack in the pavement. We were approaching the station now, and I pulled out my phone to open the Uber app.

Panic filled me as I saw there were none available. Murray was right.

I closed it and opened the Lyft app. While I waited for it to load, I toyed nervously with my necklace, pinching it tight between my fingers like a wish. We were standing at the opening to the station now, and Murray was also checking his phone—one last attempt to save me from a full-blown panic attack. His lips were pursed, and his underarm sweat painted a deep gray ring down his torso.

As the moments ticked by, my hope began to melt. I kept the subway station in my peripheral, as if it were going to lunge at me, pull me underground, and devour me.

"There's nothing, Kass. I'm sorry, but we have to go." He cupped his hand against my cheek, forcing me to look at him. It was something he often did when I began to unravel with panic. Sure, it may be cheesy, but the forced pause of looking directly into his eyes and seeing him there always settled me down. "I'm here with you. It'll be okay, I promise."

He dropped his hand, reaching for his bag. In one last ditch effort, I looked back down at my phone. In that same moment, a car appeared on the app. Relief washed over me as I requested a ride, and I held the phone up to him, triumphant.

When it arrived, we loaded our luggage into the trunk and basked in the blasting air-conditioning. My breathing steadied and my muscles relaxed as the AC cooled my skin, but as I reached for Murray's hand in his lap, I noticed his legs were shaking.

CHAPTER

4

ALTHOUGH I'D MENTALLY prepared myself for our arrival, the Sedgemont home was nothing like I'd expected.

The most jarring fact was that it was not in fact a *home*, but an *estate*, just as the invitation had said. Not in simply the size of the sprawling building and its sweeping acres of land, but in the imposition of it. Murray's family home was technically part of a gated country club community, but the mile-long driveway made it so far removed from their neighbors that it seemed to be in a county of its own.

Honestly, I should have known the house would look like this as soon as the hired chauffeur waved us down at the airport. He'd ushered us into a shining black Mercedes, and after his initial greeting, he didn't say a word.

I'd been nervous already, but as soon as I saw the house, my anxiety tripled. I tried to slow my breathing, but my stomach gurgled and my mouth was dry. I was half tempted to ask the driver to turn around.

"Don't be nervous," Murray whispered as he squeezed my hand.

"Too late." I tried to laugh but it sounded more like a whimper.

"I promise they're going to love you. This is probably the only time we'll ever visit them here. And what's the worst that could happen in one visit? We just have to get through the weekend."

He was right. Even if it went terribly wrong, Murray wasn't close with his family anyway. Even if it all went up in flames, this trip would just be an embarrassing memory that we could one day laugh about.

As if reading my mind, Murray said, "I hardly ever see them, so their opinion of us doesn't matter either way."

Despite the car's air-conditioning, nervous sweat trickled down the nape of my neck. The midday North Carolina heat was unbearable, and I swore it was penetrating the cracks of the car, seeping in through the slick, German metal. Our driver navigated the car through the shadowed drive, lined by thick-trunked trees with overbearing canopies.

The trees broke and a circular courtyard came into view. The building rose above us as if challenging the trees, the ornamented towers and spires meeting in threatening points overhead. The gray stone was nearly black in the shadows of the trees, but as the wind shifted their branches, sunlight revealed that the stone was a light gray, punctuated by copper flashing along the roof that was greening with age. The home sprawled to each side so far in every direction that the closer we got to it, the less I could see, so I snapped a picture on my phone and turned my gaze back into the car.

"Wow," I muttered. The driver's eyes met mine in the rearview mirror, and he glanced back, grinning at me.

"I know. It's a monstrosity." Murray shifted uncomfortably, embarrassed by the magnitude of his childhood home.

"It's beautiful. My Prince Charming and his castle," I teased, and he pretended to gag.

Tires crunched over the pebbly gravel, and I couldn't help but think of *Downton Abbey*. I held back a laugh as I pictured the Dowager Countess greeting us with a sly grin on her face, her cane digging into the gravel like a threat.

Murray squeezed my knee. "Hey," he whispered, drawing my attention away from the landscape and back into the car. "Just remember that we're here to celebrate us. Nothing else really matters from here on out, okay?"

It was a sweet sentiment, but it also had the undertones of a warning. I put my hand on top of his. "Okay, sweetie."

"Fuck what everyone else thinks. Just you and me."

He was staring straight at the house now, as if challenging it. I tried to focus on the sentiment, but it left me more worried than ever that his family wasn't going to like me.

Our driver pulled to a stop at the front door, climbing out of the car to help us with our bags. As we dug through the trunk, the expansive front door creaked open, and a man stepped out. He wore a dark gray suit and a dark green tie, his outfit mirroring the colors and shadows of the home he stood in front of. His hair was a stark white, and by the deep groove of wrinkles around his mouth and eyes, I guessed him to be in his mid- to late seventies.

I plastered a smile on my face, even though nervousness made my cheek twitch with the effort. "Hi, I'm Kass." I extended my hand to him after wiping it on my jeans, hoping he didn't mind the slick sweat on my palms. "Kassandra," I corrected. My shortened name somehow seemed too casual for such a grand home, and for a ridiculous moment I felt like I was trying to impress the building—to fit in.

"Nice to meet you," he said, gripping my hand. "There's no need to bother with your bags." He motioned to the bags that Murray was still struggling with, but Murray had his head lowered in concentration.

"Mur?" I asked, wondering why he was ignoring the man I assumed to be his father. "Your dad wants to help with the bags."

The older man laughed, and Murray whipped around, his cheeks flushed red.

"Silly dear, I'm not his father. I'm the butler," the man said, still without giving me his name.

Heat rose in my cheeks. I hadn't even been here for five minutes, and I'd already embarrassed myself. But how was I supposed to know? Murray had mentioned that his family was well-off, but not so rich that they had a mansion and a *butler*, for Christ's sake.

"This is William. He's worked with our family since I was young," Murray said as he handed William our bags. "How are you doing, William? Long time, no see." Murray patted him on the back.

"Worked with." My mind lingered on the words. William did seem happy to greet us, but I wondered if it was a relationship in which the word *for* would have been more appropriate.

We thanked the driver as William led us up the wide stone stairs to the front door, the stained-glass windows on it shimmering like gems in the summer sun. My heart skipped a beat as William set our bags down to open the heavy doors. I was more nervous now than I had been when we received the invitation.

When Murray called his family "rich assholes," I had expected a nice upper-middle-class home, but I hadn't expected *this*. This was a mansion. I'd been in plenty of homes out of our price range for parties and vacations, but I'd never been around this kind of wealth—the kind of wealth that made money lose its meaning.

Murray should have been more clear. I glanced down at my sneakers, the leather on them scuffed and soft with age. The laces were a dingey off-white and speckled with flecks of black paint. How did I miss that when I was packing? I should have worn something else.

William paused with the door open and ushered us in. I breathed in one final gulp of the humid summer air before stepping inside.

Holy mother of God.

We entered the foyer of the Sedgemonts' house, and my jaw went slack as I gazed around the grand space.

"Welcome to the Sedgemont Estate," William said, a hint of elitism in his voice. Although he continued to speak, I wasn't fully listening as I took in the dramatic sweep of the staircase that hugged the right side of the room, looping in a wide curve like a vine as it twisted up the wall.

I stepped forward and peeked upward. There were two more floors above us, maybe more, the staircase snaking around, creating a wide, empty space in the middle that accentuated the enormous brass chandelier that hung from the center-point of the domed glass ceiling. I imagined this room when the sun was at its highest, pouring down into the space. It must be absolutely stunning, marking the time of day like a giant sun dial.

"This is beautiful," I said to no one in particular.

"Not anywhere close to you," Murray whispered in my ear as he placed his hand against my lower back.

"Pfft," was all I could muster at his compliment. I was in my own world, like a child left to roam in a museum.

William had his shoulders swept back and stance wide, wearing pride unabashedly on his face. He clearly held himself in high esteem for working in such a grand home. I expected Murray to look the same—after all it was where he grew up—but he wasn't looking at anything but me. I wondered if he was unimpressed by the grandeur of the room or ashamed of it.

"I mean, this foyer alone is spectacular. It's enormous," I said wide-eyed.

"Entrance hall, not foyer," William gently corrected.

"Oh." I paused. "Right—sorry." *Entrance hall,* I thought. Of course the word *foyer* was too casual. That's something you would find in a normal house, not a mansion.

"Let me show you to your rooms so you can make yourselves more comfortable," William said as he began to make his way up the staircase.

"This staircase—and much of the house—was inspired by the historic Biltmore Estate. Have you heard of it?" William asked.

"Murray showed me pictures from a wedding once, but no, I've never been." On one of our earlier dates, our heads buzzing with booze and the excitement of getting to know one another, Murray had mentioned Biltmore when I'd asked him about his hometown, which was right outside of Asheville, North Carolina. He had described Asheville as a place I would love—a bustling downtown filled with artists and cafés, great restaurants and walkable streets. I hadn't seen any of that yet. All I'd seen was this neighborhood's astronomical wealth, each house hidden away in its own little kingdom.

When we reached the second-floor landing, William led us down a long hallway dotted with oil paintings, their

gilded frames shimmering in the dim lighting. With a
flurry of excitement, I noticed that they all had Murray's
golden-brown eyes, tilted downward at the edges as though
they were permanently deep in thought, ruminating over a
past memory.

"Are these all the Sedgemonts?" I asked Murray.

William answered in his place. "Yes. Each family
member has a portrait made when they get married. We
have every family portrait from the last one hundred
years."

"Does that mean Murray gets to sit for a portrait
soon?" I said with a flashy smile and waggling eyebrows.

William's face remained completely serious, as though
the ritual of having your portrait made was a rite of passage, not just a picture to hang on the wall. "Of course.
Once you two marry, he'll have his place on the wall, like
all the others."

Murray placed his palm between my shoulder blades
and planted a kiss on my forehead, clearly enamored with
the idea of us being married. "The wall would look much
better with a portrait of you up there."

I stood in front of a blank space on the wall, presum-
ably for Murray in the future, and gave him my best Mona
Lisa smile. It was strange for a family to place so much
weight on being married, especially since my own parents
only tied the knot a few months after I was born. *Every
family has their culture,* I thought. *It just takes time to decipher it.*

"So, what happens to the Sedgemonts who don't get
married?" I asked.

William ambled away. Either his old age had dulled
his hearing, or he was unwilling to answer the question.
Murray stifled a laugh and followed behind him.

The unanswered question filled me with a surprising sadness as I looked into the Sedgemonts' eyes, which stared back at me with mirrored sorrow for their lost family members. If they didn't find love, were they forgotten more and more with each passing year?

"Here is your room," William finally said as he opened a door to a bedroom and shuffled inside.

"Is this your childhood room?" I asked with a smile as I stepped inside. But there were no remnants of a boy or even a teenager. Only heavy furniture that signified money rather than comfort. Although it was beautifully decorated in lush greens and heavy, floor-length curtains, it felt rather cold and distant—more like a display at a historic home than somewhere to rest.

"Not really," Murray said. "Not anymore."

I set my purse down on an armchair and shrugged my tired shoulders.

"Oh," William said in surprise. "I'm sorry for the misunderstanding, Miss Kassandra, but this is where Mister Sedgemont will be staying. Your room is upstairs."

"You've got to be kidding me," Murray grumbled. "How about we just keep it between us? It's not like she ever comes to this side of the house anyway."

William straightened his back, clearly prepared for this battle. "I do apologize, but that's not a decision I can make," he said firmly.

"Any chance you could convince her otherwise?" Murray asked, pushing it just a little bit further.

William bowed his head in apology. "Mrs. Sedgemont's orders. You're welcome to speak to her about it in private."

Murray mumbled a string of profanities through gritted teeth.

My heartbeat quickened at the sentencing of being separated from Murray. We'd spent the night together every single night for the four months we'd been together, and the thought of being alone in a massive house, surrounded by strangers, filled me with dread.

Plus, how the hell was I supposed to find my way around this labyrinth of a house? I gulped as I pictured myself getting lost on the way to the bathroom in the middle of the night, only to end up opening someone else's bedroom door, and them screaming bloody murder. What if I walked in on someone naked? Or using the bathroom? Anxiety crept up my neck like an itchy rash.

Murray mouthed, "Sorry," with a helpless expression. I was waiting for him to push back more, to let out his little laugh that would smooth everything over and charm us out of this awkward mess. Instead, he stood at the foot of his bed with his luggage at his feet while William politely muscled me out of the room.

At the last minute, Murray gripped my hand and gave it a light squeeze. I knew this truly wasn't that big of a deal, but I couldn't fight the feeling of panic as our hands separated.

"I'll show you to your room now. It's on the third floor, where the other guests will be staying."

"The other guests?" I asked, somewhat breathless as we made our way up the sweeping staircase.

"Beatrice has invited guests from all over to celebrate your engagement. She's well-known for her parties and so far, not a single person has RSVP'd no. The phone's been ringing off the hook all week," he said proudly.

The evidence was mounting that this was going to be a far bigger deal than I was expecting—and certainly more than I would like. I preferred house parties, with friends tucked together on a sofa in a cramped apartment, drinking cheap beer and passing around a joint. I couldn't imagine anything like that would be allowed to happen in this house.

We arrived on the third floor, and I twisted my head at the endless hallways. This floor mirrored the second floor, with two long hallways extending to the left and right.

"Down this way," he said, leading us down a hallway on the left. The farther we went to the left, the more distance there was between me and Murray. I couldn't help but feel like it was on purpose.

Sconces glowed gold down the hallways, but without windows the lighting cast shadows. They danced along the floor, sending a ripple of discomfort up my spine. I wasn't one to be spooked easily, but I quickened my pace behind William as the shadows twitched behind me.

When we arrived at my bedroom, William opened the door and motioned for me to enter. He followed behind me, resting my bags on the floor by one of the wide windows.

This bedroom was much darker, the furniture wrapped in lush burgundy velvets and deep blues that mirrored the Persian rug beneath my feet. The wood floor creaked under my feet as I moved inside. I wrapped my arms around myself, a weak defense against the chill.

"I'll leave you to freshen up," William said with a slight bow. I thanked him, and he closed the door. Did I look like I need to freshen up?

I pulled out my phone, opening a text to Murray.

Uh . . . wtf? I texted, a smile on my face, but an uneasiness still sitting in my gut. I added LOL to the text before hitting "Send" so he would know I wasn't upset with him.

What the fuck is right LOL. Mom's a little strict. I'll tell you about it later.

I sent an emoji of a mind exploding and flipped over to send a group text to my mom and dad. I sent the picture I took as we arrived, the house erected like a mausoleum against the backdrop of summer sun.

My mom texted back instantaneously—I was sure she'd been nervously clutching her phone, waiting for a text since the moment I told her I'd be meeting the Sedgemonts. *How beautiful!!! Is that a museum!!! Have U met parents yet?*

There was a soft knock at the door, and I sat up, reflexively locking my phone. "May I come in?" an unfamiliar voice asked.

"Sure." I hopped off the bed.

The door opened, and a short woman stood in front of me, dressed in black slacks and a black top. She looked smart and put together, not a hair out of place or a smudge of mascara to be seen. Despite her immaculate appearance, her face was warm and kind.

"My name is Gloria—I'm the housekeeper. I wanted to drop off some extra towels for you. I know Lyle is arriving soon, and he tends to use three towels per shower. Can't have him stealing yours too," she said with a smile.

"Oh, thank you. I'm Kassandra, Murray's fiancée. Wow." I paused. "I think that's the first time I've said that word out loud. *Fiancée.*"

"Congratulations on your engagement. Please let me know if you need anything. I'm sure William said the same thing, but I'm your woman." She smiled.

Her tone hinted at a staff rivalry, and I had the curious itch to ask, but I held my tongue. "Thank you, I'll be sure to do that."

She smiled and closed the door without a noise. *Might as well get settled in,* I thought. I grabbed my suitcase and placed it on the chest of drawers. As I hung up my clothes and put my toiletries on the vanity, my mind whirred with both excitement and trepidation.

The fact that I'd only met the family's employees and none of his family worried me. I imagined them lurking somewhere in the house, hiding from my presence.

Maybe they didn't want me here at all.

Deep breaths, I told myself. Even if that was true, it didn't matter. All I had to do was make it through this party with a smile on my face.

I could survive that.

5

As I was touching up the concealer that had creased under my eyes, I practiced my introduction in my head, giving a cringe-inducing smile to my reflection.

Hi, I'm Kassandra. Thanks for having me. Nervousness rattled in my eyes as I studied my image. I looked out of place in such a grand room. The freckles that dotted along the bridge of my nose were somehow too casual for the home, and my chestnut hair was dull compared to the shine of the room's rich, dark wood.

I had no standout features like the distinctive, regal portraits of the Sedgemonts. I was too simple. These people were going to eat me alive. My introduction needed to be perfect. I cleared my throat to try again.

Hello, absolutely delightful to meet you, darling. I extended my hand out to the mirror, palm facing down and fingers limp with the exhaustion known only by eighteenth-century aristocrats.

A knock on the door made me flinch, and I bumped my fist into the mirror. The door opened, and Murray stepped in and skirted around the spot on the floor that had creaked under my weight as I entered.

"What are you doing?" he said with a grin as he looked at me, still hunched over the vanity.

He was looking at the setting powder that I'd spilled on the table when I'd jumped. *Whoops.* My gaze lingered on the white powder, the familiarity of it drawing blurry memories to the surface.

I blinked them away, turning my attention back to Murray. "Just getting ready for the big introduction to the in-laws. Any advice? Any last words?"

"Just don't take it personally if Mom doesn't give you the warm and fuzzies. She's a bit of an ice queen."

I gulped down the million other questions that rose up my throat. Nothing he told me about his family was making me any less anxious. Maybe it was best to just suck it up and get it over with.

"You'll be fine. Everyone will love you." He approached me from behind and squeezed my shoulders, lifting my hair off my neck and onto one shoulder. He kissed the bare skin at the nape of my neck. "You look very pretty."

"Hey now, don't get too handsy. I'm a lady—in my fabulous ladies' quarters." I motioned to the room with a sweeping arm.

"I'm sorry, I didn't know she was going to make us sleep separately. Really, though, I should have guessed." He didn't elaborate any further.

"Have you never brought a girlfriend home to meet your parents?"

"Nobody as special as you." He kissed the back of my bare neck once more before releasing my hair down my back. "Ready to go downstairs?"

"Nope, not even a bit." I stood from the vanity, fiddling with the hem of my light cotton sweater. It had been suffocating outside in the Southern summer heat, but the sweat had cooled on my skin as the frigid air-conditioning pumped through the house. I shivered and Murray placed his hand on my lower back, guiding me out of the room and down the hall.

"Should I take my shoes off?" I asked Murray in a whisper as I glanced down at my Vans.

"God no," he laughed.

"What? Are socks or—heaven forbid—exposed toes not classy enough?" I joked, already knowing the answer.

"Something like that," he said, snorting with laughter.

"Alright then, shoe prison it is. I guess your family won't have the pleasure of seeing my sparkly blue toenails, but whatever."

"What's that room?" I asked as we reached the second floor. I pointed at the imposing double doors, its knobs carved in gilded gold. Where the doors met was a crest, carved expertly into the dark wood. The familiarity of it made my brain itch. The crimson wax seal on our invitation, I remembered, had the same crest pressed into it. I didn't realize American families still used crests.

"That's my dad's office. He holds meetings in there, so people will be coming in and out."

I nodded, realizing I had no idea what his parents did for work—meaning I had no idea how they'd made enough money to have such a sprawling home. Why had Murray never told me about his family in more detail? What he *had* told me was widely inaccurate in its omissions. He'd said they were rich, but this was miles beyond just plain rich.

But did that constitute lying? Not necessarily, I thought, feeling defensive about my own line of thinking. He hadn't looked me dead in the eye and lied. Still, I couldn't shake the shadow of suspicion and hurt that loomed in the back of my mind, like a splinter nestled into the skin. I had to give him the benefit of the doubt—it wasn't like I didn't have my own omissions. And mine were much bigger.

"What does your dad even do in his big fancy office? Stock trading? Black market organs?"

Murray laughed. "Textiles. He's the big man in charge of Sedgemont and Company."

He said it so casually, like it was normal for a family to own a wildly successful company.

When we finally reached the bottom floor, I grabbed Murray by the arm. "Hey," I whispered. "Before I meet them, can I ask you a question?" The thought had been bothering me, and I needed to get it out before I was introduced to his parents.

He turned around. "Sure, what's up?"

"Why didn't your family greet us? We've been here for half an hour and haven't even seen them yet." I sighed. "I feel like they're not excited to meet me. Like they're hiding from me?"

"Oh, sweetie, no," he pulled me into a tight hug, and I closed my eyes against his body warmth. "They can just be thoughtless sometimes. It's got nothing to do with you."

I opened my eyes and startled at the sight of Gloria, the housekeeper I'd met only a few minutes prior. I hadn't even heard her approach. How much of our conversation had she heard?

"Mrs. Sedgemont is in the Blue Room. She's very excited to meet you, Kassandra," she said, echoing what I'd just confessed to Murray. Had she been listening?

Murray and I followed Gloria through the enormous entrance hall, closer to the Blue Room. It felt like ten minutes had passed before we entered the room. It was styled like an old-fashioned Victorian parlor, with its printed seat cushions and powdery blues, but it also had bursts of modernity—mid-century side tables with flashes of gold, a white marble coffee table. The wall was dotted with modern art in mirrored frames that glinted against the light streaming in from the full wall of windows on the left side of the room.

"Murray, dear," a voice said from behind an *Architectural Digest* magazine. She tossed the magazine down onto the end table next to her, muttering under her breath, "These modern homes are absolutely nauseating."

Her hair was a striking silver, and the light from the window set it aglow. Her skin was flawless and accentuated by soft lines that told stories of years of smiling at parties and posing for photos. Her trim figure and the soft slope of her hips were highlighted by immaculately tailored clothes.

"Hi, Mother," Murray said, approaching his mom and planting a kiss on her left and then right cheek. His hands were pale against her dark plum sweater. Before he pulled away, he whispered, "Separate rooms, Mother? Is that really necessary?" Mrs. Sedgemont ignored the barb of his question and turned her focus to me.

I took note of how he'd kissed her on both cheeks. Should I do the same? My stomach gurgled, and I pleaded with it to be quiet.

"Mrs. Sedgemont, it's so nice to finally meet you. I've heard so many wonderful things about you," I said as I stuck my hand out. When I gripped her hand, it was limp, her palm facing downward just like I'd done in my vanity mirror. I shook it awkwardly, and when she pulled her hand away, she brushed her hand against her blouse.

"Have you, now?" Mrs. Sedgemont said with a know-ing, yet somehow playful smirk.

No, I thought. *Literally nothing.*

"Welcome to your home, dear," she said as she sat back down. Murray and I sat across from her in plush reading chairs. I nearly sighed at the astonishing comfort of them. Her words rattled me, and for the first time I realized that one day this home might be handed down to us. "You're a part of the family now."

*   *   *

"Let me see this ring," Mrs. Sedgemont said as she leaned forward in her chair, her reading glasses low on her long, elegant nose—the same nose I'd admired on Murray's face many times, just without the boyish, crooked bridge.

I extended my left hand out to her. Although the ring wasn't the highlight of my engagement—that was sup-posed to be your partner, after all—I'd known she'd ask to see my ring and had prepared myself. I'd even given the stone an extra polish before leaving our apartment and painted my nails a shade of nude, innocuous pink.

"I see you decided to go with three carats? Lovely," she nodded at Murray, removing her glasses effortlessly. Her grace was mesmerizing, and she had that indescribable fac-tor that made it hard to look away.

My knowledge about diamonds was minimal, but the muscles in my shoulders lowered in relief at her approval. Now that I'd seen the estate, I couldn't help but think of how much the ring had cost if it was Beatrice-approved.

"Tell me about yourself, Kassandra. And please, call me Beatrice."

"Well, I went to NYU—uh, New York University—"

"Yes, dear, I know what NYU is," she interrupted impatiently.

"Right, of course. Well, I was lucky enough to meet your son there. I'm a set designer for off-Broadway plays, but one day I hope to maybe work in TV and film. But that'll probably require a move out to Los Angeles, and I'm not sure if I'll ever be ready to leave the city."

"How magnificent. We love the theater. And your family? Who are your people?" she asked.

Who are my people? I was beginning to feel like I was in a job interview. I straightened my back.

"My family is from Upstate New York. Shortsville, right outside Rochester. My dad owns an auto shop, and my mom's a social studies teacher."

Beatrice nodded once. "How philanthropic." She fixed her gaze on Murray, and an awkward moment passed in silence until Beatrice called out, "William, could you fetch Emmett?"

I wasn't familiar with the name, but I assumed it was Murray's brother. I swear Murray had told me his name before, but it must have slipped my mind. I should have asked more questions, and now I was kicking myself for it. Did it make me a bad partner that I didn't push harder, ask more questions? Probably.

Moments later, footsteps approached, and Murray and I twisted around in our chairs. A tall, lanky man walked in—more a boy than a man, actually—and came to stand next to his mother's chair. He faced us with an indolent grin.

"You must be Kassandra," he said, his hands still in his pockets but his face warm. He had the air of a private prep school senior stuck in a twenty-something-year-old's body, someone who thought he was the big fish but was swaddled enough so that he would never find out he was just a minnow.

I shook off the judgment. After all, I was grateful to have a more casual introduction, so I gave a little wave.

"It's great to meet you. I'm so happy to be here," I said.

Emmett's eyes glistened with sunlight slanting in through the window—the same piercing blue as Beatrice's. Those sad but endearing hazel eyes I saw in the family portraits must be from Phillip's side of the family.

"Do you want a drink?" He waved a finger at Murray and me.

It was just after lunchtime, only two o'clock. Not knowing if this was some sort of etiquette test, I looked to Murray for some guidance.

"Sure," he said. "Just a bit, though."

"A nip never hurt anyone. Kassandra? Bourbon okay?"

"Yes, thank you," I said as he began to slosh the amber liquid into the first of three thick crystal highballs.

I peeked at Beatrice, trying to catch a glimpse of her reaction to my day drinking within the first hour of our meeting. Relief washed over me as the glint of a half-full martini glass caught my eye, an olive poking out of the clear liquid like an iceberg. It was funny that day drinking for the rich was a luxurious pastime, whereas when poor people drank during the day, they were wasting their time and money. What a life.

Emmett handed Murray and me our bourbons, and although I wanted to gulp mine down like a shot, I matched Murray's cautious pace and took a small, neat sip. Emmett, on the other hand, returned to the bar cart and downed the two fingers of bourbon before pouring another and making his way to the seat next to his mother.

Had he meant for me to see that? Murray had been answering his mother's questions about work, and neither

of them seemed to have noticed. The action had been practiced and swift—the same type of motion I performed
each morning when I took my vitamins and birth control.
Muscle memory.

"And tell me about the Lucas Goedert event. Was it a
success?" Beatrice asked, bringing my attention back to the
conversation.

"Is this that Looney Tunes European artist you were
working with?" Emmett asked with a snort as he sat down
next to Beatrice.

Murray had spent months preparing for Goedert's
show at the gallery where he worked as a curator. He and
the gallery owner, Karl, had spent nearly two years trying
to convince the reclusive, yet wildly famous artist to hold a
show in their space. Murray had found his first gray hair in
the weeks before the show, as the artist had arrived in New
York City only to stop answering any form of communica-
tion. As the grunt of the gallery, Murray had been in
charge of keeping tabs on the artist and supplying him
with his every desire.

A smile crept in at the memory of being pulled from
sleep by Murray's cell phone vibrating violently on the
bedside table. It had been the owner of a karaoke bar, calling to ask Murray to come get his "son," who was incredibly intoxicated and refusing to let other customers on stage
to sing. It turned out that after hundreds of texts, calls,
and emails from Murray, Goedert had put Murray in his
contacts as Daddy.

"Yeah, he's the one from Luxembourg. It ended up
being our most successful show to date. We were at max
capacity each night, and almost all the paintings were
bought," Murray said proudly. I could tell he wanted to
impress his family, and my heart swelled.

"Tell them about the highest selling piece," I said, egging him on. He was never one to show off, and I often had to force him into telling the full truth of his successes. And I think I knew what his family's love language was: money.

"Oh, well . . ." he hesitated. "It sold for four million."

Emmett made a noise of approval, and Beatrice raised one eyebrow as she took a sip of her martini.

"And tell them what it was made of," I went on, unable to stop myself.

"Oh boy, okay. The paint was mixed with the ashes of his dead dog." He gave a nervous laugh. "Which died of natural causes, of course."

"How maudlin," Beatrice said after a pause, causing Emmett to erupt into a fit of laughter.

"Glad you're here, brother," Emmett said as he stuck out his nearly empty glass for a cheers.

Murray leaned forward and clinked his glass. "Happy to be home."

CHAPTER

6

As the sun dipped lower in the sky, so did the liquor on the bar cart. It was nearing five o'clock, and while Murray and I had only had two bourbons, the bottle was almost empty. None of us appeared to be tipsy, but I looked around with the certainty that I would see glassy eyes or unsteady feet. But I saw none, and conversation continued as it did when we'd first arrived—perfectly tidy and polite.

"Now, let's talk about the party," Beatrice said. She called in William for a fresh martini. "Everyone is absolutely dying to come," she said. "There are so many people who want to meet the newest addition to the Sedgemont clan."

I'd never been one to suffer from social anxiety, but her words gave me pause. "Exactly how many people are invited?" I asked, trying to keep my tone excited.

"There are two hundred who have RSVP'd yes. But of course, we all know that some people might not show."

The room grew hotter at the thought of two hundred strangers' bodies filling the bottom floor, their eyes on me as they took in the fresh meat.

"Oh wow, that's impressive." My voice faltered.

"We have guests coming from all over to spend time with you—family from out of state, old friends coming in from London, even a few from New York. Some of whom are arriving tonight."

"Tonight?"

"They'll be staying with us. Far more comfortable than some Airbnb," she said the word with disdain. She glanced at her watch. "They should be arriving at any moment now."

As if on cue, a chime rang, reverberating through the house with a haunting echo. I shifted in my chair, ready to stand and greet them, but nobody was making a move for the door. It must be the norm that William greeted everyone at the door instead of one of the Sedgemonts. I was grateful now that the bourbon had settled my nerves, and found I was actually excited to keep meeting new people.

While his family was distracted by the doorbell, Murray got my attention and made a quick motion like he was swinging a baseball bat. "Knocked it out of the park," he whispered. "You're doing great. I told you she'd like you."

I could tell he was slightly buzzed from the bourbon, and I was happy to see him having fun. I gave him a little thumbs-up and took a sip of my drink.

A moment later William entered the room with two guests in tow. The man was in his late sixties or early seventies, and his heavy middle stretched his dress shirt. The woman behind him was the opposite in every way—twenties, rail thin. Her sundress billowed around her delicate limbs as she moved. "And who might this beauty be?" the man asked, looking me up and down.

"This," Beatrice said as she stood unhurriedly, "is the reason we're all here. Meet Kassandra, our future daughter-in-law."

He took my hand in his, flipping my hand so my palm was facedown as he planted a wet kiss on it. "I'm Lyle Cooper. Friend of the family."

"It's so great to meet you," I said, holding back a grimace. He'd planted a glob of saliva on my hand. I put my hands behind my back, trying to hide the fact that I was wiping his spit off on the back of my sweater.

The young woman behind him cleared her throat.

Lyle flinched. "And this is my wife, Mary Margaret." He placed his bloated palm on the back of her arm, but she stepped to the side, putting space between them. Three gold Cartier bracelets jangled on her wrist as she reached her hand out. Her long, elegant fingers were surprisingly strong, and I held back a wince at the discomfort of her bony grip.

"Nice to meet you, Mary," I said.

"It's Mary Margaret," she corrected. "Congratulations on the engagement. We got married in October in Savannah, my hometown—hurricane season be damned!" She giggled. Her Southern accent was different, her drawl dripping in long vowels, like honey. "I'd be happy to put you in contact with my planner. Who's making your dress?"

"Uh . . ." I paused, my voice croaking. "We haven't started planning yet."

"But surely you've thought about it?"

I hesitated, knowing they were expecting a certain answer. Changing the subject was the only good option. Beatrice's lips were pursed, eyes watching. "Well, to be honest, I've only had time to think about this party. Beatrice, I'm sure it's been hard work. I can't imagine how you put it together with such little time." My voice was false in my own ears, but Beatrice and Mary Margaret's eyes lit up. It worked.

"I've thrown many parties and made contacts along the way. They were willing to drop their clients and work with me on this celebration." She took a sip of her martini, proud of herself. "It was a bit last minute, but we can make it work." She gave Murray a sharp look with the last comment.

"Now," Mary Margaret stage-whispered, edging closer to Beatrice, "will the Lockwoods be coming?"

"Of course, missing it would be foolish," Beatrice said. "Their daughter is still single. And nearly thirty."

Mary Margaret nodded her head knowingly, and I held back a snort. She looked like she had just had her first legal drink herself. "Is there anything I can do tomorrow to help? I'm at your disposal, Bootsie," Mary Margaret said.

Bootsie? I glanced at Beatrice—a woman so fabulous that surely no one would call her something like Bootsie. It sounded more like a pet's name than a millionaire's. I was surprised when her face softened at the nickname, her head tilting to the side as she stepped forward and looped Mary Margaret's thin arm around hers.

"Actually, yes. You wouldn't believe what the caterers suggested . . ." her voice trailed off as they turned their backs and walked into the entrance hall.

Lyle's full belly moved as he chuckled. "Women and their parties. Like clucking hens. Only a matter of time before they start pecking."

The four of us stood there in awkward silence for a moment, when two chattering men entered the room, one of them around Beatrice's age and a younger man, maybe forty years old. The younger man was tall, with broad shoulders that spoke of an active lifestyle. His dirty-blond hair was speckled with grays that framed his high cheekbones and dimpled chin. I averted my eyes as I realized I was staring.

I wasn't the only one. Lyle trained his eyes on him as they greeted him, a pleasant smile on his face as he shook the older man's hand, but it morphed into a strained grimace when he gripped hands with the younger man.

"So sorry we're late," the older man said. "Our meeting ran long. Nearly turned a lunch meeting into a dinner meeting." He laughed. He turned to Murray and embraced him in a quick hug with a booming pat on his back.

"Son," he said simply before moving onto me. "I expect this is Kassandra."

"Mr. Sedgemont," I said as I grasped his outstretched hand. His grip was strong, but his skin was soft and clammy. "Thank you so much for having me."

"Of course, dear. You can call me Phillip. This is Beau, the vice president of the family business. He's not family by blood, but he might as well be."

We exchanged greetings for a moment before Mr. Sedgemont stepped back and said, "Will you all excuse us for a moment? Beau and I have some things to clear up before dinner."

The two men left the room and once again, Murray, Emmett, and I were left standing in silence with Lyle, who was shifting awkwardly on his feet.

Instead of striking up a conversation, Lyle's eyes traveled over my body, his milky irises silently undressing me. Murray draped his arm across my lower back and cleared his throat forcefully.

Lyle's eyes met his, challenging for only a moment, before he walked out of the room without a word.

* * *

About an hour after Lyle and Mary Margaret's arrival, Gloria ushered us into the dining room. Beatrice and Phillip walked ahead of us with a slow but confident gait that said, *"Take this all in. Look at the beauty that we own."*

The formal dining room was bright and lavishly decorated. It had the regal but playful energy of a French aristocrat's chateau, like something pulled from the set of Sofia Coppola's *Marie Antoinette*. Crisp white panel molding extended up to the high ceilings, climbing the walls alongside the tall, wide windows.

"We ate dinner in here every single night when I was little. I prefer our setup," he said with a homesick smile. At home we always ate dinner on the sofa while watching TV.

Gloria herded us to our seats with practiced ease but enough command to make sure we didn't go astray. Beatrice had clearly spent time thinking about the perfect seating arrangement.

Beatrice and Phillip sat at the heads of the table, perched rigidly in their chairs. Murray sat closest to Beatrice, with myself in the middle and Mary Margaret to my right. Her husband was across from her, both of them flanking Phillip.

There were two empty seats next to Lyle and since I knew Emmett was eating with us, I imagined Beau would be joining us as well.

We all sat in a charged silence, no one knowing who should speak first or what to say.

Beatrice's chair creaked as she leaned closer to Murray and whispered, "Next time, please change into something more appropriate." Murray tugged on the hem of his gray T-shirt and snatched a white linen napkin off the table, draping it over his black jeans.

Emmett walked in, his previously crisp blue button-down now slightly ruffled, with a portion of it coming untucked. As he turned his face, I noticed with a shock that his skin was sallow, and his steely blue eyes were rimmed with red and deep plum halos. He had the clammy sheen of an ill person, and it struck me as odd that nobody in the room was saying anything about it. His father didn't even seem to notice he'd entered the room. "Are you feeling okay? Would you like me to get you a cup of coffee?" I whispered, trying not to draw attention.

"Who's this?" Emmett asked as he sat across from me at the table. He took a sip of red wine.

I laughed softly, painfully aware of my presence at the table as the newest member of the group. "Very funny," I said playfully, even though I was eager for the attention to be pointed away from me. Murray opened his mouth to speak, but Emmett interrupted.

"No, seriously. Who are you?" he said, a bit more forcefully this time. His gaze was unflinching, and I struggled to maintain eye contact. I was fine with friends and family poking fun at me, but this didn't feel playful. My mouth was dry, and I raised my glass of water, covering my fake smile that probably looked more like a wince.

Phillip glared at Emmett—he had been talking with Lyle about an upcoming meeting—and slammed his hand on the table.

"Goddammit, Kennedy. I told you to stop with the bullshit," he barked, causing me to nearly spill my glass of water. His deep, booming voice sent vibrations through the table.

I clasped my hands together in my lap, picking at the case of my phone that I'd nestled between my knees. *Who the fuck is Kennedy?*

"Enough with the *Parent Trap* nonsense," Phillip commanded.

Parent Trap nonsense? I looked around in confusion, but everyone at the table appeared annoyed and even mildly entertained, rather than confused.

"I'm just trying to entertain our guests," he retorted.

"You're such an asshole," Murray grumbled.

"Wait—I'm sorry," I interjected. "I'm so confused."

Murray said, leaning into me slightly and speaking with a hushed voice, "This isn't Emmett; this is Kennedy. My other brother."

7

"KENNEDY AND EMMETT are identical twins," Murray explained under his breath. The word *identical* whipped from his tongue like a curse.

As if on cue in a dinner theater that I *did not* buy tickets to, Emmett walked in. He strode to the table and sat in the open seat directly across from me. "But obviously I'm the more attractive one." He and Kennedy shot daggers at each other out of the corners of their eyes.

A flicker of irritation with Murray burned in my throat. How could he have simply left out the fact that he had another brother? And not just another brother, but *identical twin brothers*. I tried to go over the few times he'd talked about his family, rewinding to the rare and short stories of his brother. He had once described his brother—singular—as highly intelligent and charismatic.

But now that I thought about it, he'd also once told me in passing that his brother flunked out of college. I'd been surprised by that, since all he'd told me about his brother was how driven he was. It was clear now that he'd slipped up and had been talking about Kennedy.

I glared at Murray, but he was completely unaware as he shot his own daggers at his brothers.

Was he embarrassed by Kennedy? Did he simply dislike him that much? Or maybe in his head they were one entity despite all their differences. Either way, I didn't appreciate Murray keeping secrets and letting his brother talk to me like I was an uninvited guest.

"Why are you wearing my shirt?" Emmett asked, his chin tilted up and back, eyebrows lifted.

"I thought it looked better on me. I took it while you were showering the stink of bourbon off yourself," Kennedy said with a smirk. His teeth had a purple sheen from his wine, even though he'd only had half a glass since he sat down.

"You're delusional. And you don't smell any better," Emmett said. He turned to me, an amused expression on his face. "Don't pay him any mind."

"Can both of you shut up, please?" Murray grumbled, and Beatrice gave him a withering glare. I'd had many friends with siblings, and I'd heard them fight, angry voices levied against each other like hatchets, but only a moment later they'd be sitting next to each other, watching TV. But Murray's voice didn't sound like that. It had actual hatred burning underneath.

"You are both equally handsome," Beatrice cooed. The love in her face was surprising—I'd yet to see her look at Murray that way.

I hesitated, trying to think of what to say to reset the sour mood in the room. "Let's start over," I said to Kennedy. "I'm Kassandra, Mur's fiancée. We just got here today."

"Mur? Makes him sound like a dog. I'm Kennedy. Welcome to the estate," he said, half mumbling with a bite in the word *estate*. It was obvious he was intoxicated, but I couldn't tell if his behavior constituted more than just wine and mischief.

"Kassandra and Murray got engaged this past weekend," Beatrice said to Kennedy. There was something different about her tone when she spoke to him. Her voice softened and her face became more animated, as if she were speaking to a young child. It was nice to see a softer side of her, but it also sent a shiver down my spine to witness her talk to a grown man like that.

My phone vibrated between my knees, and the urge to peek at the screen made me itch. I took the chance and glanced down. It was another Instagram message. My heart sank as I thought of the message I'd received before we left the city. *Bitch.* My eyes stung—I hadn't blinked in quite some time.

"Kassandra, dear," Beatrice said with a schoolteacher's tone.

"Sorry—what?" I tried to say in my most polite tone as I turned away from the distraction.

"No cell phones at the dinner table. It's awfully gauche," she said as she slid the olive in her martini between her teeth, her eyes on me all the while.

"I'm so sorry." I said, trying to think of some polite phrase I'd heard on television that got someone away from a group. "May I please be excused?"

"Certainly, dear," Phillip said. He gave Beatrice a look, something that said both *"Lay off,"* and *"But you're still the boss."*

I got up, placing my napkin on my seat. As I walked out of the dining room, her eyes were hot on my skin, and I became so suddenly self-conscious that I felt removed from my body.

My limbs were jittery and stiff, as if I was relearning how to walk. I didn't know what to do with my hands, so I gripped my phone tight at my stomach and sped through the doorway.

As I entered the entrance hall, I caught a whiff of the approaching main course. Fresh rosemary and thyme made my stomach growl. The Sedgemonts' kitchen staff rounded the corner, their arms full of serving trays. With a jolt of panic, I realized that I had no idea where the first-floor bathrooms were.

"Sorry, I know your hands are full, but could you point me to the bathroom? This place is a maze," I asked, my mouth watering at the smell of roasted chicken and something herbal, maybe risotto.

The woman, who appeared to be the head chef, based on her crisp, double-breasted white jacket, pointed across the entrance hall near the Blue Room, where I'd first met Beatrice. "Through that room to your right," she said. Her smile was warm, but it was clear she was in a hurry, and my cheeks flushed with embarrassment.

"Thank you," I said. I'd wanted to introduce myself, but the staff hurried into the dining room.

Every light in the Blue Room was blazing bright. I slipped inside the half bathroom, which was nearly as big as our studio apartment. There was a seating area with an upholstered armchair and side table, and the sink had enough counter space that it could easily fit a second sink.

Quickly, I pulled out my phone and entered my password, opening Instagram in a rapid succession of practiced movements. I thumbed through the congratulatory notifications that were still rolling in and felt a pang of guilt as I ignored them.

With a shaky breath, I opened the message request notification. It was a different account this time. Another string of letters and numbers.

You don't deserve happiness.

I slammed my phone face down on the marble countertop, not caring about the slight *crack* from my phone case.

My reflection stared back at me in the mirror. My cheeks were flushed with red splotches, and heat pulsed underneath my skin. I turned on the sink and ran my wrists under the cool water, trying to focus on the frigid sting of it.

Clearly somebody had heard the news of our engagement and was less than pleased about it. I wondered if it could be an ex-boyfriend. That was actually something my friends had cautioned me about, warning me that some exes were like roaches, crawling out of the woodwork when they realized a former partner had finally found a stable, happy relationship. I thought of when my best friend Zoey posted a picture of herself and her girlfriend on social media, only for an ex to message her, threatening to ruin her relationship when she was at her happiest.

My hands were beginning to grow numb under the cool water, but I kept them there. What if this wasn't about Murray and me? What if it was just about me? The rush of the running water grew louder, and I shut it off, but I could still hear a distant ringing in my ears.

No, I told myself firmly, *it isn't possible.* The messages— my past—they're not related. I pushed the thought away, allowing anger to replace the guilt.

"Psychopaths," I muttered angrily under my breath.

I smoothed down a stray hair that had grown frizzy with the Southern humidity. Nobody was nearby, but I flushed the toilet for the sake of appearance, turned on the sink again, then swung open the door. I took deep breaths as I traipsed through the enormous Blue Room, trying to focus on my reason for being here.

Some soulless internet troll wasn't going to keep me from celebrating the happiest occasion of my life. As I neared the doorway to the entrance hall, Mary Margaret rounded the corner, the sharp points of her face only inches from mine as we nearly collided.

"Oh my God, I'm so sorry," I said, an awkward laugh escaping from my mouth in a huff.

She smoothed her dress, collecting herself. "Beatrice asked me to come check on you."

How long had I been in the bathroom? And if it was such a concern for everyone, why hadn't Murray come to check on me instead? Perhaps it was for the same reason that Beatrice had us sleep in separate wings—propriety or some other bullshit.

"I'm fine—just using the bathroom." My voice was unconvincing, and I sounded like I was up to something. I clamored for words to add that would break down the wall Mary Margaret had thrown up between us. "Just the trials and tribulations of womanhood."

She gave an understanding smile. "Let's get back to the table."

Mary Margaret and I walked back to the dining room, our shoes clicking against the floor and echoing against the tall ceiling. I glanced up through the hole created by the stairs, marveling at the dome of glass above. The stars were brighter here, but although it was beautiful, I missed the city in all of its light-polluted glory. Everything was so different here with Murray's family.

Dizziness forced me to look away, back to the room around me.

I needed to be here. To be present. Even if I hated every moment of this, I needed to do it for Murray.

*   *   *

The rest of dinner passed without a hiccup, Kennedy on his best behavior for the remainder of the evening. That mostly entailed him sipping in silence, but that seemed to appease Phillip. My head was a bit fuzzy with wine and the cordials that were brought out after dinner. I could still taste the Knocklofty coffee liqueur on my tongue, but it was turning sour as the sugar lingered in my mouth.

I was glad to finally be alone in my bedroom. I loved meeting new people and getting to know them, and usually it energized me, but the Sedgemonts left me wilted. Maybe it was because I was putting so much effort into behaving appropriately, or maybe it was this damn house that made me feel so out of place, but I was absolutely exhausted.

I lay back on my bed, feet still on the floor and laced tight in my sneakers. My bones ached and my heavy eyelids fluttered, changing the room from its golden glow to a stark black again and again.

What seemed like moments later, I opened my eyes, realizing I was awaking from a deep sleep. I blinked furiously, confused by the darkness of the room. Had I turned the light off before falling asleep? I was still lying fully clothed on the bed, both legs dangling over the edge. I sat up and groaned at the pressure of my full bladder.

The darkness was disorienting, but a sliver of light peeked out from under the doorway, helping me regain my bearings. I rose to my feet, searching for the bedside lamp, when I froze.

A shadow passed by my doorway, the outline of two feet visible as they moved down the hallway. I supposed it was one of the guests getting up for a drink of water or to use the bathroom, like myself.

But the feet grew still in front of my door.

What were they doing?

I tried to make out the size of the feet—could it be Murray coming to visit me? I grasped for my phone, thinking he might have texted me in warning. But the screen glared bright in my face with one unanswered text.

Love you. Goodnight! Murray had texted over an hour ago.

My tongue was dry from the alcohol and panic. This didn't feel right.

Lyle staring at me throughout the night came to mind, and the way he talked about women like they were thoughtless animals. Could he be the one outside my door? A shiver traveled up my neck.

"Hello?" I called out. The feet remained still.

Using my phone's flashlight, I swung the bright white light toward the door, hoping to scare whoever it was off.

The feet faltered, moving backward. I breathed a sigh of relief as whoever it was shuffled and finally moved back down the hallway, in the same way they had come. Someone had nearly passed my door—which was one of many guest bedrooms in this enormous house—before coming to a stop in front of mine.

If they had returned in the same way they came, I realized with dread filling my chest, they must have been searching for me.

8

THE NEXT MORNING Murray greeted me outside my door with a beaming smile on his face.

I gave him a quick kiss and looked him up and down with a grin. "Well, look at you!" He was wearing camel-colored khakis that I knew for certain I'd never seen before. His navy-blue T-shirt and scuffed white sneakers were familiar, making him look a bit more like himself. "Where'd you get those?" I pointed to his pants.

"They were laid out for me. I'm guessing Mother told Gloria to make me look more 'palatable.'" He waggled his fingers in air quotes and rolled his eyes.

"Do a little spin for me."

He spun around, pausing and looking back. "Nice, right?"

We laughed as we made our way down to the dining room, where some of the Sedgemonts were already eating.

We all sat at the dining room table, soaking in the morning sun that streamed in the tall windows while we ate our breakfast. The Sedgemonts' chef must have gotten up at five AM to make such a large meal. There was fresh fruit, bacon, and eggs cooked individually to each guest's liking, and I counted at least six kinds of fresh pastries arranged on platters in the center of the table. The Sedgemonts were unfazed by it all, but I was ecstatic, and the instinct to stuff my pockets with pastries, like I did at hotels, was nearly too strong to resist.

I heaped my plate with food and thanked Gloria as she passed silently behind us. I took a seat, leaving a few empty chairs between my future in-laws and me, to act as a buffer. A phone rang in another room, the metallic din ricocheting off the walls. Gloria rushed out of the dining room, and silence soon returned.

"Where are Kennedy and Emmett?" I asked.

"Probably sleeping it off." Murray chuckled under his breath, adding, "As always."

Beatrice and Phillip gave him a sharp glare, but I could tell that the comment annoyed them because it was true.

"The boys do tend to sleep a bit too late. At one point we had William try to wake them each morning, but that proved . . . perilous," Beatrice said.

William, who stood by the dining room door, lifted his hand reflexively to a dented scar on his forehead that I hadn't noticed before. It was red and angry, like it was only weeks old.

Had one of the twins done that to him? I pictured them fumbling around on their nightstand as William tried to wake them up, grabbing whatever they could— their phone, an empty bottle—and launching it at the poor man's head.

As if on cue, they both entered, the stale smell of booze noxiously trailing behind them. It was rank, so I lifted my coffee to my lips and inhaled deeply. The energy in the room changed instantaneously. The Sedgemonts and their guests shifted in their seats, turning ever so slightly away from them. William shrank in on himself, his wide frame caving in.

Could he really be that scared of these waif-like, alcohol-soaked twenty-somethings? They sat down, Kennedy on the other side of me, and Emmett directly across. They moved in tandem with each other, yet somehow always opposite.

The twins' plates were full of greasy bacon and buttery toast. Despite his clear disdain for the pair, William promptly brought over a tray of two black coffees and two powdery waters.

Murray leaned in and whispered, "Their holy grail hangover cure: Pedialyte and a shot of vodka."

I stifled a laugh. "Nice."

I looked up to see Beatrice staring at me, her face eerily expressionless. My smile dropped and heat rose in my cheeks. Murray squeezed my knee, giving me a playful look that said, *"Oops."*

The doorbell rang, echoing faintly through the room, and William slipped out to answer it. The rest of us continued eating. Nobody spoke as the sound of footsteps approached.

William walked in with Beau trailing behind, and announced, "Sir, ma'am, Beau Andersen has arrived. Unannounced." The disdain for Beau in his voice was unmistakable, and Beau responded with a snarl of a smile. What had happened between them to make them so openly hostile at nine in the morning?

"Phillip, can I have a moment? Sorry to interrupt your breakfast," Beau said. His body was twitchy, and he ran his fingers over his lips repeatedly, as if he were trying to clamp his mouth shut. "Good morning, everyone." He greeted those seated at the table by name, with a smile—everyone except for the twins.

"Ever heard of a phone?" Kennedy mumbled.

Beau's eyes passed over him for the first time, completely unimpressed by Kennedy's bravado. His twisted snarl of a mouth shifted into a perfectly polite mask. "Sorry, Kennedy. I nearly didn't see you."

As Phillip took one last sip of coffee and rose from his chair, Beau straightened his tie, and his eyes fluttered around the room nervously.

The twins snickered to each other as Beau and Phillip retreated up the stairs to Phillip's office.

Beatrice spoke. "There will be more guests arriving to town today. Some of them may pay us an early visit, schedules allowing."

Murray asked who was in town, and Beatrice rattled off unfamiliar names, providing no explanation as to who these people were, while Murray nodded, unimpressed.

"We'll also have caterers and planners coming in and out of the house." Her eyes sparkled with excitement. This party was the highlight of her year. Not our engagement— just the party.

A phone rang again. Beatrice's jaw set, her lips curling in on themselves into thin, crimson slashes. "William! Gloria! Will someone answer the godforsaken phone?"

Murray flinched against her raised voice. He gripped the napkin in his lap, and I reached out for his hand.

William rushed out of the room, nearly crashing into Gloria on the way out. What was he more driven by—the desire to please Beatrice? Or fear of her?

Beatrice's lips unfurled back into their usual relaxed semi-smile. "That cursed phone. Only five more guests left to RSVP. And I am counting down the seconds."

Beatrice picked off the remains of her small meal and eventually left Murray and me to sip our coffees. William had delivered a fresh latte as soon as I'd finished my first. Heaven.

The pretense of a family this obsessed with their wealth was repulsive, but as much as I hated to admit it, I could get used to certain aspects of this lifestyle—mostly just the food.

*   *   *

A commotion of new arrivals echoed in the entrance hall. There were three sets of feet, all scurrying into the Blue Room.

The party was tomorrow, and it had been looming like a thick, dark cloud over the house since we got here. With each hour that ticked by, the cloud became more violent, with lightning bolts striking out at any moment. Beatrice was the lightning.

We had been lounging in the Blue Room since break-fast, sipping coffees and chatting. Beatrice had been answering calls, back to back, for an hour, holding up her long, bony finger in the air mid-conversation, no matter the topic. I'd heard the names of the two poor party plan-ners who had just entered the house many times, hissed under breath and shouted through the phone at heights of Beatrice's frustration. Ricky and Sue. I pitied them.

From the racket of their conversation, they were going through the final details and arranging the arrivals of caterers, florists, and the rest of the motley crew of Bea-trice's worker bees. Ricky and Sue's employees were meant to be following behind them with two vans full of tables, chairs, and other party-related furniture, but apparently one van had taken a wrong turn after stopping to get gas. The planners were trying to calm Beatrice, whose voice had risen from a stressed bark to a panicked shriek.

"Is she always like this?" I asked Murray under my breath.

"Sort of. Planning parties just brings out the worst in her."

We both flinched as Beatrice shouted at Ricky and Sue. "Now what the hell am I supposed to do with table-cloths, but no tables?"

Murray shot up from his seat and hustled to the kitchen door. I followed behind reluctantly, not wanting to get caught in the crossfire of Beatrice's anger.

A group of unfamiliar people stood in the kitchen, all dressed in white and black. They were setting up catering materials and equipment—extra hotplates, even though the range in this kitchen already had eight burners and two ovens. A trail of silver and brass chafing dishes and food warmers was being paraded in and set down, covering every surface of the kitchen.

Beatrice was barking orders, and when a caterer dropped a box of napkins, she raised her voice another octave. I flinched as her anger cut through the air like a closed fist.

"Want to get changed and go on a walk?" Murray asked, ushering me out of the way and back into the Blue Room.

I drained the last of my coffee, eager to get away from the party talk and thrum of electric anxiety. I grabbed my crumpled napkin and my mug, ready to take them to the kitchen. It was our unspoken rule as a couple—we either cleaned as we cooked or we cleaned immediately after. No exceptions.

Murray stood in the doorway, waiting for me. His coffee sat on the side table, next to a small plate with an untouched chocolate croissant.

"Murray?" I said, pointing at his dishes.

He shrugged. "I don't want to get in the way of the caterers."

I tried to resist it, but my face contorted in judgment. It didn't matter, though, because he'd already turned his back.

"You comin', babe?" he called out.

Wordlessly I followed, fighting off the disappointment as I pictured Gloria tossing his untouched pastry in the trash, frowning at his wastefulness.

We were halfway to the second floor when Beatrice shouted up the staircase at us. "Darlings, would you please get your party outfits to Gloria? She'll be doing some steaming today." She had one arm wrapped in front of her chest, with her other hand waving her reading glasses like a conductor's wand as she spoke.

"Sure, Mother," Murray called back.

I wasn't sure if it was his wastefulness or the way he said *mother* that made my skin crawl. Two sides of my mind battled with each other, one frustrated with Murray's rich-boy lifestyle and one defending Murray. The defensive side of myself said, *No, it's not him that's creeping you out. It's just him calling her that.*

My mom was a real mother—loving, kind, caring, but hard on me when I needed a kick in the ass. Yet I never called her mother. She was Mom. Whenever Murray and his brothers said *mother*, all I heard was *mommy dearest*.

"Of course," I finally said. I'd been staring blankly at her.

"Lovely," she said as she turned on her heels and glided into the Blue Room.

Murray was already marching up the stairs, the pockets of his khaki pants staring me in the face. I glanced down at my jeans. They were worn in the knees from work, and while I liked the distressed look of it, I was now the only one wearing denim. A small difference, but still another one separating me from the Sedgemonts.

We parted ways when we got to the second floor, Murray making his way to his room and me up another flight to mine. I was finally getting the hang of where things were, no longer disoriented by the matching dark wood doors that splayed out down the long hallways.

A heated discussion was bleeding from Phillip's office. Phillip rarely spoke, but it sounded like he was letting Beau have it. I wasn't sure what the disagreement was, but it didn't sound good.

The weather app on my phone said it was already eighty degrees, with the humidity of a Swedish sauna, despite it only being ten in the morning. I opted for a thin sundress and peeled off my jeans, throwing them in a pile on the other side of the bed. I hoped that if Gloria came in, she wouldn't see them. I liked Gloria and William, but the idea of anyone coming into my bedroom while I was away gave me the creeps.

I opened the double-door closet, marveling at the size of it compared to our city apartment's cubbyhole. When I'd arrived, I'd hung up my favorite yellow maxi dress, pleased at the thought of how I would look and feel in it on the night of the party—it would be like a comfort blanket, the contrast of the yellow against the dark house like a beam of afternoon sun.

I turned on the closet light and scanned the closet, flipping through the hangers. My yellow dress wasn't there.

I slid a garment bag to the middle, opening it up. Empty.

Pushing past a group of empty velvet wire hangers, I stepped inside, searching the deepest corner of the closet. All of my sweaters and tops were hung up, but the most important piece of clothing for this trip was nowhere to be seen. My dress was gone.

*   *   *

My heart sank and I grabbed my phone to text Murray.

My dress is missing??

How would Beatrice react when I told her I didn't have anything to wear to the party? Would she use the chilling, passive anger I'd witnessed, or would she would burn me to a crisp with her fury, like she had with her party planners? My hands shook as I waited for Murray to respond.

Moments passed at a creeping pace as I stalked back and forth across the room, the hardwood floor creaking loudly under my weight.

There was a knock on the door, and I yanked it open, one finger in my mouth as I gnawed on my freshly painted fingernails that were now ruined. I could taste the chemical tang of nail polish flakes on my tongue.

Murray was standing there, wide-eyed, with his suit draped over his arm.

"Where do you think it could be?" he asked nervously.

"I don't know. I hung it up right when we got here. I haven't touched it since."

"Mother can figure this out. Let's go downstairs," he said with a sudden resolve.

"No, no. Please no. She's going to be so pissed. Murray, she may actually kill me," I begged.

He laughed nervously, and I stared at him, speechless. But what other option did I have?

As I followed him listlessly down the stairs to the Blue Room, my eyes stung with the threat of tears. The lump in my throat threatened to suffocate me. I felt like a little girl being marched to the principal's office. I tried to match Murray's calm and took a gulp of air before we entered the Blue Room.

Here we go. Complete and total obliteration.

"Mother," Murray said, knocking on the doorframe. I gritted my teeth. "I've got my suit, but it seems like Kass's dress has gone missing."

"Missing? Did it grow legs and trot away?" she said, looking up from a stack of menu samples for the party. She lowered her reading glasses to the tip of her long, elegant nose.

"I'm sorry. I hung it up right when we got here, but now I can't find it." My voice warbled a bit. I cleared my throat.

"Not to worry. I'm sure we can find you something just as good, if not better." Her smile was calm, completely unbothered. She rose from her chair, and her smooth, deliberate moments were making me more anxious, like a snake coiled, measuring the distance to its prey, readying itself to strike.

"I can't really afford to buy—" I began to say, my voice still shaky.

"Nonsense," she said, waving her hand dismissively. "You two, come with me. Let's see what we can find in my closet." She ushered us out the door and into the entrance hall.

Murray and I cast a glance at each other. "See? All good, babe," he whispered.

Beatrice led us to the second floor, where she opened the first door to the left of Phillip's office. The door opened into a seating area with bookshelves and two windows with cushioned seats nestled beneath them.

We trailed behind her wordlessly, turning left into an enormous bedroom. The size of their primary suite was at least four times bigger than Murray's and my apartment. Beatrice approached a door to the left of the bed, which was even larger than a king size, and punched in a code on a security pad.

When the door swung open, I gasped. It was a closet that was just as large as the bedroom, with floor-to-ceiling shelves of designer clothes, shoes, and bags.

Directly across from the door was a glass case filled with sparkling jewelry, each piece nestled into its own display box. There was even a seating area with a chair, table, and full-length mirror, where I imagined Beatrice sat each morning, painting on her signature slash of red lipstick.

"This is amazing," I whispered in awe.

Beatrice nodded. "Isn't it?" She combed through the rack of hanging dresses while I stood dumbly, taking in the sight of the room.

"Ah, here we are. I think this would be lovely." She turned, holding a silver gown embroidered with gold embellishments that glittered in the light like stars. Beatrice held the gown up to her chest. "Isn't this perfection? You'll surely turn heads in this."

That was just it. I didn't *want* to turn heads. I wanted to be comfortable in my own clothes—it was the only thing I could ask for when I was so uncomfortable around all these new people with their lifestyle that was worlds apart from my own.

"Wow." My voice rang false. I cleared my throat. "It's beautiful." It was in fact a beautiful gown. It was surely outrageously expensive, like it had been designed to be worn to the Met Gala. It was beautiful—it just didn't look like *me*.

"You'll look great in that. You'd look good in anything," said Murray.

She handed the dress to me, and I picked up the long hem so it didn't drag on the floor. I rooted around in the fabric for a tag, searching for a size. Beatrice and I had extraordinarily different body types; despite both being thin and somewhat tall, everything else was different. My hips were narrow and my chest was flat, while she had a proper hourglass figure with a waist as cinched in as her manners. There was no way one of her dresses would fit me. It would look terrible on me without proper tailoring.

"It's a four. If you're wondering," she said.

"Oh, that's perfect. That's my size," I trailed off while I thumbed the embroidery. Why would she have a brand-new dress in this size? I glanced at her, thinking she would be more of an eight.

"Now for jewelry . . ." She unlocked the glass case and studied her collection before tutting and opening a drawer below it.

A small silver revolver lay on a padded velvet pillow. It had Victorian-looking engravings along the sides, and the handle was a sleek mother-of-pearl that sparkled just like her jewelry. Next to it were necklaces that I assumed were less expensive than the ones in the locked glass case. She plucked one from the drawer and held it up to the dress. It was a simple design of silver and clear stones—I tried not to imagine what the stones were and how much they cost.

"Stunning, isn't it?"

"It really is, thank you so much," I said.

"Let's get this down to Gloria to steam."

We walked back down the stairs and in the direction of the kitchen, but at the last minute Beatrice yanked open a door on the right and flipped on a light switch. I glanced down to the basement, and for a fleeting moment, I was sure Beatrice was going to push me down, leaving me to rot away in a prison where she kept her worst etiquette-oblivious enemies.

The stairs were finished in a richly colored Persian runner, with brass rods nestled into the crooks of the stairs to keep it in place. We followed Beatrice down the stairs, and when we rounded the corner, I was surprised to see that this wasn't just a basement. It was someone's fully finished apartment tucked away behind the immaculate and enormous laundry room.

We stood in a laundry room that had a small circular table littered with needles, thread, and various bottles of stain remover. A button-down shirt lay draped across the table, a red wine stain from Kennedy's sloppy hand marinating in cleaner. Through the open door was a kitchenette and a tiny living room with a loveseat and television.

"What's through there?" I asked, pointing.

"That's where Gloria stays," Beatrice said as she walked over to a rod of hanging clothing. She began thumbing through the garments, pulling them out to inspect Gloria's handiwork.

"She lives here?"

"Mm-hmm," Beatrice affirmed with a mumble.

The apartment was too small to house more than one person. It wasn't much bigger than our Brooklyn studio. "She doesn't have a family?"

She turned so only her profile was visible. "*We* are her family, dear."

The cold, territorial ferocity in her voice made me take a step back. That was a warning shot. Gloria was none of my business. I wanted to ask if William stayed at the estate too, but I kept my mouth shut. Self-preservation.

Beatrice hung the dress on a rack next to the washing machine. "Well, I believe we're done here. Feeling better, dear?"

"Yes. You're a lifesaver," I added with a smile. "Thank you again. Is there anything we can do to help with the party?"

"Not at all. Run along and get your beauty rest," she ordered before reaching out one last time to touch my new gown. "With this outfit, you'll be the star of the show."

9

THE SEDGEMONTS' PROPERTY was sprawling—a demonstration of the distance they put between themselves and those around them.

As Murray ushered me out the front door, I took a deep breath, inhaling the thick morning air. Fog still nestled in the tops of the trees, in a battle with the hot sun that glared bright despite the early hour.

So much had already happened today, and I was already eager for it to be over. I'd hoped this walk would be a reset, but as we traipsed through the perfectly landscaped gardens, it only served to remind me where we were and how out of place I felt.

As we walked through an herb garden that hummed with the feverish activity of bees and butterflies, Murray began to talk about work.

"Got an email this morning. Every painting has officially sold—the gallery is empty." He did finger guns, blew on them, then holstered his imaginary weapons.

I whacked him on the arm, and he grabbed it as though I'd inflicted a mortal wound. "That's amazing!" I said. "Why didn't you tell me at breakfast?"

"It's hard to think with so many people around."

"You're tellin' me. I'm proud of you." I reached over and squeezed his hand. "You worked really hard, and it paid off."

I listened contently as Murray talked about future artists they might host while we skirted around the gated pool. It was dotted with canopied lounges so large they could only be called daybeds. The sun grew hotter by the minute, and out of the corner of my eye, I saw a bead of sweat drip down Murray's temple.

"Let's sit down for a second," he said, pointing to a greenhouse nestled among the hedges. The glass of the pitched roof gleamed in the sun, and as we approached the door, I was relieved to see that it wasn't just a run-down greenhouse filled with plants and toppled-over bags of soil, but it was also a finished sunroom with places to sit. Two large fans were already spinning, nestled into the white wood beams that jutted across the glass ceiling.

A ripe lemon tree towered overhead, and I ran my fingers along its leaves as we walked to a small table in the middle of the room. Everything but the plants was a stark white, and I squinted against the brightness before giving up and pushing my sunglasses onto my face.

"Isn't this nice?" Murray asked as he sat down on a cushioned chair. He tilted his head back and closed his eyes as the fan whipped the hairs around his face into a frenzy.

"Murray," I said softly, "why didn't you tell me about your family?"

He opened his eyes and said, "I did."

"No, all you ever told me was that you had *one* brother"—I held up one finger to emphasize the omission—"and that your family were rich assholes. I think we have a wildly different definition of *rich*."

"Okay, I guess you're right. I'm sorry." He tilted his chair onto the back two legs, and it creaked pitifully. I tensed, waiting for it to collapse. "It's just not relevant to my life now. *Our* life now. I've moved past who I was when I was involved with my family. I'm not that person anymore."

I nodded, trying to be empathetic. "I think I would understand what you're saying more if you were completely estranged from them, but Murray, we're here with your family right now. You *are* involved. Whether you like it or not."

He gave a sad, knowing nod. "I don't want our friends—I don't want *you*—to think I'm some little rich boy who doesn't work hard. I bust my ass at the gallery, and it's taken me years to get where I am. I think I deserve credit for that. Not my parents."

I didn't know how to feel about our new situation—on the one hand, I didn't fit in with his family, and I wouldn't be upset with Murray if he decided to pull further away from them. On the other hand, the fact-oriented part of my brain was telling me that we'd be stupid to cut ties with them. What if we had some sort of catastrophic health scare and were up to our eyeballs in medical debt? His parents could at least throw a mahogany wood ladder down into the pit we'd dug for ourselves. Or if we decided to have kids—his parents could leave them money for college that we otherwise wouldn't be able to contribute with our minuscule salaries.

This type of money-minded politics left me feeling greedy and conniving. But if anyone in my position said they didn't think about these possibilities, they were lying.

"I mean, think of all our friends. Last time we hung out with Zoey, she was wearing a shirt that said 'Eat the Rich.'" He laughed and combed his fingers through his hair, leaving it disheveled and slick with sweat. "If she knew, she would hate me. I can't have your best friend hate me, Kass. And I didn't want you to respect me less."

I opened my mouth to soothe him, but he continued more frantically. "Imagine if we go through with the kind of wedding Mother wants. Can you even picture our friends and coworkers at a five-hundred-thousand-dollar wedding? That's what she told me she wanted to spend on us. That's half a million dollars for a *party*, Kass—a party that we don't even really want. I don't even know if you'd want to have a bridal party, but assuming you picked Zoey as your maid of honor, can you imagine her being in that situation? She would literally want to burn the building down."

I stifled a laugh at the thought of my best friend pulling a lighter out of her combat boot and setting fire to a tablecloth that cost more than my entire wardrobe. She would never do it, but she'd definitely think about it. "If your mom wants to plan another wedding, she and your dad can have a vow renewal."

Murray gave me a pointed look, urging me to take him seriously.

"Alright, I can kind of see your point," I conceded. "But you could have at least told *me*." I couldn't deny the possibility that our friends might treat him differently. And to be honest, I found it admirable that technically he never needed to work a day in his life, but he chose not to take his parents' money and, instead, to work hard, scraping by and saving every penny to build the life he wanted.

"I know I can trust you not to tell our friends about this, at least for now. You can let them know how weird and stuck-up my family is, but please keep the money stuff out of it. Just a white lie. For me."

I blushed. "I already texted a picture of the house to my parents," I confessed.

A flash of tension in his jaw, then it disappeared. "That's fine. They can know. I guess they'll all figure it out at the wedding anyway."

"Guess we just have to elope." I shrugged.

"I'd rather have a fake Elvis at my wedding than my mother."

We talked a while longer, and it was mostly me assuring him that I wouldn't tell our friends, as hard as that would be. I desperately wanted to talk to Zoey about this; otherwise, I was going to burst at the seams with the ridiculousness of it all. And I wasn't yet sure if I could poke fun at Murray's family *to Murray*. I was still feeling that out.

I looked around at my unfamiliar surroundings—the lush grass outside the greenhouse was mowed into perfect stripes, and not a petal on a single flower was out of place. I missed home and the city, and the imperfection of it all. Soon we would be home in our everyday routine, and I wouldn't ever take it for granted again. While I hoped we could return to that stability, I wasn't sure. Would Murray's family change the way I looked at him? Would this huge omission make me constantly wonder if there was something else he was hiding?

It's not like I don't have secrets of my own, I thought guiltily.

"Alright, you ready to go back in?" he said as he wiped away a trickle of sweat that was beading at his hairline.

I was relieved. Despite the fans whirring, the air that they stirred was still hot and thick, and it clung to my skin. I was damp all over, and my skin itched underneath my clothes.

Murray opened the greenhouse doors, and I began to follow him out. My phone vibrated, and muscle memory made me bring the screen to my face.

It was another message. I stopped in my tracks. Murray continued walking—he was talking, his voice light and playful, but I couldn't make out the words.

Does the guilt keep you up at night? Or have you forgotten her?

I stumbled backward, my shoe catching on a crack in the floorboards. My hand reached out, fumbling for something to grab onto. It landed on a pot of lavender, which came crashing down, causing a domino effect of smashing pots next to it. I winced as clay cracked against the wood floor.

Murray rushed back into the greenhouse. "Kass? You okay?"

"Shit," I said flatly. One more thing to make this family hate me.

"Oh, it's fine. They're just pots." He pointed at a stack of empty clay pots, ready for use.

He was right: the cost of the pots was insignificant, but I didn't need to make more work for someone else. As I dropped to one knee to clean up some of the shards of clay, Murray stopped me.

"No, someone else will do that," he said.

But it was my mess. I was fed up with being told someone would trail behind me at all times, fixing whatever I'd done wrong. I ignored him, continuing to pick up the shards, pinching them carefully between two fingers. My hand shook as the words of the text repeated in my head like a mantra.

Yes, I answered silently, *the guilt does keep me up at night. But I could never forget her.*

10

THE HOUSE BUZZED with activity. Today was the last day before the party, and uniform-clad strangers darted through the house with clipboards and cameras, noting every inch of the house, to plan its transformation. I should be thinking about the party, looking forward to the food and drink, the celebration of Murray's and my engagement.

But all I could think about was my phone, which sat heavy in my hand, like a brick. I waited for it to vibrate again, to show another message from the stranger. But its stillness was somehow worse—the waiting making tension build in my body as I wondered who could be sending the messages.

Murray walked me to my room, leaving me to take a quick shower and change into clean clothes. I was nearly done reapplying my makeup when a deep, booming voice cut through the air, undercut by the frantic words of other men. I paused, mascara wand wavering in front of my face as I tried to make out the words.

"Disloyal scumbag . . ." someone shouted. I screwed the mascara cap back on and stepped away from the vanity. I looked off-kilter, one eye wide awake with mascara; the other bare eye, puny and tired. I perched at the door, holding my breath to listen.

"Calm down," a deeper, older voice hissed.

"Don't fucking tell me to calm down."

The twins. Like their bone structure, their voices were so similar that it was impossible to tell them apart from a distance.

I bit my nails. I wanted to crack open the door, to peak down the hallway and see if I could make out the conversation. My heart raced as I gave in, turning the knob as quietly as possible. With the door cracked open, I positioned my ear in the open space, careful not to stick my head out too far.

The hushed voices continued, but the younger, louder voice of one of the twins broke through. "This is wrong, and you know it. He's not family!" He was shouting unabashedly now, but I still couldn't tell who it was. I realized with guilt that I was picturing Kennedy's sallow, tired face spitting out the words.

Without thinking, I stuck my head out far enough so I could see down the hallway. There was nobody there. They must be a floor below, in Phillip's office. I pulled the door open further, sliding out as silently as I could manage.

I tiptoed down the hall, body tight against the wall in case there was anybody on the other wing.

Only occasional hisses were audible now, harsh consonants against gritted teeth. I reached the carved handrail of the staircase and peeked my head over, heart racing.

A sweep of movement made me flinch backward. A messy head of hair appeared below, jerking as its owner made his way to the stairs. A carbon copy soon followed.

"We know you won't tell Father what kind of man you really are, Beau. You're too much of a pussy," one of the twins spat.

I leaned back further, only a sliver of the floor below visible now.

Beau appeared, his dark, slicked back hair gleaming in the light from the chandelier. "Wait," he pleaded. "We have to talk about this. We can figure something out."

One of the twins—god, which one was it?—raised his long middle finger to him as he walked down the stairs. With each step down the curved staircase, their bodies turned, and they were nearly facing me now.

I got one last peek at Beau, Phillip now approaching behind him with a weary look on his face. One of the twins sped up his descent on the staircase, and I flinched, hitting my chin hard on the guardrail with a loud *crack* as I floundered to the floor, my belly pressed stiff against the hardwood. My hip bones ached with the force of the impact, and I held in a groan of pain as my body protested.

"What was that?" one of the twins said as they paused on the staircase. The wood creaked under the weight of them on the same step, the noise sounding unmistakably like an animal's scream.

Worried that even the sound of my panicked breath would alert them to my position, I clamped my lips shut. They began moving again, their footsteps angry and hard against the stairs. All was silent, and I was just beginning to get to my feet when Beau muttered, "Jesus Christ."

Phillip's voice was soft and kind, far different from how he spoke to his twin sons. "Listen, I don't know what it is they think you did, but I need you to ignore them and focus on what's important. They're just slinging dirt and seeing what sticks."

"Phillip, I—"

"They're just not ready for the responsibility. You're our only option. Our best option."

"They're never going to let this go. Thank God Murray is distracted, or he would throw his hat in the ring too."

Distracted. The word was loaded. Distracted by me, I supposed, and our engagement. As far as I knew, his family had no sway over our relationship or the timing of our engagement, but the way he said the word *distracted*, with so much relief, gave me pause.

My curiosity about the twins' involvement in the family business was piqued. Kennedy surely wasn't capable of running a multimillion-dollar corporation, but it was possible that Emmett eventually could.

They were a showy family on the outside, the home their pride and glory, their shell. But on the inside, it was secretive, cloistered, and protected.

I lifted myself up carefully, my scrawny arms shaking under the weight of my body. Once again, I crept down the hallway back to my room, wishing to be invisible.

* * *

After enough time had passed since the twins' dramatic exit, I made my way downstairs to meet Murray. "Why don't I give you a tour of the town?" he said.

"Yes, please," I cried out, almost before he'd finished speaking. The prospect of getting out of the house for a bit was enticing.

Murray's father passed by with William in tow, and Murray stopped them. "I'm going to take Kass out and show her around town. Could I borrow one of the cars?"

"How fun! Of course," he said, smiling. "William, could you pull my car around to the front?"

William disappeared down the hall, only to open the front door minutes later, ushering us outside into the courtyard. The pebbled driveway radiated heat, and it made me gasp for air, as did the sight of the car in front of me.

The sun beamed down on a black Bentley and I held back a laugh at how ridiculous my life had suddenly become. I gawped at Murray with an incredulous smile on my face, but only the edges of his lips lifted into a half smile, as if this were an everyday occurrence. He said he hated his family's lifestyle, but he certainly seemed to enjoy the benefits.

I studied him as he went around the car into the driver's seat, and I slid into the already-open passenger seat. I'd become so confused by the Murray I'd known for years versus this man in khaki pants who was comfortable driving a Bentley. The heat made my thighs stick to the leather seats, and the thought of tainting the car with my sweat made me sweat even more. Murray started the car, the dash with three analog clocks clicked, and the display flipped open, startling me. A digital screen now lit up the dash.

"Sweet Jesus," I muttered. Murray laughed.

The gate opened automatically—likely some sort of sensor on the car—and Murray pulled out of the courtyard confidently. NPR played low on the radio, and I was tempted to turn it up, but kept my hands in my lap, afraid to touch anything.

We began our drive with Murray pointing out the homes of family friends. Dense trees created a curtain of privacy between the enormous homes. They were beautiful, but none were quite as large as the Sedgemont Estate. Thick oak trees canopied the road protectively, and sun peeked through in a flurry of pinpricks. The dance of light was mesmerizing, and the roofs of the expansive homes rose in intimidating points behind the trees.

Murray proudly pointed to an Edwardian-style manor that was not a home at all, but his private high school, which he had attended his junior and senior years. He seemed to have had a better high school experience than I had, despite his transfer, as he regaled me with stories about his lacrosse team and his motley crew of friends as we drove down the road.

Murray's pleasant chatter came to a halt when we turned at a stop sign and left the exclusive country club village for the real world. The homes shrunk by the mile, going from two-story homes to ranches, to cottages. Some people were in their yards, carefully pruning their flowers and shrubs, their skin pink and gleaming with the summer heat. A few of them ignored us as we drove slowly by, but most followed the car with their watchful eyes, their faces set in steely frowns that sent a cold shiver down my body. All their screen doors and windows were open, and I felt a pang of sympathy for them at how hot it must be in their houses without air-conditioning. I'd lived without an AC unit until I moved in with Murray, and every summer day had been a vicious punishment.

We turned onto unfamiliar roads, me smiling and listening as Murray pointed out locations that held memories. Gradually, his smile faded as the homes became smaller, and boarded-up commercial buildings became more common.

"This all used to be a lot nicer," Murray said quietly.

Murray slowed the car to a creep as he pointed at an industrial park. Gray metal and concrete buildings engulfed the landscape. Dry, flaking paint littered the ground alongside shattered glass. From a distance I could barely make out a word that had been spray-painted along one wall in red: *Traitors*. Someone had attempted to paint over the graffiti in white, but the red seeped through like a wound covered in gauze.

Tall chain-link fences topped with barbed wire encased the enormous industrial park. It was clear someone wanted to keep trespassers out, but the ghostly appearance of the buildings made it look like something just as dangerous was being trapped inside.

"That used to be my family's. We sold all the American factories about six months ago and outsourced everything to China. The town went downhill really quickly." He paused, looking at me tentatively. "I feel a little guilty about it."

He'd used *we* despite the fact that he had no involvement in the family business. Or at least that was what he'd told me.

"Thank God Murray is distracted," Beau had said, *"or he would throw his hat in the ring too."* What would make him think Murray wanted to be involved in the family business?

"What are those buildings?" I asked, still thinking of the argument I'd overheard earlier. "Do your brothers work for the company?"

"Textile factory. And in their heads they do."

Murray sped up, leaving the decrepit factory behind us as we entered a run-down neighborhood. Smaller, unkempt homes sat among mobile homes, with long, wild grass creeping up over the tires, all the way up to the windows.

It looked like it had once been a nice neighborhood and that all it would take to make it nice again would be some fresh paint and clearing debris from the yards. People sitting on their lawns in yellowed plastic chairs watched us drive by in our flashy car, their eyes narrowing in disgust.

I resisted the urge to sink down in the leather seat and hide my face. I was embarrassed to be involved in such an exorbitant display of wealth as Murray drove through this neighborhood—a neighborhood that Murray admitted his family had ruined. If the Sedgemonts had so much wealth, surely they could do something kind with it, something helpful. Instead, they spent it on flashy parties and cars that cost more than every house in this neighborhood.

"What exactly happened?" I finally asked. Could the Sedgemonts really be the reason everything aside from their exclusive village was so impoverished?

Murray's eyes were glazed over as he looked out the driver's window. "Father didn't give any of the workers notice," Murray began to explain.

I gasped at the sight of something in the road, straight ahead. "Murray! Stop!" I shouted, as a man stepped into our path and we barreled toward him. The car came to a halt only inches away from the man's legs, but he didn't flinch. He stood, legs and shoulders wide in his faded blue jeans and black T-shirt. His baseball cap shadowed the top half of his face so that all that was visible was the grimace of his chapped, flaking lips.

"What the fuck?" Murray grumbled as he put the car in reverse. But the man raised his hand with a pointed finger, aimed right at us, and the command was clear. Murray shifted the car back into park and raised both hands above his shoulders to silently repeat his earlier question, *"What the fuck?"*

My heart quickened as the man lurched to my side of the car. I jammed on the lock button and the car clicked loudly again and again. He was closer now, only inches of metal and glass separating us now. I leaned toward Murray, half my body atop the center console, my seat belt clip digging into my hip.

"Roll the window down," the man barked.

"No. Who the hell do you think you are? I almost hit you, dumb ass." Murray had a fire in his voice that I wasn't familiar with.

"Get out of the car, and say that again."

We both sat there, our breath coming out in quick gasps. Murray put his hand to his seat-belt clip.

"What are you doing? Stop, Murray. Stop!" I ripped his hand away from his seat belt, and he gripped the steering wheel, his knuckles turning white and the leather creaking as he clenched his hands.

"I lost my job because of you. Our whole town can't afford to live because of your fuckin' family." The man spat on the window, and the remains of the food in my stomach curdled as the mix of saliva and chewing tobacco dripped down the glass.

My eyes were brimming with tears, and I blinked, refusing to let this man see me cry.

"Get the fuck out of here, and go back to your castle, little boy," the man snarled, his lips nearly touching my window.

Murray's hand whizzed by my head and I flinched backward as he shoved his middle finger toward the man, unshaken and confident. He knew this man couldn't hurt him, that because of his family if he even so much as breathed on Murray, the Sedgemont lawyers would be on this man like vultures on a carcass.

The man was screaming, spittle and fists beating against my window, and I was fully crying now, whimpering with each thump of his knuckles. Murray put the car into drive and stomped on the gas, the car lurching as the engine growled. My heart pounded wildly, adrenaline electrifying every cell in my body as I tried to calm my breath.

We drove away, Murray fuming as I tried to stop crying.

"Murray, slow down," I said through tears.

Murray eased off the accelerator. "I'm sorry," he said. "People like that just make me so angry."

People like that. I wondered if he meant aggressive people or people without money.

"It's okay." I held my hand out in front of the center console, and he took it in his. I was glad he did it quickly so he didn't see that my hand was shaking.

Murray drove us back to the house. He took extra turns and drove so slowly that I could tell he was delaying our inevitable return to the estate, but I didn't say a word.

11

FOR DINNER, BEATRICE had shuffled our former seating arrangement to accommodate Beau joining us. I sat directly across from Mary Margaret, who had the pleasure of sitting next to Murray while I was stuck next to Lyle. Oddly, there was an additional empty seat at the table.

I'd been taking fortifying sips of wine to try to chase away the awkward energy in the dining room, and I welcomed the familiar warmth in my stomach, the buzz of alcohol spreading through my body.

"What did you two get up to today?" Lyle asked us.

"Murray drove me around and gave me the lay of the land," I said.

"Did you see the factories?" Lyle asked me.

I paused, confused by the excitement in his voice. "Yes."

"You wouldn't believe how much the Sedgemonts have done for this town," Lyle said. "And for the towns surrounding us, to be quite frank." He took a sip of his drink, wetting his tongue for more gossip.

"How so?" I asked, actually listening now. What could he say that would convince me after all the evidence otherwise?

"Well, just take old William. He's a prime example. He used to work in the Sedgemonts' old textile factory for years and years, as did his daddy and his daddy before him. Well, when the factory came under hard times, Bill, as the townsfolk used to call him, lost his job. The Sedgemonts took pity on him and took him on as help around the house. And that's how Bill became William. It's just a shame that people in town treat him differently now. Poor man."

Came under hard times? Murray had said they'd sold the factories, but he hadn't said the factories were struggling. If a factory needed financial help, the Sedgemonts surely had enough to help one of their own factories— their own employees. And how sickening to force an employee to change his name.

"Why was the factory struggling?" I asked.

"And Gloria," he continued, ignoring my question. I swore that every person I'd met this trip didn't even hear me speak. It was like they were talking to a mirror. "She never worked in the factories, but her husband did."

Husband? Beatrice had said she didn't have a family of her own.

Lyle droned on. "Needless to say, things took a turn for them when he lost his job at the factory. Thank the Lord they never had children, because when he . . . well, he's in a better place now."

My stomach dropped. Had Gloria's husband killed himself because of the Sedgemonts shutting down the factory? The Sedgemonts had made it seem like Gloria and William owed a great debt to the family for being treated and paid so well. But the reality might be the opposite—the Sedgemonts may have been using a high salary and a free room in a fancy house to pay them off. Keep them prisoner.

"I'm sorry to pry, but what happened to the factory?" I asked again.

"Did I hear the word *factory*?" I flinched as Beatrice's voice chimed from the head of the table. "This is no time for business talk, Lyle. Don't get this poor girl all wrapped up in your economical whimsies."

"Of course, Beatrice," he capitulated. "My apologies."

"Bootsie, who is the extra seat for?" Mary Margaret asked.

"Just a family friend. He's a very busy man—works magic with our finances, so he's always caught up in meetings. He's surely being wined and dined by the Fitzsimmons or the Rutherfords this evening, but should be arriving at some point tonight to stay until the party. We're saving him a seat just in case he can make it."

Beatrice drew the conversation back to herself, and dinner progressed without any dramatics from the twins or off-color comments from Lyle. Conversation was easy, although I was mostly just listening in, and it felt like no time at all had passed when William began bringing in dessert—mango-basil vacherin, whatever that was. William set the elaborate dish in front of me, and I was busy restraining myself from diving in when Phillip tapped his wineglass with his knife.

We all gave him our attention except the twins, who scowled down at their empty drinks. Phillip forcefully cleared his throat, and they conceded, fixing their eyes on him. They radiated tension, and I felt like a bomb was about to go off.

"This is such a special night, with our closest friends and family—including our newest member—that I felt it was an apt time for an announcement," Phillip said proudly. "It is with great pleasure that I announce my retirement."

Mary Margaret and Lyle gave an encouraging coo. The twins' eyes were alight, and they both leaned forward expectantly, with their elbows on the table. Emmett wiped the corner of his mouth and straightened his back.

"I cannot think of anyone more suited to take over this company," Phillip said with glistening eyes. "Everyone, please congratulate the new head of Sedgemont and Company, Beau Andersen."

My eyes flicked to Murray, whose lips were slightly parted in shock. He met my eye and mouthed, "Uh-oh." He leaned back and watched his brothers, waiting for them to explode. He looked like he was enjoying himself.

We all applauded Beau, who flashed a bright white smile at us while the twins stared daggers at him. Their cheeks were flushed with rage and embarrassment. This must have been what the argument was about, I realized.

Beau stood and began to thank the Sedgemonts, when a shrill alarm screeched its interruption. Everyone looked around in shock and annoyance. Mary Margaret and I pressed our hands against our ears.

"What is going on?" Phillip roared over the alarm.

Mary Margaret leaped from her chair and nestled herself between Lyle and Beau, her fingers gripping tightly on both their shoulders. Lyle frankly looked more scared than she did.

Murray stood, positioning himself between my chair and the doorway. "You okay?" he peered down at me, his forehead wrinkled with concern.

I nodded shakily.

The twins were still incandescent with envy but now had an amused smirk on their faces. They were clearly pleased that Beau's golden moment had been ruined. Beatrice, on the other hand, was completely stoic—nearly unreadable except for the slight twitch at the corner of her perfectly painted lips.

William rushed out of the room, Phillip and Beau following close on his heels. Mary Margaret protested weakly, urging them to stay and call the police, but she soon gave up and took a seat in Beau's chair, next to her husband, wringing her hands in her lap. Moments later the noise stopped, but the ringing in my ears remained, high and whining.

Phillip appeared in the doorway and said, "Everything's okay—we're just checking something." He disappeared again.

Emmett finished the last of his drink and pointed at Murray. "You two should be pissed about this too."

Murray said, "I don't want anything to do with this."

At the same time I asked, "Why?"

"If Beau takes over, we've lost all bargaining power in the company. You can kiss any future involvement goodbye."

Phillip and Beau stormed into the room, with William close on their heels.

"Someone has gotten past the gate," Phillip announced.

A chorus of questions erupted. *What? How? Who?*

Phillip held up his hand. "We have them on camera, and we don't know where they are now, but the house is secure. There's nothing to worry about. They can't get in." Without another word he left the room.

"Would anyone like more wine?" William offered, and unsurprisingly most of us accepted.

We drank our wine, pretending to be consumed by our forced conversations, but tension lingered as we eagerly awaited Phillip and Beau's return. Kennedy dragged his finger around the rim of his crystal wineglass, the high-pitched hum becoming the underlying tone of our conversations. Eventually, Beatrice gave him a look, then smiled at him sweetly when he stopped.

Maybe ten minutes passed before Beau and Phillip returned.

Emmett turned around in his chair. "What's the deal—"

Phillip raised a hand, wordlessly shushing his son, who immediately turned back around and looked down at his plate.

Kennedy blushed as if he were the one who'd been silenced. He glared at his father and Beau. "What happened?" His tone was prodding and sharp.

"None of this concerns you," Phillip said.

"It kinda does since this is my house too," Kennedy sniped back.

"You inhabit this space, but this is not your house," Phillip said through gritted teeth.

The twins snorted in unison. Kennedy threw his napkin down on the table. "Got it. Not my house. Not my family business. What, are you gonna write this dickhead into the will? You already turned the business over to him—why not the property too?"

"Don't speak to your father like that," Beau demanded.

"Who the fuck do you think you are? With everything we know, you should tread lightly," Kennedy said. He stood quickly, his chair teetering backward before William grabbed it, resting it back on the floor. Kennedy stormed out of the room and Emmett followed calmly behind, the air of resignation thick around him.

Beau watched the twins leave with a smug grin. He said something under his breath to Phillip, who gave a huff of laughter through his nose and took a gulp of his wine.

"Alright," Phillip said, placing his napkin back in his lap. "Shall we continue?"

We began to eat our desserts, and there was a cacophony of scraping forks and gulps of sweet wine while conversations sparked back up, the energy in the room slowly returning to normal.

Despite the sense of normalcy, I also sensed something else as soon as the twins left, something that seeped out of the pores of everyone in the room.

It was relief.

* * *

As I lay in bed, body heavy under the thick down comforter, I couldn't find sleep. No position was comfortable as I tossed and turned from my side to my back, and even into a ball with my face buried deep in my pillow. My brain was restless, and tiny pinpricks of energy jolted through my legs and arms. It was late into the night, probably three AM by now, but I was utterly restless.

My legs were hot, so I threw the covers off, my skin rippling as the cold air washed over me. No matter what room or time of day, this house was freezing cold. I couldn't imagine the energy bills. Not like the Sedgemonts cared about that kind of thing, though.

My eyes slowly adjusted to the dark room as I swung my legs over the side of the bed. I could barely make out the shadows of the looming furniture, and I shuddered at the open closet doors, pulled aside like a grimace showing the dark depths of its mouth.

I stood and walked to the window, drawing back the heavy curtains. Moonlight spilled inside, casting a blue tint over the room, making all the lurking shapes friendly and unassuming. My cardigan was draped over the armchair, and I pulled it on, rubbing the goose bumps from my arms.

My body propelled me, unthinking, to the door. With a deep breath, I put my hand on the doorknob and opened the door.

I was going to see Murray.

The hallway was dim, and I shivered with adrenaline. Someone was snoring, probably one of the new guests who had wandered in sometime after dinner, without an intro- duction. The house was full of sleeping bodies, but I could still feel the energy of someone stirring deep within the house. Was someone lurking around like me?

The thick runner was soft against my bare feet as I carefully avoided the bare, creaking floorboards. I made my way down the stairs, moonlight beaming down through the glass-domed ceiling. The effect was mesmerizing— dust particles moving through the air drifted like snow, but in the wrong directions, moving left to right and rising to the top.

When I got to the second floor, I paused at the sound of a creak above me. Careful footsteps were sneaking down the staircase, and I dipped into the dark shadow at the entrance to Phillip's office and pressed my back into the corner, holding my breath as the footsteps got closer.

Mary Margaret appeared in the blue light of the moon, wrapped in a satin robe that drifted behind her as she moved purposefully through the house, showing the bare skin of her thighs.

My breath hitched with worry that she would see me, but she moved past me without noticing, further into the depths of the dark hallway. I waited a moment, trying to remember who was staying in that wing of the house. I believed it was the twins and Murray, and perhaps Beau, who had drunk too much at dinner to drive home. Her bedroom was certainly not there, as I had passed it on the third floor when leaving my room, Lyle's booming snore rattling the doorknob.

When I was sure she was gone, I emerged from the shadow and tiptoed in the opposite direction from Mary Margaret.

The doors were all the same, but I'd made a point to count the doors so I didn't walk in on some unsuspecting guest. Murray's was door number five on the right.

I knocked lightly, my knuckles barely making a noise against the thick, dark wood. There was a rustle inside, and I stood there waiting, shivering with anticipation of seeing him. I knocked again, but instead of waiting, I cracked open the door and stuck my head inside. Murray was a night owl, and as expected, he was in bed, his phone casting a circle of light around him like some sort of technological campfire.

He snapped his head to me in surprise and quickly rose from bed. His face was tense with surprise, but his smile became wide and playful when he realized it was me. "What are you doing?" he said when he got to the door.

"I couldn't sleep." I pushed my way past him and sat on his bed, wrapping myself in a blanket that was balled up at the foot of the bed. "You'll never believe who I saw skulking around the house in the dark."

"What, just like you?"

I grinned. He was right. Maybe Mary Margaret wandering through the house was innocent—a trip to the bathroom or to the kitchen to get water. Or maybe she was like me, sneaking through the house to go meet someone. But whom?

He sat on the bed with me and slipped his hand under the blanket to rub my feet. "I'm sorry about keeping things from you," he said, his voice soft and low.

"I think I get it." I paused. It was true—I really did understand why he'd remove himself from his family. But the secrecy of it still hurt. His apology was like a salve, and I was grateful for it. "It's okay."

His phone sat idle on the bed while we whispered, the screen still radiating light. I was overcome by the absurd romanticism of it, our faces close and aglow with the soft light of what appeared to be Twitter. It was a makeshift candle, a private dinner for two. Time for just us.

Our murmurs drifted to a stop, words no longer needed as we looked at one another. A charge was building between us, intensifying with each silent second passing.

His hand rushed to my neck and his lips crashed into mine. The charge had overflowed, the excess had nowhere to go.

My lips throbbed at the force of his kiss, a soft tenderness soon replaced by a rough eagerness. When he pulled away, I raised a fingertip to my lips and touched where his stubble had rubbed against my flesh, the contrast of the coarse hair against his smooth lips pleasant.

Our eyes were on each other, our bodies still separated by a gap that felt like miles. The silence was electric between us, saying more than we could with words. His eyes were glassy with lust, but his eyebrows were knitted together. He looked worried, almost repentant.

I understood.

Crawling forward onto the bed, I knocked his phone out of the way with my knees. I needed to be closer to him. Show him it was okay. That we could feel like home wherever we were together.

I reached for his face, and he met me halfway, our lips and teeth colliding, hands moving hastily, trying to take it all in. This was a stolen moment—something we knew we shouldn't be doing. The illicitness of it sent a thrill through me, a part of my brain awakening that I used to feed with bad behavior. It wasn't the time or the place, but our bodies drew each other in, nonetheless.

He pushed me onto my back, and I was grasping at him, clawing into his body, desperate for the feeling of home to be closer to me. The loneliness and worry that had been sitting heavy in my chest was distant now, replaced by the warm aching between my legs.

Our breath was heavy and quick as we gripped at each other's skin like it was the first time, our fingers digging into each other's soft flesh as though any distance between us would be anguish.

His breath was hot and wet in my ear. "I love you," he said, and the words made my flesh ripple down my neck, all the way from my ear to deep into my belly.

I breathed him in, taking in the smell of him like I hadn't had oxygen for days. He smelled clean, but also of the woods on a cold morning—natural and wild. I never cared much about smell until I met him. Now I wanted to bottle it up, huff it in search of the high I felt now, electric shocks jolting through my body.

"I love you too," I began to say, but the words were muffled as a moan escaped my lips. He placed his hand over my mouth, not threatening in its act of silencing me.

It felt right, as if no one else deserved to hear the sound but him.

Some distant part of my brain not driven by desire heard a creak in the distance, but we continued, heat building between our bodies like fire.

He kept his hand pressed tenderly to my lips and between our panting breaths, I swore I heard the sound of slow, deliberate breaths outside the door.

CHAPTER

12

THE SYNTHETIC TANG of setting spray made me recoil
as I spritzed it over my freshly made-up face. It was
going to be a long night, and I needed my mask of makeup
to last. I'd painted on a lipstick smile and intended to
make it convincing.

Just make it through tonight.

Tonight was just like any other party, I told myself, but
as I stood to face the metallic gown in the closet, I knew it
was a lie. I took out the dress and caressed the intricate
beading. It was so beautiful, too beautiful for someone like
me to wear. I dug my fingernails into it, wanting to rip out
the stitching and wander down in my robe instead.

I untied my robe and paused in front of the mirror,
studying my naked body. I admired the floral tattoo
that snaked up from my upper thigh to my ribcage and
wondered what the Sedgemonts would think of me if
they knew what was etched into my skin, hidden
beneath my clothes. I slipped my dress on, struggling to
slide the zipper up my back and fasten it at my neck. I
rushed to the mirror, desperate to see if I looked anything like myself.

My hair was swept to the side, the curls I'd spent an hour crafting, soft and romantic. I'd initially put on the flashy necklace Beatrice had given me, but had soon replaced it with the warped gold pendant I always wore. My hair and makeup were just how I liked them—as low-key as possible. Manufactured effortlessness. Everything was to my liking. Except the dress.

It hugged my body tight along every inch, showing off each curve in a way that I wasn't used to. The jut of my hip bones peeked out of the fabric. I wished I'd brought some sort of shapewear to blur the curves of my body under this unfamiliar gown—to act as a barrier between me and the dress I was being forced to wear. I had to admit that it was flattering. But to anyone who knew me—actually knew me—it was clear I'd never pick this for myself. I looked like a discount Disney princess.

I pulled out my phone to text Murray. We'd agreed to let each other know when we were ready, and have a stiff drink beforehand to soften the edges.

Cinderella has arrived . . . :(

My dress's beaded fabric scratched against itself as I sat down in the armchair, setting my teeth on edge. The already-tight fabric was even more constricting sitting down, and as it dug into my underarms and hips, I gave up and stood, beginning to pace. While I waited for Murray, I made my rounds through various social media apps on my phone.

As friends' Instagram photos floated by, I mindlessly liked their posts and scrolled, not really paying attention. One big flick with my thumb and the screen flew by like a slot machine, and I was eager to see what I'd landed on. Hopefully an animal video. Or maybe one of those vans that people gut and make into a tiny home.

My stomach lurched when I saw it.

Jacqueline.

It was her familiar smiling face, swarmed by her wavy platinum hair that looked silver in black and white. Her mother had followed me on social media after the funeral, and each year on the anniversary of her death, she posted a photo of her daughter. There were no posts in between, as if the only thing left in her life was mourning.

Jacqueline's parents had been the only ones to speak to me at her funeral. Her brother refused to come near me. He'd stood in front of me at the service and hadn't come to the wake because he couldn't bear to be in the same room as me. I'd never even seen his face.

I tapped into the post and zoomed in on her face, holding my breath at the sight of her perfect nose that was rippled across the bridge from her smile. No matter what we did together, she'd always had that goofy smile plastered on her face.

And no matter what I told myself, I felt responsible for the fact that the only way I could see that smile was through old photos that were meted out by her family each year, like gruel.

I closed Instagram and opened my calendar. August fifteenth. I hadn't noticed when we'd received the invitation. I had been too blinded by the thrill of our good news, and I had forgotten it was the anniversary of the worst day of my life. The realization made this party even more of a sick joke.

A knock at the door made me jump. I was tired of being so skittish, and I wished for at least one hour when I could relax. That hour wouldn't come until at least tomorrow night, as I planned to get so obliterated that my hangover would destroy me for a full twenty-four hours.

"Is she here?" he said, his eyes darting around the room.

"What?" My eyebrows went up, nostrils flaring.

"Your text? Cinderella?"

He must be messing with me. "Yeah, Murray, Cinderella is here, dressed in your mother's finest," I said sarcastically.

Murray's face lit up in a grin, but he was nervous. Twitchy. He pointed at me, an awkward mix of finger guns and jazz hands. "You scared me, I didn't know if Cinderella was a code name or something."

"Uh, no. It's clearly me. I look like a fucking princess." I put my hands on my hips and puckered my lips.

"You look beautiful. Wanna go get a drink?"

"You bet your sweet little ass I do," I gave him a little pat on the pocket of his tuxedo pants. "You're very handsome in your suit. Like James Bond, but hotter."

He grinned at me and led me down the stairs.

"Wow," I muttered. The entrance hall, which before had been relatively bare, was now filled, floor to ceiling, with greenery and pastel flowers. Green vines wound their way up the banisters, dotted with flowers, almost as if a vortex of nature had swirled into the house with the mission of softening the hard, cold stone and dark wood. And nature had succeeded—the house looked beautiful, romantic even.

I wasn't sure how the party planners had set all this up so quickly. When I'd gone up to get ready, only the tiny glass candles had been hung all the way from the top floor ceiling, giving the room a magical atmosphere as they dangled from clear fishing line.

Although no new guests had yet arrived, there was still a frenzied thrum throughout the house as party planners and caterers bustled through the rooms, carrying food and flowers, making final changes. Beatrice stormed from the kitchen into the entrance hall, and Ricky and Sue fluttered behind her, wearing headsets.

Two young assistants listened as Ricky and Sue gave last-minute notes on one of the flower arrangements. It towered over them in a spectacular arch of white and light pink, and Ricky climbed atop a tall ladder to point out a single misplaced bloom. The arch framed a vintage velvet loveseat, and across from it a photographer was setting up a tripod.

Despite the beauty of the fully decorated home, panic crept into my body. This was more extravagant than any wedding I'd ever attended, and if this was just our engagement party, I couldn't imagine what Beatrice was going to talk us into for our actual wedding day. I wondered if my parents would be upset by the Sedgemonts' insistence that they cover the costs, but as soon as my dad met Beatrice, he would step down. Something about her was so intimidating, and I knew she could convince anyone, even my dad, to do her bidding. I glanced down at my over-the-top gown and thought of how easily she'd persuaded me to wear it.

About twenty minutes later, all the caterers were hidden away in the kitchen or behind the bar, and guests began to stream in. A waiter stood at the door in a black suit, handing out glasses of chilled champagne to entering guests, and some of them walked straight to the floral arch for photos, like celebrities at a red-carpet event.

Soon the bottom floor was full of finely dressed guests, and my head spun with introductions. At first, I tried my best to keep track of the names, but soon I found myself forgetting the second they were told to me.

A middle-aged couple greeted Murray and me, but after a moment the conversation drifted to family memories, a subject for which I obviously had nothing to add, so I stood there smiling and nodding without taking in a single word.

My phone vibrated in my clutch, and Murray was talking to someone, so I took a step back and discretely pulled it out of my handbag. I had one Instagram DM.

Don't have too much fun. We know what happens when you do.

I stared at the username, my breath halted by the muscles constricting my throat: anon20188. It was a slightly different username than for the previous messages, but I was certain it was the same person. What could they possibly get out of this? And why would they start harassing me now? My brain tried to string together reasoning—maybe I'd upset someone at work, or perhaps it could be an ex, like I'd previously thought. But all my exes were mild-mannered, and I was still in touch with most of them in a friendly, albeit distant way.

Someone said my name, pulling me into the conversation. But all I could think of was the only two options that made sense.

Either these messages were because of my engagement to Murray or because of the anniversary of Jacqueline's death.

* * *

Beatrice's stern voice tore me away from my thoughts, and I fumbled with my bag, trying to slide my phone back in. My fingers were clammy, and my body flushed with heat, but I took a deep breath and allowed her to introduce me to the couple that stood in front of me.

"This is Mayor Erstine," Beatrice said, motioning to the man as if I couldn't see him right in front of me. I plastered on a smile and shook his hand diligently.

"Cold hands," he said flatly.

I flexed my fingers self-consciously. "Sorry—it must be my drink." I lifted my glass, and he smiled slightly, apparently endeared by a woman drinking bourbon on the rocks, as if it was some sort of skill. I'd switched from champagne to liquor and was going to regret it tomorrow, but I didn't care. He raised his own glass, topped high with amber liquid.

"I used to work with your future father-in-law before I went into politics," he said, pride making his voice a bit more theatrical. A guest to my left turned her head slightly, unabashedly eavesdropping.

"Is that right?" I asked. Truth be told, I could care less about his rise from riches and power to even more riches and power, but I'd quickly learned that sometimes the easiest thing to do was just to smile and nod. After all, if he was talking about himself, nobody could ask me pointed questions about my low-earning job or lack of money. To be fair, rich people love donating to the arts, but that's less about supporting artists and more for the tax deductions.

I wondered, though, if these people saw me as a penniless city girl working in the arts, or if all they saw was the Sedgemonts' money standing behind me like an army. Did they respect me because of it? Without it, would they even speak to me?

A ripple of laughter turned heads, interrupting the mayor's monologue. He'd begun giving me a not-so-brief history of the Sedgemonts' company, and while it was incredibly boring, I was glad that someone was finally telling me how the hell they'd made so much money from textiles. Until now, the source of their wealth had only been vaguely talked about, almost as if it were an autonomous creature of its own, locked somewhere to churn out funds and never rest.

"Phillip took over for his father when he was only twenty, in the early seventies. Can you imagine a twenty-year-old today in charge of sixteen textile factories throughout the state? And now, even more factories in China? You all would never get anything done with your Twitters and Instagrams." He smiled, flashing driftwood-colored teeth.

He paused and took a gulp of his drink, enjoying the attention he was getting. Beatrice, however, seemed to be crawling in her skin. It was clear that the talk of money made her uncomfortable, but she didn't want to interrupt the mayor.

"They were already the most powerful family in Western North Carolina, employing nearly one hundred thousand people, but when they sold those factories"—he paused, looking around at the group of people who'd slid into the conversation—"they became the richest family in all of the Carolinas."

"Tim, you've always been one to exaggerate," Beatrice said.

The mayor glanced at a woman who was calling his name, a petite woman with a chic brown bob. She was surrounded by a group of impatient-looking people, as if this were a meeting that the mayor was late for, instead of a party.

"Duty calls. Must make the rounds," he said and walked away without another word.

The group quickly broke up, and Beatrice began to wind me throughout the room, darting from new face to new face, like a show pony.

"Let's top up our drinks," she whispered to me after one particularly dull conversation with one of their company's shareholders. "I always need a stiff martini after talking to that dolt." I enjoyed the mischief behind her eyes, but I was still on guard.

We arrived at the bar, bumping into Phillip, who was ordering another gin and tonic. Beatrice interrupted. "Make that just a tonic," she said to the bartender. Phillip jumped, turning to face us. His cheeks were flushed a ruddy red, and he had a sparkle in his eye that I had yet to see.

"Oh, I didn't see you there!" he said. "Silly me." He took his tonic water and walked back into the crowd, his gait loosened with gin.

"He can be a lush sometimes, but at least he's harmless," she said.

I couldn't help but laugh at her loosened lips, and smiled as I ordered our drinks while she greeted more guests. As I waited at the bar, I noticed that the volume in the house had gradually grown louder, the air thicker. These perfectly coiffed guests were starting to become a bit untethered, their smiles more genuine. Maybe the night wouldn't be so bad after all. Parties could be weird until people had polished off a few drinks.

The bartender handed me our drinks, and I walked away with Beatrice, each of us sipping our cocktail like it was medicine.

"Beatrice, can I ask you a question?" I asked in a surprisingly confident voice. I'd been questioning whether I should ask or not, and let the words spill out without additional thought.

"Go on, dear," she said, turning to me. Her blue eyes were trained on mine, and while her face was soft, her eyes were sharp and wary.

"How did you have the invitations ready if Murray hadn't told you we were engaged yet?"

The softness in her face disappeared. "Guests should never peer behind the curtain. It takes the magic out of the moment, dear." Her voice was saccharine, and the contrast of it to her expression was eerie.

"Yes," I said, "you're right. Of course." I took a gulp of my drink as she watched me.

"Perfect." She placed a hand between my shoulder blades, and I shivered as her cold hands touched my bare skin. She pressed against me, ushering me forward. Her fingers crept up my back and stopped on the clasp of my necklace.

We came to a screeching halt, and she spun me around, eyeing my appearance. Her eyes landing on my necklace, and my hand reflexively floated to it. "I really wish you'd left off that tawdry charm and worn what I selected. I don't get my jewels out for just anyone. But oh well. Here, another guest for you to meet."

Beatrice motioned to the front door, at two women about my age, both beautiful in their own way. One had a face like a picture-book character, her proportions almost whimsical in their exaggeration. Her wide eyes swept around the room, confident and commanding as she batted her long lashes. The other woman was more mysterious, with gothic styling, but the self-assured aura and demeanor of an heiress. Beatrice waved them over, her gesture subtle but commanding.

"Cindy Lockwood, my love." Beatrice beamed. The fairy-tale princess turned her head, her serious gaze turning into a smile, her big, light eyes sparkling with joy.

The name Lockwood sounded familiar, I thought. I fumbled through my mental notes, remembering the young woman Mary Margaret and Beatrice had mentioned the day we arrived. Unmarried and, heaven forbid, almost thirty.

"Bootsie," Cindy exclaimed, swiping a glass of champagne from a waiter in a practiced motion.

I took a sip of my drink at the same moment Cindy did, our eyes locking. She must have noticed me drain the last dregs of my drink, because she snatched another glass and handed it to me.

"Cindy, meet Kassandra," Beatrice said, performing her duties as a hostess.

"Kassandra, great to meet you," she said.

"Nice to meet you too. You can call me Kass, if you want. So, how do you know the Sedgemonts?"

"Mm," Cindy murmured, motioning to her glass with one manicured finger. "This is fantastic, Bootsie." She turned to me. "Sorry, what was that?"

"Are you a friend of Murray's? Of . . . Bootsie?" Beatrice stiffened next to me. I took my shot at the nickname, and she clearly did not approve. Oh well, worth a try.

"Well," Cindy said, taking another drink. Her glass was already close to empty. "I'm Mur's ex-girlfriend."

13

*M*UR. The nickname I whispered into his ear as I hugged him before work, my coffee breath disgusting, but he didn't care. I'd never heard anyone else call him that before.

Until now.

He was never a nickname kind of guy and always corrected anyone who called him anything except Murray. I had special permission, he'd said.

My lips cracked at the corners with the tug of my forced smile. All my lipstick had come off with my drinks, and my lips burned with dryness. The alcohol wasn't alleviating any of that, but I couldn't help myself and took another sip. Champagne now.

It was a reflex. I didn't know what to do with my hands. Or my face. My body was completely removed from my mind, and I swore I could see myself from across the room, hunched over and bland, standing next to a gorgeous pair of women, both of them looking me up and down like they were doing me a favor by breathing the same air as me.

I wanted to look away—to run away, even. But I pushed my shoulder blades down my back and stared Cindy straight in the eye.

"It's great you're still close with the Sedgemonts," I lied. "I'm Murray's fiancée." The inflection of my voice made me recoil, the emphasis on *fiancée* too strong. But it had landed the way I wanted. Her upper lip quivered, the same as my own. She may have looked perfect, but I'd made a tiny crack in the veneer.

"Ohh," she said, dragging out the word to feign an epiphany. "You're *the* Kassandra Baptiste from the invitation."

It's not like there are many Kassandras, I thought. But I played along, "That's me. I go by Kass, though."

"How special. You must be thrilled—you both deserve all the happiness in the world," she said, her voice creamy and sweet, her smile pageant perfect.

The phrase made my heart skip a beat, and I forced another smile onto my face. My teeth gnashed together, grinding under the effort.

"You don't deserve happiness."

The message appeared in my mind, the gray, faceless icon of the anonymous sender filling my mind.

I studied her face, searching it for any hint of malice—a twitch, a grimace. But she was a picture of composure, her flash of a red lip framing her perfectly straight, white teeth.

Her hair was strawberry blond, pulled up to the crown of her head in a loose, elegant chignon that was fastened by a sparkling pin. Her skin glowed in the soft lighting, and I was becoming more self-conscious by the minute. It struck me in that moment that she looked like a younger version of Beatrice.

I smoothed my dress over my stomach, wanting to peel the expensive, itchy fabric off my skin and leave. I felt like a finely decorated husk of a human, here only for show, the audience not caring about what was under the veneer.

Cindy waved to another young woman, and now I stood alone. Beatrice had wandered away, engrossed in a conversation. Cindy was now standing with a woman in a long backless dress who hadn't bothered to introduce herself. Her hair fell down her bare back in thick, glossy waves like a Hollywood starlet from the 1940s.

"Cinderellie, you look so good!" the woman cooed. "Bathroom time?"

The pair wandered off, heads turning as they walked through the room. They didn't make it two feet before a group of men stopped them, clamoring for attention.

Cinderellie. I resisted the urge to roll my eyes and forced myself to regain control. The withering heat of anger built in my body as I wondered why Beatrice had invited Murray's ex-girlfriend to our engagement party. The alcohol wasn't helping, and I felt like soon I would combust if I didn't get out of here.

Cindy bounced from group to group, slowly but surely making her way to Beatrice's Blue Room. She moved about the room with a practiced grace, her beautiful face turning left and right to greet the other guests. I couldn't keep my eyes off her, but the jealousy in the pit of my stomach begged me to look away.

I never wanted to be the center of attention at this party—I didn't even want this party in the first place—yet as my future in-laws and the other guests fawned over her like *she* was the one getting engaged to Murray, unexpected waves of envy roiled in my chest.

I took a sip of my champagne and held it in my mouth, letting the bubbles roll over my tongue until it became flat, before I swallowed with a grimace.

The funny thing was that Murray didn't even seem to realize she was here. I tried to exhale the jealousy, expelling it like rot from my lungs. He was the only one who mattered, I reminded myself. None of it mattered. Not as long as we had each other.

I scanned the room for him until I finally found him. He was beaming at a fabulously dressed woman in her seventies. I caught his attention, and the woman gave me a delighted wave and excused herself to speak to another guest.

He made his way through the crowd to me and rested his hand on my lower back. "May I?" he said dramatically with a flourish of his hand toward the dancing guests. He was clearly enjoying himself, and it soothed my anxiety.

"But of course," I accepted, mirroring his theatricality.

We moved into the crowd of couples, and I rested my hands on his shoulders as the band began to play swing music.

"How the hell do you dance to this?" I asked, looking around as the other guests began to spin and swing around one another. "Oh God."

"Just swivel around," he said with a laugh. "You look beautiful."

See, I reminded myself, *he doesn't care about Cindy. I shouldn't care about her either.*

"Thank you," I said. "You look quite pretty yourself."

"Are you having a good time?"

"Oh!" I squeaked in surprise as a couple bumped into us, pushing me into Murray so forcefully that we almost knocked heads.

"Oops. These new Manolos are a bit slippery," Cindy said with a sparkling smile. Her dance partner swung her around, and they disappeared among the dancing guests.

"Ignore her," he grumbled. "I have no idea why Mother invited her. I saw you talking to her earlier. Did she tell you who she is?" His mouth twitched at the corner.

"She most definitely did. I can't say I'm surprised you're no longer together. Why did you break up?" I surprised myself by asking. Maybe I should slow down on the drinks.

"She cared more about money than actual human connection. She's not like you—she doesn't care about people the way you do."

"You're sweet." I kissed his cheek and tried to be present in the moment, even though I knew people were watching us.

The song ended, transitioning into a calm waltz. Murray pulled me closer, and I began to nestle into him when his father tapped him on the shoulder.

"So sorry, Murray, but could you come say hello to an investor? He's about to leave, and I want you to meet him."

It was a bit odd that Phillip would interrupt our dance just to introduce him to some investor. Murray would probably never speak to this man again since he himself had no involvement in the company.

"Sorry, sweetie. You should go grab some food. Keep up your energy for another dance." He smiled encouragingly before being pulled away by his father.

I watched the crowd, trying to determine the easiest way to get to the dining room without having to be introduced to another family friend.

Cindy was dancing closely with a new dance partner, but she was watching Murray and Phillip walk through the crowd. She had a princess-perfect face, but something about her eyes looked hard and cold, like she had her sights set on one thing, and nothing else mattered. It was clear she still had feelings for Murray, I realized as dread flooded over me.

Cinderella, I thought, now remembering Murray's strange reaction to me when he first saw me in my dress.

Before the party, I had jokingly texted him that Cinderella had arrived, meaning me in this ridiculous gown. Instead of him showing up with a smile, he looked like a criminal on the run from the police at the accidental mention of her.

Cindy.

My teeth gnashed together with jealousy. He had been thinking of her earlier. Had he known she was invited, and not warned me?

It was like I was on the outside of a joke, but I was the punch line.

Surely he wouldn't do that to me.

There had to be a harmless explanation to Beatrice inviting Murray's ex-girlfriend.

I just wasn't sure if that explanation was going to be the truth.

* * *

I stood in the corner of the dining room, my glass of champagne thick with condensation and dripping down onto my hand. I wanted to stay by Murray's side and was growing increasingly unsettled with all the guests who stopped me to introduce themselves.

I remembered perhaps names of the first five people when we were introduced, but after that, I found I'd completely stopped listening the moment their names left their lips. Maybe that made me an asshole as I stood here at this party meant to celebrate our engagement, when meanwhile I couldn't even be bothered to listen to people's names.

But would they even remember my name? No, likely not. Soon I would just be Mrs. Murray Sedgemont to them. Even if I decided to keep my surname, that wouldn't matter either. *Mrs. Murray Sedgemont.* The noise of it ricocheted in my head, and I was astonished by the bitter taste it left in my mouth. I knew I wasn't upset with Murray, but the idea of these people lumping my identity in with his—with this family—made me flush with stubborn anger.

This wasn't me. This party, this house, the fancy hors d'oeuvres.

I won't be taking his last name, I suddenly decided. This whole charade was the final nail in the coffin. When we got home, we would have a *real* celebration. One with lukewarm Pabst Blue Ribbon tallboys, Zoey's dry vegan cookies, and overly strong weed.

The thought of it gave me a pang in my chest of utter, hopeless homesickness. I wanted the city. I needed my friends.

I unclasped my bag and took out my phone, thumbing out a quick text to Zoey.

"You'll never guess who his mom invited. His EX!"

In almost an instant, she began texting me back. She was the type to leave her phone on silent under a couch cushion for a week, but if one of her friends was going through something big, like being introduced to their future in-laws, she was always on-call and ready. God, I missed her.

WTF? Drop the address. I just need a word with this Sedgemont woman. 🐱 🔪

I typed back a skull emoji and three little knives and turned to the bar. I'd told myself to slow down, but I desperately needed another drink. Something stronger than my champagne, which I promptly downed in one gulp. The bubbles fought their way back up, burning my throat.

The bar was fully stocked, and the caterers had brought in tall shelves to display the expensive bottles that guests downed without any consideration of the cost. Guests were even leaving half-drunk glasses scattered about, never to be returned to. What a waste.

"What can I get you?" one of the four bartenders asked me as he brandished a cocktail shaker with a flourish. The brass cap of the shaker matched the brass and glass liquor shelves, and I couldn't help but applaud Beatrice's attention to detail. She might be completely over the top, but she did it well.

"Blanton's, please," I asked a little too breathlessly, and watched him pour my bourbon.

I lifted my drink in thanks and turned back to the crowd of people. I took a deep breath, holding it full in my chest before taking a gulp of my drink. I exhaled the fumes after I swallowed. It seemed like a crime to drink such an expensive bourbon so quickly, but it was my silent middle finger to Beatrice and everyone here who had given me a sideways glance tonight.

People passed by, some of them whirring like traffic, others circling the room like vultures. Some of the faces were recognizable, but there were still so many I hadn't met yet. I tried to remember how many people Beatrice had invited. Was it two hundred? I wondered how many had actually showed up.

A flash of familiar platinum-blonde hair stopped me in my tracks, and I wobbled as my heel caught the hem of my dress. I glanced down and yanked it out from under me, not caring about the sound of ripping fabric. I was too lost in memories to care.

My eyes searched for the person who had caught my attention. I shuffled away from the bar and into the formal dining room, where guests buzzed around the food.

The familiar warmth from the bourbon I'd tossed back rushed through me. It seemed I wasn't the only one growing hot with drink. Suit jackets were slowly being removed, and faces were growing flushed with liquor and dancing.

As I entered the room, I spun around wildly, searching for the woman I'd glimpsed. Then I spotted her. It wasn't Jacqueline at all—of course it wasn't, it couldn't be—but an older woman with snow-white hair that fell down her back in soft waves.

Still, the fantasy I'd conjured that she was here on the anniversary of her death left me shaken. I needed a breath of fresh air, or maybe the opposite.

Through the French doors, I eyed a group of guests standing outside, smoking cigarettes and talking. With a huff, I made my way to them, eager for a rush of nicotine to dull my senses that were too sharp. Too punishing.

"Where are you going, dear? I have some more guests I would like you to meet," a voice said from behind me. I flinched as a bony hand grasped my shoulder.

I turned to face Beatrice, her hand still clutching me as I whipped around. Her fingers dug in deeper as I tried to step back. Not enough to hurt. Just enough to make it clear who was in charge.

"I was just going to—"

"Come with me," she interrupted. "I realize it might be overwhelming, but there's a certain decorum we must follow as hosts. I have a rather long list of people I need you to meet—people who have done our family well in the past."

It was odd to me that Mur and I weren't being introduced together. Us being constantly separated added another tally to my theory that this party wasn't to celebrate our engagement, but just an excuse to show off and get drunk.

She ushered me to a group of unfamiliar faces for the hundredth time this evening. I hadn't enjoyed it the first time, then grew tired, but now I was numb to it.

Show me off, I thought. *Paint me how you want. I don't care anymore.*

"Janice, dear," Beatrice parked me in front of a tall, foreboding woman. She towered over the others she was talking to, and her black pantsuit looked stiff enough to cut someone if they got too close. "This is Kassandra Baptiste. Kassandra, this is Janice Becker, district attorney and old friend."

Janice raised her glass in greeting, and I muttered something in response. I wasn't even sure what was escaping my mouth at this point. All conversations were blurring together, and I was growing certain that I would be stuck in this time loop forever.

"Murray has told me about you and your feminist friends, so who better for you to meet than the most powerful woman in Western North Carolina?"

I laughed despite the barb in her voice as she spat out the word *feminist*. Janice had a curious expression on her face. She was studying me.

"Tell us about yourself, Kassandra," she instructed.

I told her about my work, living in the city, my engagement to Murray.

"I studied law at Columbia. A bit before your time, but I did work in the city briefly after I graduated. What was that—maybe five or six years ago? I loved the city when I was young, but I doubt I'll ever live there again."

We talked for a few minutes about our favorite restaurants in the city and the shows she should see if she were to visit again. As I spoke, her focus on me was intense, and while I appreciated that she was actively listening to me— one of the only guests to do that so far this evening—her gaze gradually became hardened.

When I finished speaking, she didn't ask me another question like she had before, and the conversation came to a screeching halt. I stood awkwardly, raking my tongue along the back of my teeth.

The heavily pregnant woman next to her took pity and asked, "So, Kassandra, do you intend to move to North Carolina?"

I had to repress the urge to laugh. The state itself was beautiful, but the thought of being closer to Murray's family and farther from mine made me itch with anxiety. "I hadn't considered the possibility yet," I lied.

The woman began to speak, understanding, but eager to brag about the beauty of her hometown. Janice interrupted and the woman's smile faltered. She took a nearly imperceptible step backward, and Janice's daunting form towered over her. "I swear I know you from somewhere," Janice said.

"I don't think so, unless we saw each other in passing in the city." Her eyes were narrowed, but her deep brown eyes remained piercing.

She crossed her arms. "You ever been in trouble with the law?"

"What?"

The long summer of investigations came to mind, along with the police interviews that centered around me but had somehow also passed me by. The police had interviewed me a handful of times, drawn out over the course of my junior year at NYU.

The first interview had been the longest thirty minutes of my life. I could still feel myself shivering in the doorway of my student housing, with my roommates standing close behind me, waiting for me to crumble like support beams on a ruined, collapsing home. None of my friends ever questioned me. They rallied behind me, helping me get back on my feet and return to a normal life.

I thought of the weeks I'd spent talking to police and grimaced as the image of the detective entered my mind. All the nights I'd spent answering questions about where I'd been that night, what I'd been doing. About my relationship with Jacqueline and the men we'd been spending time with. The people we'd been using just so we could use.

The people surrounding me looked mildly amused except for one man. He stood tall above the rest of the guests, and his hand rested gently on the pregnant woman's lower back. His skin glistened with drink and the heat of the room, but his eyes were sobered with focus as he studied me.

Janice's serious expression broke, and she barked out a laugh, giving me a playful shove on my shoulder. Her skin was fiery warm and knocked me off balance. I tried to mirror a playful expression, but the question had dredged up the feeling of panic and dread that I'd buried after all these years.

I laughed off the question, forcing a smile. I gripped my drink so hard that the glass might crack at any moment.

The messages I'd been receiving had sent me over the edge of paranoia.

"Would anyone like a refill?" I asked.

"How sweet of you," Janice said, and I was relieved for the lighter tone. "I don't need one, but your glass is empty. Better go top that off."

I smiled back and walked toward the bar. Once I knew Janice wasn't paying me any attention, I turned in the opposite direction and skirted around the edge of the crowd.

14

I NEEDED TO BREATHE. The bodies swarming around me were increasingly warm, heat rolling off their intoxicated bodies as they danced and meandered through the house. I pushed my way past a group of men animatedly talking about cryptocurrency and a young couple kissing against the wall, and made my way to the Blue Room. I'd found solace in that bathroom before and felt drawn to the space.

Although the Blue Room wasn't closed off to guests, it seemed that almost everyone sensed the power emanating from the room, as if Beatrice had marked the room with the scent of her perfume, warding off most guests. I entered anyway.

"Excuse me," I said to the group standing in the doorway of Beatrice's lounge. It was three women and one man, the man clearly enjoying the heavy-handed attention he was receiving from the women. His tie was loose and his eyes were red and glassy as he looked me up and down. One of the women pursed her lips and shot daggers at me. None of them bothered moving an inch as I shuffled between them.

Although I wanted to rush to the bathroom door, I pushed my shoulders back and walked calmly, feeling the heat of their eyes on my back. It seemed like these people wanted me to be uncomfortable. I wasn't one of them, and some of the guests were making it damn well clear. But I didn't care.

The doorknob didn't budge under my grip as I tried to twist it open. It felt like someone was on the other side holding it still. I rapped on the door, and it cracked open to reveal a younger woman, probably around my age. She was the woman I'd seen earlier in the evening, floating through the house with Cindy in her black gown that served as an extension to her jet-black hair. Even her eyes were black as her pupils swallowed any color in her irises.

I let out a strangled gasp as she reached out her hand and pulled me into the bathroom by my forearm, banging my shoulder into the doorframe in the process.

"What the fuck?" I grunted when I was in the bathroom. The black-haired woman shut the door behind me and pushed me out of the way. She leaned against the door, blocking my way out, and anyone else's way in.

"Cindy, look who it is," she sneered, showing all her teeth.

I froze at the sight of Murray's ex-girlfriend sitting cross-legged, one hand holding a credit card. It hovered over a pocket mirror that was dusted with white.

"Kassie." Cindy smiled. The nickname made my stomach drop. "I knew you were the type to come looking for the real party." She began chopping up the powder, arranging it in three neat lines. One for each of us.

"I . . ." I paused, my voice gravelly. *Kassie*—the nickname set my teeth on edge, making it hard to think. "I was just trying to go to the bathroom. I didn't know you were in here."

Was she right? Could I sense it? Seek it out like a bloodhound despite leaving my past behind?

"Oh, come on. Everyone knows what's done in this bathroom during Beatrice's big soirees. Why else would she have this little seating arrangement and all that counter space? She knows what she's doing."

Cindy rolled a twenty-dollar bill up and bent over the mirror, snorting the line in one quick, seasoned movement. She delicately patted around her nostrils with her ring finger and handed the bill to her friend, who took it eagerly. She pulled her dark hair back with one hand and snorted the line, leaving one more row of fine white powder.

"Evie's a real pro," she stage-whispered, pointing theatrically at her friend. Her eyes were wide and sharp, and the sparkle that was in them when I'd first met her was now a burning hot flame. I looked away, unable to hold her gaze.

"Here you go," Evie said, holding out the bill to me. Her nails were long and crimson—the only color that stood out from her black outfit other than her pale skin.

Her hand hovered there, waiting. I was enraptured by the feeling that I'd lived this moment before. In a way, I had many times. I'd had a pale hand reach out to me with the same sweep of red nail polish, offering me a reprieve from my day.

But a reprieve from the day became a crutch. And then it all ended in a furious storm.

"No thanks," I finally said, my voice unconvincing, almost scared.

"Don't be a party pooper, Kassie," Evie said, pushing the bill closer to me.

"It's Kass," I said firmly.

Evie raised an eyebrow. I'd breached etiquette. As my friend Zoey said, if someone offers you drugs, be grateful, because they're expensive.

I blinked slowly, letting myself give into the sense of déjà vu. I could picture Jacqueline's bright hair in front of me instead of Evie's dark locks, her hand stretching out, inviting.

I reached my hand out to her, taking the rolled-up bill.

Cindy beamed. "There we go. Murray always had a soft spot for the good stuff. Figures you would too."

My cheeks twitched, battling my grimace. I'd never seen Murray do anything harder than a bong rip. He hadn't known me when I went through my party phase— if you can even call it that—and I'd confessed to him what had happened. What I'd done, or most of it. But he'd never told me he'd experimented too.

I bent over the mirror and nestled the bill into my nose. A sense of calm washed over me at the ritual of it, but beneath it pulsed a dark, frenetic excitement, like a part of me was waking up—a part of me that I'd pushed down into an artificial sleep.

Someone pounded on the door and the three of us jumped, my hand flinching and blanketing the mirror with white. Cindy letting out a little yip like a small dog.

"Just a second," she said with no trace of anxiety in her voice.

A man's voice outside mumbled, "For fuck's sake," followed by a trail of a woman's giggle as they walked away.

"Sorry, I didn't mean to," I grumbled defensively, my heart racing at the near spill of the powder. I hated hearing the words as they came out of my mouth, but for some reason I felt like I needed to appease them. Their energy was volatile, balled up in this tiny room.

Cindy picked up a credit card and tidied the powder back into a neat, straight line. With quick, practiced movements, she grabbed the bill from my hand and cleaned the mirror in one swift inhale. She licked her finger and dragged it over the mirror before sliding her finger into her mouth, puckering her lips out as to not smudge her lipstick.

She popped the compact mirror into her clutch and fumbled for a bit to close the clasp against the fullness of her purse. Evie and Cindy admired their reflections, checking for any trace of their bathroom activities.

"See ya later, Kassie," Cindy cooed as she opened the door and they sauntered out.

Standing alone in the bathroom, I listened to the muffled commotion of the party. It sounded as though I were underwater, slowly drifting further as my head clouded.

The armchair cushion sighed as I crumpled into it. I didn't want to go back out there, but the thought of Murray and Cindy mingling in the same room without me made my chest burn. It didn't seem like there was anything between them, but it sure as hell seemed like Beatrice wanted there to be.

My head drooped against the back of the armchair, and I tried to force myself to take a moment to clear my head. That's when I noticed something fallen between the cushion, wedged tightly in the depths of the cushion. I reached down to grab it and held it in front of my face. It was a little baggy, filled to the brim with white powder.

I put it in my clutch and walked back into the fray.

15

AFTER LEAVING THE bathroom, I'd intended to return to my robotic introductions, but my body had other plans. I gripped my clutch tightly to my side and walked right out the front door.

I gulped in the night air—it was less thick than during the daytime, but there was still a wet warmth to it. I welcomed it against my exposed, chilled skin.

"Hello," a man said from the edge of the front portico. He had a cigarette hanging from his lips, and the amber glow lit up his eyes. He looked at me like I was on fire.

"Hi," I said. "Can I have one of those?"

He wordlessly pulled a cigarette from his pack, trying to hold back a grin. It was hard to tell in the dark, but he appeared to be in his fifties. I hadn't yet met him, but there was a familiarity to him that I couldn't place. But perhaps that was because everyone at this party looked the same. Well-dressed, dripping in wealth, and smug.

He handed me the cigarette, and I put it between my lips.

"May I?" He flipped open an antique brass lighter, and I nodded, the designs and engravings becoming clearer as it approached. But I couldn't make out what it said.

I took a long drag and said "thank you" quietly, staring out into the night. He began to speak, but I interrupted.

"Okay, thank you very much. Bye." It was rude, but I didn't care.

There was a mumbled protest as I walked away, followed by a weak "Whatever." I kept moving.

Turning off the cobbled path, my heels began to sink into the cool grass. I tugged them off my feet and carried them in my hand—one hand gripping my clutch and shoes, the other my cigarette. I knew I looked utterly classless.

Good.

I continued around the house the way Murray had shown me yesterday. All I needed was a little air, a little time. Then I'd be fine and I could keep pretending.

The underwater lights of the pool turned the water into a lagoon of jade and turquoise, a sunken chest of precious gems. I thought about peeling off my dress and slipping in. What I really wanted was to sit in the greenhouse, to tilt my head back and blow smoke up at the stars peeking in through the glass roof. I picked up my pace, eager to get to my little hideout.

I passed a small patio that dipped down into the earth. It appeared to be an exit for the basement, perhaps Gloria's living area. I hadn't noticed it before, mostly because it was partially shrouded by stout shrubs and flowers. I could see the glow of a cell phone, but whoever was holding it was obscured.

What did Gloria and William think of all this? Were they proud of the beauty of this party and all the work they put in for this family, even after their lives were ruined by the Sedgemont business?

A twig snapped behind me. My toes dug into the grass as I waited a moment for another sound, but nothing came. Probably a deer in the woods that hugged the perimeter of the property. The light moisture on the grass had brought a chill to my body, creeping up from my feet. Whereas previously it had been cool and refreshing, now it made me clammy and shivery.

I began walking again, slower this time, my breath quiet and measured. There were no more sounds behind me aside from the murmur of the party inside, a joyful, chaotic clamoring of music and conversation. I took in the view of the estate—all the windows were lit up, even the guest bedrooms, and they twinkled against the dark, inviting but somehow boastful. Surely not every single guest left their bedroom lights on—I definitely didn't—and I wondered if Gloria and William were tasked with going through each room to light up the house like an advertisement of the Sedgemonts' success.

Despite only hearing the party, I had that distinct feeling of heat across my back like someone was staring me down. It was probably the booze swimming in my head, warming my body and twisting my thoughts, but I could feel someone—*something* near me.

I turned around just to make sure, my bare feet twisting slowly against the grass. Blades of grass broke between my toes, and my heels dug into the turf beneath me.

A swift shadow moved closer to the house. I couldn't make out anything about the shadow besides a wisp of smoke trailing behind them. I thought of the man who lit my cigarette and shivered, picking up my pace as I continued toward the greenhouse.

The path branched ahead of me, and I ventured toward the right side as the greenhouse came into view. The moon was high and full in the sky, and gave the glass an opaque quality, but as I got closer, I noticed the glass panels were fogged from the day's humidity.

There was a stirring in the air around me, and I whipped my head around, checking if anyone was behind me again. There was no one there. I turned to face the greenhouse, and my eyes glazed over as I took a deep inhale from my cigarette, which was nearing the filter. The smoke hovered in my lungs, and I let it burn and build. When it became unbearable, I exhaled, the discomfort clearing my muddled mind for a moment.

The smoke drifted in front of my face, then cleared, drifting away like morning fog. It floated upward, revealing movement inside the greenhouse. My muscles stiffened, and I worried that whoever was inside would think I was a creep standing out here motionless in the dark.

There were two dense shrubs to the right side of the greenhouse, and I darted toward them, desperate not to be seen and to smoke my cigarette in peace. I stood behind them, the burst of adrenaline sending violent shivers through my muscles.

Well done, I thought. *This isn't suspicious at all.*

I crossed my arms around myself, trying to stop the shivering, and winced as I clumsily brushed the cigarette against my bicep. I flung it away from me and watched in horror as it landed in a bed of dry mulch. I scuttled toward it, using the shoe in my hand to stomp out the ember.

I was no longer covered by the shrub. The bottom of one of the glass panels was clear, and I sucked in a breath as I made out the form of the person inside.

It took a moment for my brain to comprehend what I saw, but the person inside was unmistakable. It was Mary Margaret, her thin frame wrapped in a tight crimson dress.

She was on top of someone, her legs straddled across their lap. The fogged glass obscured the person's face, but I could tell it was a man by the contrasted black and white of his suit. I dipped down to one knee, carelessly smudging my dress with dirt.

It was dark inside and the glass was still a bit foggy, but I was absolutely certain it wasn't her husband, Lyle, based on the muscular, hairless chest exposed by the man's open shirt. Mary Margaret tilted her head back, and her mouth opened wide in a moan. Her long neck was porcelain in the moonlight.

She tilted her head to the side, letting her hair fall partially over her face. All her features were obscured except for her eyes, which were looking right at me. Her body grinded up and down on the man, her eyes trained on me.

"Fuck, fuck, fuck," I muttered under my breath as I teetered onto both feet. My head spun as I stood upright, and I tumbled out into the open, hoping the darkness was enough to obscure me from sight. Surely there was no way she could see me out here in the dark. She must have just been looking in my direction, her mind elsewhere. But what if she had?

The noises from inside were muffled, but they were clearly having a great time. I tried to soothe myself; if she had seen me, she would have frozen, but she'd kept moving like nothing happened.

I needed to get back into the house without being seen, but my limbs were clumsy, and despite the adrenaline, my vision was spinning ever so slightly.

I skirted all the way around the house, as the path to the back door was a bit darker, and I was less likely to be seen, but unfortunately it was more treacherous. The cobbled path stopped halfway there, and the landscape dipped down into a decline. I picked up my pace involuntarily, and before I knew it, my bare feet were slick with moisture, and my stupid, drunken limbs were giving out on me, and my body was sliding, slipping downward.

My tailbone smacked hard into the ground, and a pained groan escaped my lips. I tried to get up and pick up my shoes and clutch that I'd flung away from me in a last-ditch effort to regain my balance, but I toppled over, slipping this time into a prickly hedge that lined the side of the house.

The obscenities I muttered under my breath could have set fire to a church. I stood one last time, slowly and deliberately, and collected my things.

My tailbone ached, my heartbeat sending throbs of pain throughout my back every second. And that wasn't the worst of it. My forearms and cheek stung, and I raised one arm in front of me to see it covered in scratches, as though I'd fought off a pack of wild cats.

I was a mess.

*　*　*

By the time I'd made it to the back door, smokers and revelers had littered the manicured lawn with kicked-off Louboutins and half-smoked Cuban cigars.

Nobody paid me any attention except for a few men, but I was almost certain that they were so drunk that their eyeballs were simply floating in their skulls, following my form as I walked to the back door.

I passed through the open door and was greeted with a shot of body heat. The scent of stale perfume and body odor was overwhelming. Within seconds, my nose became accustomed to it, and it made me wonder what else I could get used to against my will. What was that saying? Put a frog in slowly boiling water, and it won't notice until it's too late?

I slinked my way through the raucous crowd, overhearing snippets of conversations as I passed.

"Have you seen the work she got done? She looks ten years older, not younger!"

"I remember them vacationing in Côte d'Azur during quarantine, don't you? Not a mask in sight."

"I hear she has to pay him alimony. Is that what the feminists wanted? Well, they got it."

The conversations were all different in subject, but somehow all the same. Each group was dissecting someone else's life.

I was nearing the end of the hallway, the crowded entrance hall in sight, when a large form blocked the entryway, darkening my view of the crowd.

"Did you get in a fight with a bush?" Kennedy said, not an ounce of emotion in his voice or face. He had a sheen to his skin and eyes like he was oozing alcohol, but he had a surprising amount of composure.

Lots of practice, I thought.

"No," I said, clasping my hands behind my back, trying to hide my stinging arm. Beau slunk into the hallway from the back entrance, looking disheveled. He ran his fingers through his hair and disappeared into the crowd.

"Right." Kennedy nodded, drawing out the word in disbelief. Then he just walked away, disappearing into the fold.

I moved listlessly into the same crowd, bumping into people without Kennedy's unlikely grace. Nobody seemed to notice or be bothered by it.

The volume in the house was booming. Conversations were being shouted over the music, and hoarseness rattled in everyone's voices.

Beatrice appeared out of the corner of my eye, and she drifted into view with the grace of a specter.

"Kassandra," Beatrice stood gawping at me, mouth agape. "You look positively dreadful. I'd say you were rolling around in the bushes with someone, but Murray appears to be unscathed."

Her suspicious eyes traveled over my face, as if she were waiting for me to crack and confess something terrible. She looked behind me with a raised eyebrow, and out of the corner of my eye I saw Beau crossing the entrance hall, straightening his lapel. Silently, she took me by the arm to inspect my scratches. She raised her hand and touched one bony finger to the scratch on my cheek.

"You need to clean yourself up. Go on upstairs and then come right back down." She put her hand on my back, right in between my shoulder blades. "Oh, and darling, put on the necklace I picked out for you. That one is an absolute travesty." She gave me the lightest of shoves.

At first, I let my body be propelled by Beatrice's shove; then I thought, *Screw it*, and made my way to the bar first. I ordered another bourbon while the bartender looked at me with concern.

"Oh, I'm fine. Don't worry about me, Beatrice. Thanks for asking how I am, *Bootsie*," I muttered under my breath, my teeth clasped together in anger. The bartenders cast glances at each other but continued about their business. I knew full well that I looked like a mad woman, but I didn't care. All the guests were so drunk and high that if they were looking at me, they wouldn't even remember it in the morning.

I propped myself against the bar and surveyed the room. The formerly picture-perfect elegance was in a state of chaos. Professionally done hair was limp with sweat, clinging to the necks of the town's elite as they danced wildly to the live band.

A flash of red caught my attention. It was Mary Margaret entering through the back door. Just as Beau had. She smoothed down her hair and made her way through the crowd. Her gaze was fixed on something, eyes narrowing with focus. She had the look of a woman scorned, but one who knew she couldn't show it.

I followed her gaze only to find Beau talking to the young woman who'd interrupted my conversation with Cindy earlier—the one who looked like a Hollywood starlet. They were standing close together, their hips angled so that they were nearly touching. The woman leaned in to whisper something, and her red-painted lips grazed his earlobe. Beau's fingers grazed lightly down her back.

I looked back at Mary Margaret, but she was gone.

I gave up on following the drama and went up to my room, per Beatrice's orders. I took a cotton pad out of my toiletry bag and dabbed it on my arm, wincing at the pain.

I plucked the pins from my disheveled hair and switched my part, pulling my hair to the side so it covered the scratch near my ear.

Then I tackled my arm, breaking out the green color corrector and heavy-duty foundation I used for bad break-outs. I dabbed the makeup over my scratches and set it with powder. Although I worked in set design, I'd learned a lot from observing other departments at school, picking up makeup tips and tricks that came in handy every so often.

Finally, I unlatched my battered gold pendant and slipped on the necklace Beatrice had picked out for me. As per her orders.

I stared at myself in the mirror, watching as I drained the last of my bourbon. Whenever I was at parties, I was always taken in by bathroom mirrors, unable to look away. It wasn't because I thought I was beautiful or anything like that—I wasn't really sure why it happened. It was like the alcohol loosened up my mind enough that I was able to take in the fact that the person in the reflection was *me*. That's what other people saw when they looked at me. Not the badass tough girl I pictured in my own head.

I was plain. Pretty, but just another boring white girl. With the look of someone easily manipulated, maybe.

Perhaps I wasn't as tough as my favorite pair of combat boots, and people had known that my whole life—that it's just a facade.

And maybe they were right all along.

16

As I DID my best to make myself presentable, my phone buzzed on the vanity.

The notification told me I'd been tagged in a photo. I opened Instagram and went to my notifications page, which was still littered with congratulatory comments on our engagement announcement from a few days ago. I would have to remember to go back and thank everyone. I hadn't had a moment's rest to just sit and enjoy our engagement. I wished this party could have been a few weeks later. Better yet, Beatrice and Phillip could have actually warned us that it would happen—maybe asked for our input. *Yeah right,* I thought.

When I found the photo I was tagged in, my stomach lurched.

StrawberryJacquiri tagged you in a post.

My muscles froze in fear. That was Jacqueline's username—my best friend from years ago. Bile rose in my throat, and I tapped into the photo. It was a black and white shot of Eighth Street Station. There were no people in the photo, and I could practically hear the silence followed by a deafening roar, just like back then.

I searched for other details in the photo—any ads on the walls to determine when the picture was taken. But there was nothing. All I could see was the empty train track, exposed like a metallic spine that ran under the flesh of the city.

The caption on the photo read, "This can't be buried underground."

There were no likes or comments, since it had only been posted two minutes ago. Soon, our old friends and her family would stumble on the post, confused as to who had access to her account. I'd never been able to guess her passwords, much to her family's dismay. I'd told them to contact Instagram to see if it could be taken down, but they'd balked at the possibility, wanting it to serve as some sort of permanent digital mausoleum.

But it was clear that someone had known the password all along. So why had they waited all this time to log in and post something? There was no denying that this post was directed at the lowest moment of my life. Others knew where she died, and seeing my name tagged in the photo was a blatant accusation.

My finger shook so much as I tapped my tagged username that I missed multiple times. I read the menu and pressed down hard on the option to remove myself from the post. Would whoever had access to Jacqueline's account get a notification?

For good measure I checked my notifications and messages once more. There was nothing new, only the previous anonymous messages that I'd quickly blocked.

Moments later, I found myself sickly curious to see if the subway photograph had been taken down after I'd untagged myself, or if anyone had liked or commented on it. I opened the app and tapped through to Jacqueline's profile. Her bio had been erased, only to be replaced by a single engagement ring emoji. The black and white photograph was still there, and I clicked into it to see that there were two likes: user12312 and user789. Those were the same people who'd sent me messages, I thought, my breath coming in panicked bursts now.

Two people had commented, but they appeared to be real profiles. One user simply commented three question marks and the second said, *"Wtf is this?"*

Unable to look at the photo anymore, I locked my phone. They hadn't retagged me, and I was relieved that the people who'd commented likely hadn't seen me tagged at all.

I'm sure that back then, people had heard about the investigation through trails of whispered gossip. But even then, they could only know so much. Jacqueline's family and Murray were the only ones who knew the truth. Well, not the full truth—just the truth that I presented.

My phone buzzed and the screen told me I'd been tagged in another photo by Jacqueline—or more accurately whoever had control over her account—and my eyes welled with tears. I blinked them away as I opened the notification. It was the same photo of the subway.

My phone vibrated once again, then multiple times, so quickly that there were no breaks in between. It rattled in my hand like a hive of angry bees, notifications pulsing faster than my racing heart. The screen was full—and growing fuller—of tagged photo notifications. I studied them through teary eyes, my vision blurred.

Even through the tears, it was clear that someone had gone through her photos, all the way back to 2010, and tagged me in every single one of them.

* * *

A knock on the door pulled me back into the present. How long had I been sitting there, staring at my panicked reflection in the mirror?

I'd put myself back together, fixing my hair and covering all my scratches. My eyes, however, gave me away, glassy and streaked with red. I wasn't some glamorous, elegant woman. I was drunk. Frazzled and exhausted.

The door cracked open, and I watched in the mirror as Gloria's head poked through. I smiled as her kind eyes met mine in the mirror.

"Are you okay?" she asked. She entered the room and handed me a glass of ice water. Her suspicious eyes lingered on my phone.

The question hit me like a shock of winter wind, not because it was a particularly moving question, but because nobody had asked me that all day—not even Murray. But to be fair, we hadn't seen each other in nearly an hour, and he probably had no idea that I'd left the party at all. Which was mostly my fault since I'd slipped out without a word.

My eyes burned as tears built behind them, and I struggled to regain control. "Yes, I'm fine." I smiled weakly, and I could tell by her face that she felt sorry for me. I took a long drink of water. "Thank you for the water. I clearly needed it."

"You look like you've had quite a night." She was looking at my arm. While I'd been able to conceal the redness, the raised and puckered skin was still visible when the light hit it at a certain angle.

I wondered how much she'd heard—how much she'd seen that she wasn't meant to. Not just during parties such as this, but every day. Did Gloria silently observe the twins' secret pours of liquor as they got sloppier throughout the day? Did she witness guests screwing people that were *not* their spouses?

If so, how could she keep all that information locked inside herself?

I was about to burst at the seams with questions. I considered blurting it all out to Gloria, telling her what I'd seen and overheard since I'd arrived at this house.

I parted my lips to speak, but bit it back. It wasn't her responsibility—she didn't need another problem. Just because it was her job to pretend to care didn't mean she actually did.

"Mrs. Sedgemont wanted me to bring you back down to the party. Would you like me to walk you down?"

I stood from the vanity stool, picked up my clutch, and walked to the door. "That would be great."

She made small talk as we walked down the long, dark hallway. How did I like the food? Had I had enough water?

Instead of leading me to the top of the grand staircase, she said, "Why don't we go down the back staircase? It's a bit more private."

I mumbled in affirmation, all the while wondering what she was talking about. I hadn't noticed any staircase other than the sweeping carved wood spiral that led down into the booming party.

She led me to what I'd presumed to be just another panel on the dark wood wall. She pushed her palm against the panel, and it popped. As it opened, it displayed a narrow landing and the first few narrow steps of a hidden staircase. The rest of the steps were enveloped in darkness.

A surprised "Oh!" escaped my lips. I was enthralled with the little secret staircase. I'd read enough moody Victorian novels in my college days that I'd always dreamed of something like this.

Gloria gave me a cheeky smile. "How do you think I dart about the house so easily?"

There was an adorably small doorway to the left. It came up to my knees and had a small brass latch. "Where does that go?"

"It's just storage," she chirped as she flipped a light switch and began down the stairs.

The passage was narrow, and I gripped my arms close to my sides. As we made our way down the winding stairs, I noticed the outlines of other panels that I assumed led to other rooms, but Gloria paid them no mind.

It wasn't some dusty old passageway from the detective novels I'd read as a child. It was fully functioning, if not hastily designed and built, with lights above and air vents pumping in the same frigid air as was in the rest of the house.

It felt like the staircase had wound around nearly twenty times, and I tried to picture where we were in the house, but I'd lost track.

Finally, Gloria pushed against a portion of the wall, and it opened into the bottom floor hallway. There were a few straggling revelers, one man pressed tightly against a woman who stiffened in disgust at his touch, but the hallway was mostly empty, and our arrival went unnoticed.

I was completely disoriented and turned my head left and right to gain my bearings. To the right were the wide French doors that were slung open, wafts of warm summer air drifting in. The scent of cigarette smoke also drifted in, mixed with the sweet, skunky scent of strong weed.

Down the hallway to my left was the entrance hall, and bodies vibrated around the room, some dancing, some gesturing in excitement as they spoke to other guests. The party was in full swing still, the energy more frenetic than ever.

I sighed deeply and Gloria squeezed the back of my arm. I inhaled once more and turned to thank her for escorting me down, but she'd already disappeared into the winding depths of the house. I desperately wanted to go with her—to vanish into her complex web of passageways that she used to disappear and reappear so quickly.

As I entered the entrance hall, there was an undefinable change in energy. There was a reckless charge to the crowd, like a stadium during a sporting event. Everyone was undeniably drunk, and the previously put-together guests now looked disheveled and feral.

I spotted Murray as he shifted the tides of the crowd and made his way toward me. His face was shimmering with a sheen of drunken sweat, but the way he looked at me with so much love made me briefly forget where we were.

"You look so pretty," he slurred, complimenting me for the hundredth time tonight. "Where have you been?"

I began to explain, when the band came to a halt and a voice boomed over the microphone. It was Phillip, his voice low and surprisingly carefree. He was clearly celebrating his impending retirement—maybe a bit too much.

"Uh-oh," Murray said as he looped his arm around my back.

Phillip cleared his throat. "I want to thank everyone for coming tonight to celebrate the engagement of Murray and Kassandra."

He paused as the guests clapped and whistled, and motioned for Murray and me to join him near the microphone. We made our way through the crowd, and my heartbeat quickened knowing that all these eyes were about to be on me. All the bodies in the room shifted toward us as we passed, their eyes unashamedly scanning over us, ranking our importance to them. Everyone was watching us, their bright white teeth flashing against the lights. Their eyes glistened with exhilaration as they all stood, waiting.

Murray wrapped his arm around my waist, pulling me into him. He knew I hated the attention, and his touch brought some semblance of comfort as everyone stared at us.

Phillip continued with a small hiccup. "It means so much to us that many of you traveled far and wide to be here tonight, especially on such short notice. True love is not something we come by easily. Many of us may never find it, but I can tell my boy has found it with Kassandra. You better hold on to it, son."

He pointed a finger at us, and Murray smiled, but I could tell by the rise of his shoulders that he was uncomfortable. The crowd let out a saccharine *aw*, quieting as Phillip began to speak once more.

"Murray, may you have a beautiful marriage like your mother's and mine, and like Beatrice, may your future wife prove to one day be a powerful Sedgemont woman. With that being said, everyone, please raise your glasses to Murray and Cindy!"

*　　*　　*

My breath caught in my throat and there was a collective gasp from the crowd. Murray tugged his father away from the microphone and a pitiful *"What?"* echoed throughout the room as Phillip looked around in confusion, still smiling at the success of his toast.

"To Murray and Cindy," Kennedy and Emmett cheered in unison, raising their glasses with identical smirks on their faces.

Little shits, I thought. My skin seemed to be engulfed in flames, embarrassment coursing through me like poison. Had it been an honest, drunken mistake? Maybe she caught his eye at the last minute, and it had been an innocent slip.

I found her in the crowd, unsure of what emotion I'd find on her face. She stared back at me with an insolent grin. We held each other's gaze for a few seconds until her friend Evie whispered something in her ear and they erupted into a fit of laughter.

Beatrice had noticed Cindy's reaction as well. She was observing her in the same way I was, but she was titillated, leaning forward in anticipation of Cindy's next move. Beatrice brought one hand in a loose fist to her lips as though she were about to cough, but really because she was covering a smirk.

Murray returned to my side, taking my hand in his. His grip was tight and his palm was damp with sweat, but I welcomed it, nonetheless. I needed it to ground me.

Beau stepped to the microphone and cleared his throat. "I think what Mr. Sedgemont meant was please extend congratulations to Murray and his new fiancée, Kassandra. To Murray and Kassandra!" I knew the forced cheerfulness in his voice was a sad attempt to distract from Phillip's mistake, but it felt like it only made it worse. Something was bubbling in the crowd—an eagerness that verged on anxiety, a demand to be entertained.

Lyle and Mary Margaret stood at the front of the crowd. Lyle's gut had expanded with the rich food and drink throughout the night, untucking some of his shirt. One button was hanging on by a thread. He had a firm grip on his wife's arm.

Mary Margaret's hair was tousled and her makeup slightly smudged, but she was still beautiful. The messiness looked purposeful, but I was one of the only people who knew it wasn't. She spoke to Beau as he left the microphone, and it looked like she was complimenting his attempt to smooth over Phillip's blunder.

I noticed a barely perceptible twitch in the corner of Lyle's mouth, his teeth and the inside of his lips ringed dark with red wine as he flashed a false smile at Beau.

An incredibly drunk couple walked by me, unaware I was there. "Well, to be fair, everyone thought he and Cindy would be the ones who'd get married. I mean, who the hell is this girl anyway? I've never heard of the Baptistes. Have you?"

The woman responded with a mumbled "No," and they disappeared into the crowd. Murray let go of my hand and stepped in front of me, blocking me from the gossiping guests. I'd never been this embarrassed in my life, and although I wanted to run, I was completely stiff with self-consciousness.

"I'm so sorry," Murray said, pulling me in for a hug. "I'm so fucking sorry. He didn't mean anything by it. But it shouldn't have happened."

Tears began to sting my eyes. "Let's drop it, please. I don't want to cry in front of these people. They would love it."

The noise of the party was beginning to pick back up as people began conversations and ordered more drinks. Their attention span weakened with drugs and drink, some wandered off, already bored with the gossip. By the time an hour passed, it seemed like everyone had completely forgotten that it'd happened. Murray did his best to distract me with his clumsy dance moves, and I tried to ignore the itch of discontent at the back of my brain.

I was just beginning to enjoy myself when a scream ripped through the entrance hall. A violent shiver crept up my spine. The guests were mingling, their grins still wide, their eyes increasingly glazed with liquor. How could they not have heard that?

The band was between songs, but the sound of all the guests talking and laughing was nearly loud enough to cover the scream. My head snapped to Murray, his eyes already on me.

"Did you hear that?" I asked, panic making my voice tremble.

"Yes," he said with a gulp as a low moan reverberated off the walls. A few heads in the crowd turned, but all the other people were still joyously talking, swigging their drinks, and taking photos.

Beatrice walked over and began to speak, but Murray quickly interrupted her.

"We'll be right back," Murray said, looping his arm around mine and guiding me out of the crowd. My heart swelled as he took action. He was going to fix it. He always did.

Beatrice reached for my arm, and her long nails raked into my skin. "Excuse me, where do you think you're going?"

Murray ignored her and we continued weaving through the crowd and out of the room. When we entered the kitchen, the room was chaotic with the caterers cooking and arranging plates, but without the low buzz of excitement from the guests, my ears hummed. It was disorienting, and I raised a hand to furiously rub one ear, desperate for the ringing to stop.

Murray looked around furiously before spinning around again and leading me out of the kitchen. "Where is that coming from?"

We reentered the booming entrance hall, the band now picking up their instruments and plucking a few chords. They started to play a spirited song, and a few couples began to dance, too drunk to remember Phillip's botched toast and still oblivious to the scream that had ripped through the air only moments before.

The crowd was swarming, bodies cascading so quickly it blurred my vision, but the one unmoving constant was Beatrice as she watched us intently.

Another scream, softer now, nearly a wail, tried to pierce through the noise of the party. I could tell now that it was a woman. As Murray pulled me toward the winding stairs, I peered around the room. Everything was whirring by in slow motion, the garish smiles of guests bouncing around the dance floor looking sick—smudged lipstick and mascara. They were oblivious in their joy, and I couldn't decide whether I was disgusted or envious.

We ran up the stairs, Murray no longer holding my hand, but instead sprinting up the stairs two at a time. I struggled behind him, my ridiculous dress snagging on my stiletto heels.

He reached the second-floor landing, panting, but still moving quickly. I arrived behind him as he paused, listening for a clue as to where the noise came from. He craned his head left and right down the long hallways, but it snapped straight ahead, to the large, brooding doors of his father's office, as a woman softly wailed. I had never seen the doors cracked open before; the family crest was now split in half.

Murray lurched forward, wrenching open the doors with both hands. The lighting in the room was all wrong, the glow coming up from the floor, casting looming shadows onto the ceiling. A lamp had been knocked from the massive wood desk, and its shade was popped off and snapped in two, leaving the bulb bare and harsh. I turned from it and blinked away the colors that danced behind my eyes.

When I opened them, I looked toward the woman who was kneeling on the floor in front of something—I couldn't tell what. My vision was still reeling from the bare bulb, but some primal part of my mind knew what it was.

It was Beau's body. His upper torso was outlined by a crimson halo that seeped from the letter opener jammed in his gut.

His head was cradled in the hands of the crying woman; I now realized she was the woman in the backless dress who had been flirting with Beau earlier in the evening. They had both been pictures of perfection. Now that illusion was forever ruined.

The woman screamed again. No more sadness this time, but a full, terrified roar. Murray turned to me, and the woman on the floor peered up with swollen eyes, face dripping with ruined makeup. I didn't understand why they were staring at me. They should be looking at the body, at this person lying dead on the floor. And then I realized.

The scream wasn't coming from the woman.

It was coming from me.

17

THE POLICE ARRIVED quickly, and over a dozen uni-formed officers were attempting to usher drunk and disoriented guests out of the way as paramedics carried a gurney up the stairs. I watched as a uniformed officer moved through the crowd, guests automatically giving him space as he split the sea of booze and glamor. His khaki and brown uniform looked dull and lifeless against the sequins and silk of the guests. Once he emerged from the crowd, he turned around and broadened his already-wide shoulders.

"My name is Sheriff Penn. Everyone, please remain calm and stay where you are. There has been a suspicious death, and we will be investigating. We appreciate your cooperation." He lowered his voice and turned to Beatrice. "Can I have a word?" The sheriff gestured to the empty hallway, and Beatrice nodded. They began to walk, and although the sheriff had barely spoken to Phillip, he hob-bled after them, his head on a swivel between the officer and the crowd of guests.

"Sheriff, I believe we can come to some sort of arrange-ment here . . ." her voice trailed off as they disappeared.

A murmur rippled through the crowd like a disturbed hive protecting their queen. Murray wrapped his arm around me, encasing my body with his.

The house was in a complete state of chaos. Someone had dropped a glass on the dance floor, and an oblivious woman had kept dancing until the moment the police arrived, heels in hand, before noticing the gore below her. A splattered trail of blood followed her to where she was sitting, her friend holding her hand while her husband attempted to pluck a large shard of glass out of her foot as she cried.

A third of the guests had fled immediately after the body was discovered, but the rest congregated in the middle of the entrance hall, peering up the stairs with a morbid curiosity. Some, however, had stumbled over to the bar, demanding drinks, even though the bartenders were packing up, ready to flee so that they weren't stuck here any longer. One man snatched one of the unpacked bottles of booze and meandered away, the bartender scowling, but not caring enough to do anything about it. I thought perhaps the drinkers were trying to soothe their nerves, but instead of huddling together in fear, they struck up joyous conversations with their drunken cohorts. I remembered those nights of my own where if you were drunk enough or high enough, you could pretend nothing bad had ever happened.

Beatrice was back in the entrance hall attempting and failing to sooth the nerves of the frightened guests.

"What the hell are we supposed to do now?" someone shouted from the middle of the crowd. Mumbles of affirmation arose throughout the room, one louder than the next as they bolstered one another's confidence.

"I'm not staying," a man declared. "Come on, honey." He gripped his wife's wrist and dragged her through the crowd, jostling people as they went. A police officer tried half-heartedly to convince them to stay, but the couple brushed past him. The front door creaked open, and they didn't bother closing it, the whole process a theatrical middle finger to the rest of us.

"Well, if they can leave, we can too, right?" a younger man said to Murray, looking for approval. I hadn't seen him before, but he spoke to Murray familiarly, as if he were a beacon of authority just because he was a Sedgemont.

Murray opened his mouth to respond, when the sheriff called for the attention of the guests. Beatrice and Phillip stood next to him, their faces sour. Phillip's eyes were red and swollen. A wave of sadness tightened my throat—he must have been close with Beau after working with him for so long. Beatrice was whispering in Phillip's ear, and whatever she was saying gave him the expression of a kicked dog.

"Folks, listen up and try to remain calm," Sheriff Penn barked. The crowd collectively flinched in response. "This is clearly a very serious situation, and we appreciate your cooperation. That being said, we will be speaking to each and every one of you at some point. Again, we encourage everyone to stay on the property for the time being, as we will begin conducting interviews right away."

Panic undulated through the crowd, heads dipping as guests discussed their plans.

My heart sank in my chest at the prospect of the house being packed with guests long after the party was over. I was also dreading being interviewed by the police. In this case I hadn't done anything wrong, and I had nothing to worry about, but it was something I'd gone through before, and I didn't want to go through the trauma of being interrogated again. I tried to remind myself that there was no way they could doubt my alibi because I was clearly present at the party and had been paraded around to each guest. But the more I thought about it, the more it was clear that wasn't true.

Blood pumped through my body, pulsing in my ears as I realized just how much of my time was unaccounted for. I was sure others could hear my heartbeat.

There was my time in the bathroom with Cindy and Eve. And then my walk outside, followed by my trip to my bedroom to freshen up. Now I wished with every fiber of my being that I had just stuck it out and stopped trying to wander away from the party. The Sedgemonts had been asking me to perform, and I should have played along. Instead, I'd acted like a sulking teenager, traipsing around the house, searching for any corner to hide in while the rest of the guests had fun.

Murray was chewing on the inside of his cheek, staring blankly across the room. He was gripping my hand, hard and desperate, and sweat built between our palms. I followed his gaze, only to see Cindy. Cindy and Eve's heads were ducked together, and they were furiously whispering. I wondered what they were saying.

Beatrice raised her voice over the noise of the crowd. "I know many of you traveled far and wide to be here tonight. Since Sheriff Penn has urged everyone to remain on the estate, we will be opening up our home to anyone who needs a place to stay while these fine officers conduct their investigation." She looked proud of herself, as if she'd done us all such a favor, when in reality it didn't seem we had much of a choice.

"Not a chance. I have a flight to Dubai in the morning," a woman grumbled to her friend.

"Screw this. They can't legally make us stay here. What are they going to do, arrest us?" a man said loud enough for the people around him to nod in agreement. The murmur of panic grew louder as more of the guests protested against the sheriff's instructions. The man and his wife stomped out of the room, bolstering the other guests' bravery.

There was movement above me. On the second landing stood the twins, their forearms draped over the banister, utterly casual. When our eyes met, Kennedy's pale face spread into a lopsided grimace. He said something to Emmett, whose face remained stoic as they continued to stare right at me. I looked away, a shiver raising the hairs on my forearms.

I wanted to turn and walk out, disappearing with the other guests, but I knew there were eyes on me because I was an outsider. They were watching.

As soon as the sheriff left the room, many more guests left despite his request. The guests that were too afraid to disobey him remained, including those of us who were stuck here, no matter what.

*　*　*

When the guests who were leaving had departed the house, I pulled Murray out of the entrance hall, dragging him by his hand. Now that the initial shock of Beau's murder was wearing off, I was left with the intrusive mental image of Cindy's beautiful, smirking face and the rest of the guests slack-jawed with shock and titillation. Phillip's bungled toast had been a betrayal, even if accidental, and although the murder had shaken us all, that stupid toast was still on my mind.

We were standing in the formal dining room among half-eaten plates of finger foods. An empty glass of champagne, ringed with red lipstick, was toppled on the table. It left a puddle of sticky liquid around it, soaking through the table linen, and a crumpled cocktail napkin lay beside it. Thoughts blew through my mind in quick flashes and bursts. The most invasive was of Beau, toppled over like the glass, his helpless, lifeless body on the office floor.

It's just a glass, I told myself. I tried to focus on the details in front of me, but now Cindy encroached on my thoughts. She wore that same lipstick tonight on her perfect princess smile. It would be like her to toss a glass onto a table, not caring to even empty it first.

Every time I shifted on my feet, crumbs crunched beneath my heels. I was surprised by how messy it was, considering the number of caterers the Sedgemonts had hired on top of already having a butler and a housekeeper. Maybe they were busy cleaning up something else.

My mind was moving too feverishly for me to take control. I wanted nothing more than to take a bottle of champagne to my room and drink the rest as quickly as I could until I passed out. I was slipping back into old patterns—the mildest inconvenience the best excuse to get obliterated. But this wasn't a mild inconvenience. This was a dead man. I saw him every time I closed my eyes.

The twins entered the room, the two of them wide-eyed and twitchy. Each of them clung onto their drink of choice—whiskey for Emmett and red wine for Kennedy, as always—with such force that their fingertips were turning white.

"Dude, can you believe this?" Emmett said to Murray, who shook his head dejectedly. A piece of Emmett's gelled hair had separated from the rest and dangled stiffly on his forehead like a lone claw. He kept flicking it away, just for it to fall back to the same place. Kennedy was surprisingly put together, but he had the telltale purple ring around his inner lip like a bruise, making him look even more ill. I wouldn't know if his teeth were purple because he was pressing his lips together in a tight smirk.

"Whoa, Kass. You been rolling around in the grass?" Kennedy winked at Murray. Murray took a step behind me and studied the slight smudge of dirt on my backside from the fall. In the dim light of my bedroom, I thought I'd gotten it all off. My cheeks burned fiery hot.

"Your hair looks different too," Emmett said matter-of-factly.

Murray was scanning me and said, "Yeah, it does," in a huff just as Beatrice and Phillip entered the room.

"Why is your dress so dirty?" Murray asked under his breath.

Emmett and Kennedy were whispering to each other, their eyes flicking to me occasionally.

Murray stepped closer to me and inhaled. "Have you been smoking?" My hackles raised at his accusatory tone.

I started to answer him, my gut reaction to lie and tell him I'd just gone outside to get a breath of fresh air and slipped—which technically wasn't a *lie*—when Beatrice cleared her throat theatrically. She had the authoritative air of a schoolteacher staring down a misbehaving classroom.

A memory popped invasively into my head. I remembered in second grade, when my class was out playing on the playground and I noticed a small group of my classmates standing by the trees, poking something with a stick. I had wandered over—I was always a curious child— and stood in shock as they prodded a bird's nest that had fallen out of a tall tree. They had broken the eggs and were laughing to each other as they took turns poking the muck. I'd begun to silently cry, and moments later our teacher stormed up behind us. Since I was the first student she'd reached, she had somehow placed all the blame on me, and I'd borne the brunt of the punishment despite having nothing to do with it.

That's exactly how I felt now. On the periphery of the situation, yet somehow placed right in the middle, the spotlight shining hot on my skin and blinding my eyes.

"The police will be interviewing Phillip and me first. They have kindly agreed to wait until the morning for the rest of the interviews. Off to bed—you need a clear head for tomorrow," Beatrice commanded. "Wash up," she added, looking at me.

It was almost one in the morning, and although I was desperate to change into something more comfortable, I dreaded being alone. We marched in a single file line up the stairs like children, each of us shuffling off to our own beds. Emmett and Kennedy were on the second floor with Murray in their childhood bedrooms, leaving me isolated on the third floor with strangers.

"Mur," I whispered, grabbing his hand. "I'm scared. Can I stay with you?"

"I don't want to upset Mother," he said after a moment of hesitation. His eyes darted from me to his brothers, who were still watching us from the hallway.

His lack of concern for me was like a punch in the gut. I should have been angry at his complete dismissal of me, but all I felt was the heaviness of disappointment.

"Murray, whoever killed Beau could be in the house right now," I said. I was trying to get him to realize how serious this was, but all he could think about was if his mom would be upset that we slept in the same bed together.

"You're safe. The house is full of police," he assured me. Murray gave me a perfunctory kiss on the cheek as Emmett and Kennedy snickered in the dark hallway. Murray was clearly embarrassed.

At Sedgemont Estate, all affection was given in the shadows.

18

IT WAS ANOTHER night that I lay restless in this bed. The house was fuller than I'd ever seen it. Every bedroom had a guest from the party, some of the younger guests without a bedroom were even asleep on the couches and chairs throughout the house. I swore I could hear a hundred conversations at once, guests whispering to each other about the events of the night. But in reality, it was now three in the morning, and most guests had been in a shallow, boozy sleep for hours. I wondered if any of the guests were sitting awake in bed like I was, picturing Beau's dead body. Had any of them realized that one of the people in the house could be the murderer? I felt like the only one who was taking this seriously.

Beatrice had ushered us all to our bedrooms around one in the morning, but I hadn't been able to lie still in my bed, much less sleep. My eyes fluttered in an effort to stay open, despite my best wishes.

As I'd walked to my bedroom, I'd passed Lyle and Mary Margaret's room, next to mine, and overheard them spitting venom at one another, consonants piercing the night like hisses through their teeth. They'd clearly never liked each other that much, but the energy between them had amplified over the course of the night, and now they were like two bombs threatening to destroy one another. I wished they would leave. I couldn't stand feeling that anymore. In fact, I wanted everyone to leave. There was too much energy in the house. It felt claustrophobic despite the grandiosity of the estate.

My mind continued reeling in spite of my best efforts, playing memories on shuffle without my permission. Images flitted across the back of my restless eyelids, and I thought of Mary Margaret in the greenhouse, in the throes of ecstasy, unaware that I was only feet away. Or had she been aware?

There were so many men at the party that it could have been anyone, and even though the possibilities were endless, I couldn't help but try to transpose someone's face onto the obscured man beneath her. I had seen her in the middle of the night, floating through the house like a Victorian ghost, drifting down the stairs to the second floor. My mind played with the puzzle pieces—who was staying on the second floor? Tonight it was completely full of guests, but that night it had been only one—Beau, the vice president of the family company.

My thoughts were blurred with the remnants of alcohol, but I was sure there had been something between them at the party. Beau and Mary Margaret had both disappeared from the party briefly, only to come in separately later, looking slightly disheveled. And later Mary Margaret had stared daggers at the young woman flirting with Beau. The woman who had found his body.

My skin was suddenly boiling hot under the layers of blankets, and I threw them off me, swinging my legs off the side of the bed. The bed was tall and my legs dangled, making me feel like a child. I wondered if this entire house had that effect on Murray—something so big and foreboding that it shrunk him down, stunting him and throwing him back to his childhood, when he'd lived here.

He could be pacing his room or curled up under a bedsheet with his phone, like a kid with a flashlight and a book. I ached at the thought. This house and his family were not good for him. I had the urge to comfort him, but the idea of moving through the dark house, past the crime scene, filled my limbs with cement.

I thought of the police tape wrapped across the office doors, the bright yellow jarring against the dark, shining wood. They had quickly removed the body. It had been done almost too quickly, at least compared to how it happened in the crime documentaries I'd watched. They'd taken a few pictures, dusted a few items, and then *poof*—it had never happened. The doors were closed, and the Sedgemonts had wiped it all clean. The only thing remaining was the tape.

I got out of bed, like I had every night I'd been here, and began to pace. Although it was still dark out, the sky tinted with the steely gray of sun threatening to wake and begin its slow ascent.

I needed to be there for Murray like he'd been there for me these past months. If I was going to go see him, I had to do it now.

I opened the door and stepped into the hallway.

* * *

By the time I'd reached the second floor, I was shivering with adrenaline and the incredible shock of cold that blew through the house. I'd nearly turned around to grab a sweater, but I knew that any second someone could wake from sleep and catch me lurking in the hallways. There was a chance it could be Beatrice, ready to chastise me for breeching etiquette by visiting Murray. Or it could be someone much more dangerous.

I moved quickly, now growing accustomed to the quirks of the house—the creaks in the floorboards to avoid and the frayed, lifted edges of Turkish runners to step over.

When I reached the second-floor landing, I hesitated briefly, something in my body telling me to turn around when I saw the police tape. It was too perfect, like it was arranged just right for the set of a film. I didn't remember it looking like that and wondered if Beatrice asked Gloria to style it according to her taste. As if a murder scene was some sort of decorative accessory.

I inhaled deeply, puffing my chest out as though it would make me braver.

A sinister noise drifted through the hallway—I couldn't quite make out what it was. It sounded like someone was running their palm across the wall, but soon I realized it wasn't coming from the hallway's walls, but rather the floor above me. I froze, unable to convince my body to do anything.

Somebody was dragging something, the scrape of fabric followed by the thump of heavy footsteps. My imagination ran wild, and I pressed my back against the wall as the sound traveled closer, descending the stairs to the second floor.

The moment they reached this floor, they would see me, pressed against the wall right next to the office doors. What would they think of me? That I was a criminal returning to the scene of the crime to revel in the chaos I'd caused?

There was no choice. I had to hide. With my breath held burning in my lungs, I slipped into the shadowy alcove that housed the office doors, emblazoned with the Sedgemont family crest. With a shaking hand, I twisted the knob as quietly as possible and slipped under the caution tape into the darkness.

The footsteps were closer now. I couldn't shut the door without them hearing, so I left it cracked and scrambled deeper into the pitch-black of the office.

The wood floor was hard against my boney knees, and I winced as they audibly crunched under my weight, but I kept moving.

"Huh?" a deep voice mumbled, raspy with sleep. They must have seen the office door cracked open. Had I ripped the caution tape?

The darkness of the room was suffocating, pressing down on me like it wanted to keep me here forever. My heart beat wildly against my sternum. I began to crawl, my body on autopilot, like an animal rushing to find shelter before a storm. I couldn't cut right through the room—it was still littered with numbered placards from the investigation, indicating pieces of potential evidence. I hadn't seen the room since I had been dragged out screaming, Murray draping my arm across his shoulders and hoisting my limp body downstairs.

The image of the letter opener jutting out from Beau's abdomen exploded in my mind, replacing the jet-black room with the scene. Still on my hands and knees, my arms shaking, elbows buckling under my weight, I fumbled my way further into the room. My hand knocked into a placard and sent it skittering across the floor. The noise was atomic in the silence, and a whimper escaped my mouth. I should have brought my phone—I badly needed the flashlight app.

I reached out and felt the rug in the middle of the room. I hardly remembered it being there, but I was grateful for the reprieve of pain in my knees from crawling on the hardwood.

My palm touched something damp, and I recoiled. I tried to skirt around the damp portion of the rug, but it was all soaked.

Footsteps boomed toward the office doors, purposeful and quick. I rushed forward blindly, ignoring the damp rug now. I reached out in the dark every few seconds, desperate to orient myself. My fingers grazed wood. It was the desk. I scrambled forward, pushing the chair out of the way and wedged myself under the desk. I pulled the chair toward me, hiding me from view.

The double doors creaked open seconds later. I pressed my hands into my mouth, and my breath was hot and panicked against my hand.

Please leave, I silently begged.

A creaking footstep moved forward defiantly. I listened as someone drew back the curtains, the metal rings screeching against the curtain rod. The beginnings of dawn cast a gray light over the room, a sickly mixture of gray, blue, and orange, like a landscape in the aftermath of a disaster. *Not far off,* I thought with a grimace.

The person at the door was breathing quickly, and their energy was so intense that I swore I could feel their eyes sweeping wall to wall, floor to ceiling.

It was still dark, but I could now make out the vague shapes and colors of the items around me. If I could see more clearly now, so could they. My chest ached as I paused between each breath, fearful that even a slow, pained exhale would be booming in the silence. I didn't want to breathe the air in the room, as if the dust particles drifting through the room might contain a portion of Beau's spirit. It was nonsense, but I swore I could still smell the iron tang of his blood.

Wetness creeped through my pajama bottoms as I sat below the desk, shivering in silence. I thought maybe in my fear I'd wet myself, and I flushed with shame as I touched the moisture building in the fabric. When I pulled my hand away, even in the dim predawn light, I could see it was covered in something, dark and thick like syrup.

Beau's blood. The realization of it nearly made me gag, but I forced myself to sit still, the remains of Beau's blood seeping up from the rug through my pajama pants. Touching my skin.

The person stood still before turning on their heel, a breathy *humph* escaping from their lips before they shambled away.

I remained still under the desk, curled in a ball as the slow, shuffling footsteps continued down the hall. When they sounded far enough away, I pushed the chair away from the desk and cautiously peeked out. The room was empty, still shadowed in the liminal state between dark and light, but inching ever closer to dawn. I crawled out from under the desk, bumping into a framed painting on the wall as I crept out. I tiptoed to the office doors, working up the courage to flee back to my room.

The footsteps of the person outside were finally distant enough for comfort, and I peeked my head out slowly, taking in the shadowy corridor. All the lights were off, and the early dawn light shining through the glass ceiling tinted everything monochromatic.

I stuck my head further out, suddenly conscious of how vulnerable my neck was in this position. I flinched at the sight of a ghostly white figure shuffling down the hall.

The figure was misshapen, their form large and jittering, with white trailing behind them like a wedding gown.

I blinked hard. It wasn't a gown, but a white duvet being dragged behind a sleepy figure.

Based on the height and shape of the man, the only person it could be was Lyle. Despite how repulsive I found his personality, I felt a pang of sympathy for him. I imagined he'd been kicked out of bed by Mary Margaret, his adulterous wife.

Or perhaps he'd grown angry, unable to stand the thought of sleeping next to her at night, touching the same body that had been draped over another man.

Perhaps he was just angry enough to kill.

*   *   *

I was about to slip out into the hallway, when I turned to look at the office, trying to remember whether I'd left any trace of my impromptu visit.

My eyes landed on the heavy wooden desk, the items on it in disarray in the aftermath of Beau's murder. On the right side of the room, there was a seating area with yet another bar cart full of top-shelf liquor. This room was like all the rest in the house, small touches of decor and expensive art on the walls, picked by Beatrice with painstaking care.

I was disgusted with myself that I liked Beatrice's taste in the artwork dotting the walls. One of the paintings behind the desk was crooked. There was something familiar to it that made me approach it, and I studied it as I leveled out the frame. It was a bit unconventional, but with something undeniable that made you stop and admire.

As the sun began to rise outside, the room was still dim, but slightly more illuminated. I needed to get out, but I couldn't stop staring at the two paintings behind Phillip's desk.

The painting on the left was of two boys, a jarring mix of photorealism and a splash of disjointed cartoonish figures transposed across the top. I stepped closer, drawn in by the familiarity. The other portrait was similar in style, the background a sweeping hill with a castle nestled atop of it, but dotted throughout the fields were neon figures that were almost robotic in their cyberpunk clothing. It had a neurotic, enticing aura that I was familiar with.

I inched closer, my nose almost touching the canvas as I studied the small figure in the field, a frayed red cape draping behind it in the wind. A memory gripped me. Murray and I standing in front of this canvas, me pointing at this very figure. "Do you think this little girl is storming the castle, or saving it?" I'd asked.

"Well, since this other guy is holding a bayonet and that woman has a pitchfork, I'm going to assume the correct answer is storming," Murray said, laughing.

These were Lucas Goedert's paintings from the gallery that had commanded so much of Murray's time but pushed Murray's career to success. The same artist we had once dragged off a karaoke stage in the middle of the night, just to flop him on our couch with a trash can under his drooling face.

Murray had never said anything about his parents buying Goedert's paintings. These had sold for hundreds of thousands of dollars, one of them for millions. Surely it would have been worth mentioning.

I turned to face the desk, the heat of frustration in my cheeks. He had been so proud of himself, selling to some hotshot art collector who'd skyrocketed Murray's career. Just this morning an article had been written about him in the *New Yorker* that deemed him the up-and-coming darling of the New York City art world.

I wasn't sure what I was searching for, but I wrenched open the top drawers on the desk. Pens and highlighters rattled forward with the force of it, but the sound was dampened by stacks of loose papers underneath. I yanked open another drawer, leaving the previous one open. I stared down at the papers in the drawer, my eyes straining in the darkness. This whole time I hadn't known what I was looking for, yet here it was, staring me in the face.

I pulled the stack of papers from the drawer and gripped them in my hands, the paper crinkling under the pressure as I read.

Murray Sedgemont
57 Herkimer Street, Apartment 12B
Brooklyn, NY 11216

My eyes hurried down the paper, trying to make sense of why our bills were sitting in Phillip's desk. I looked further down the page to see "$2,500 monthly rent" highlighted, with "$1,250 paid" scrawled next to it in an unfamiliar hand.

It must be Phillip's handwriting. On our bills. The bills that Murray and I split so diligently right down the middle. I remembered us sitting down to talk to each other about the serious step of moving in together. He'd been the one who was adamant about splitting things fifty–fifty. *"Equality,"* he'd said. I'd been fine with it. It was completely reasonable since we weren't married, and we both had about the same salary. Plenty of our friends did it.

We'd played around with the idea of us both having our own accounts and one shared account for our joint expenses, but in the end Murray decided it would be best to keep everything separate for now. I'd been fine with the decision, but I wondered why he even bothered playing along when he knew he was never going to agree to it anyway.

I flipped to the next page to see the previous month's rent, again paid by Phillip, along with our Wi-Fi bill, which was one of the utilities Murray was responsible for.

Anger built in my muscles, making my body so rigid that my bones felt like they'd snap under the pressure. While I struggled every month to scrape together my half of the bills, Murray sat back and let his family do it for him. If he wasn't paying the bills, what was he doing with his salary?

A bitter laugh nearly escaped as I thought of Murray's personal checking account getting fatter by the day while his parents paid his half of the bills. In the meantime, I'd taken on more shows than I could handle just to barely scrape by. I'd bought myself a new bike, but I hadn't been able to buy myself any new clothes for nearly a year. I thought of all the nights out with friends that I'd had to skip because I couldn't afford it.

I pictured Murray sitting at the kitchen counter as I packed my bag for this godforsaken trip, furrowing his brow at the rental portal online like he was crunching numbers. What a great actor he was to fool me, when in reality he was just sitting there plugging in the free money his daddy gave him.

In the heat of my anger, I tossed the papers into the drawer, but missed entirely. The papers fluttered to the floor, the left side of each paper blotted with red. My stomach dropped. I'd forgotten about my hands covered in Beau's blood. I wiped my hands on the tops of my thighs, panic taking over. Logic escaped me, and the urge to flee was pulling at me. I returned the papers to the drawer and used the hem of my top to wipe the handle.

I peeked my head out into the hallway, ready to run up the stairs and into the bathroom to wash away the scarlet stains all over my skin and clothes. I took one step forward, gripping for the doorknob behind me when a wall further down the hallway twitched, cracking open like a beast's menacing grin.

My eyes widened in fear as the wall opened further, a door appearing out of nowhere.

The staff passageway.

The passage door was now gaping open, and the outline of a person became visible in the dark shadows. They stepped out slowly, and a face became visible in the twilight.

The butler's profile was clear in the light from the glass ceiling, but the gray light shadowed his face, making his cheekbones look sharp and gaunt. He no longer looked like the soft, kind man he had seemed before, but more like a cold slab of marble that a sculptor had abandoned mid-project.

William paused and slowly turned his head, and I froze as his eyes landed on me. I urged myself to dip back into the office and close the door, pretend he hadn't seen me, but my muscles refused to obey. He looked threatening in the half-darkness, and I expected him to come creeping toward me at any moment.

Instead, his lips twitched into a limp grin, and he turned away from me, disappearing back into the shadows.

19

I LAY AWAKE THE rest of the night, my mind spinning until the sun peeked its head nervously above the trees. My body ached, and the skin on my hands and knees burned from crawling around in the dark office. I was wildly hungover, not only from the—what was it, eight drinks?—but from my late night snooping. My head ached, and my heart pulsed lazily in my temples.

I'd tried to scrub the blood stains off my pajamas for what felt like hours in the bathroom sink and they now hung limp and damp over a drawer I'd pulled out from the dresser. The still-obvious ruddy stain served as a terrible reminder of last night. I would have to throw them away later.

When I finally dragged myself out of bed, I stretched stiffly. I glanced at my suitcase and frowned at the explosion of wrinkled clothes that spilled out of it. I shuffled to the closet and pulled it open. When I looked inside, I blinked away the sleepiness in my eyes, sure that I was mistaken. I turned on the closet light and my head throbbed as my pulse quickened. It was my missing dress. The one I was supposed to wear to the party.

How convenient, I thought sarcastically. *What a miracle that it was found, just a day too late.*

I didn't stop to think about who had snuck it into my room and when. I yanked it off the hanger and pulled it over my head. I sure as hell wasn't going to let anyone tell me how to dress today.

I made my way to Murray's room, hoping to have a moment to talk to him. Many of the guest bedroom doors were open, the rooms inside empty and in partial disarray after a restless night's sleep. I said hello to Gloria as she finished making the bed in the final guest bedroom on this floor. Her smile was bright, but I could tell she'd been up all night, cleaning.

When I arrived on the second floor, Cindy passed by me, her shoulder bumping into mine. I clenched my teeth and kept moving until I heard her speak. "He's not in his room. I just checked. See ya downstairs," she chirped.

My face burned with anger. Why in the hell was she looking for Murray in his room? I wanted to spew venom back at her and tell her exactly what I thought she should do to herself, but I ground my teeth together. I knocked on Murray's door and waited a moment before cracking it open to look around. She was right. He wasn't here.

I pulled out my phone and began to text him, but I recoiled at the brightness of my phone screen. I turned the brightness down and berated my past self for drinking so much.

I texted Murray: *I'm up. Where are you?*

A few minutes passed as I waited for a response, listening to the sounds of the house settling against the wind outside. There was an undercurrent of conversation as a guest came out of the Blue Room and exited through the front door in a hurry. Eventually I gave up waiting on Murray and made my way downstairs.

A din came from the dining room, silverware clanging against plates, boisterous retellings of last night's events. There were many voices and multiple strings of conversation, but I couldn't make out the words or who was saying them.

I stood outside the door and took a deep breath, trying to settle my nerves and gurgling stomach. I paused when I heard someone say my name in the dining room. Their voices were low, and I could just barely hear what they were saying.

"None of us know anything about her, so why should we trust her?" a woman said. Her accent gave her away: Mary Margaret. "And they haven't even been together that long. You think she's in it for the money?"

"Obviously. And for half the party she was nowhere to be found. She could have been doing anything. Do you understand what I'm saying?" It sounded like Cindy, her voice low and conspiratorial. I would expect nothing less from her. How could she even imply something like that? I hardly knew Beau at all—what reason would I have to hurt him?

Anger tightened my throat. I wanted them to know I'd heard them, but show them I didn't give a damn what they thought about me. I turned the corner and walked casually into the dining room, forcing a smile on my face.

When I entered, Mary Margaret immediately met my eye, a fake smile plastered on her face. I was not in the mood to talk to any of these duplicitous people, and I was tempted to grab a croissant and run. She didn't get the hint and ushered me over. There was no plate in front of her, only a steaming black coffee. "Kass, there's an open seat here." She pointed across from her at a chair next to Cindy.

My stomach lurched. I didn't want to move. And I absolutely did not want to sit next to Cindy. Invisible daggers pressed into my skin just from Cindy's glare, and I was sure if I sat within inches of her that I would be sliced in half. Her friend Eve sat next to her, staring sullenly at me as she sipped her espresso.

I surrendered, floating in a haze across the room, and sat in the open seat. The sun shone in through the tall window directly on my seat like a spotlight, and I couldn't help but feel like I was being punished as I winced against the glare.

"What a pretty dress," Mary Margaret said. It sounded insincere, like a reflex. Cindy and Eve tittered before Cindy cleared her throat.

"Yes, so bright and cheerful," Cindy sneered.

I ignored her and thanked Mary Margaret as I pulled a cloth napkin into my lap. I gripped my hands in my lap and tried to keep them from trembling.

William smiled and offered me a cup of coffee in a mug that was much larger than everyone else's. I guess my hangover was that obvious. Either way, I was grateful. As he handed me my coffee, I couldn't quite meet his eye, knowing that he'd seen me lurking around in the office. But then again, what had he been doing?

I thanked him and took a fortifying gulp before I dared to face the table full of guests. They were all talking happily between bites and sips of coffee. Lyle was drinking a Bloody Mary and crunching loudly on the vodka-soaked celery stick. I couldn't believe how happy they were all acting. I wasn't sure what I had expected—tears and voiced worries, perhaps. But certainly not this.

William set down a steaming mass of scrambled eggs in front of Janice, scooting aside her other plate, which was piled high with sausage, hash browns, and a biscuit drowning in gravy. The sight of the food nearly made me retch. Janice was dressed in dark jeans and a light gray wool sweater and looked to have avoided any lingering effects from the party.

Murray was nowhere to be seen. It was uncomfortable being around his family without him, but I wasn't sure if I even wanted to see him right now. I couldn't stop thinking about his dismissal of me last night when I'd asked him if I could stay with him.

"Can I get you some toast and bacon?" William asked.

I nodded pitifully, nursing my coffee. I'd had many mornings like this before. Hangovers much worse than this. I thought of those nights years ago, clenching my teeth at the possibility that I'd found myself in this situation again—a night of partying followed by a harrowing loss. I just needed to eat.

"How did you sleep, Kassandra?" Janice asked with a mouthful of eggs. She was an animated chewer to say the least—someone who took great pleasure in everything she was tasting. I didn't often find myself in a state of blinding rage, but when I did, it was probably because someone was chewing with their mouth open. Janice slurped down some coffee, which she also managed to do loudly. She was so put together and powerful, so to see her eschew table manners so enthusiastically took me by surprise.

"Not well," I said. I glanced at her with a weak smile and thanked William as he set down my plate. The shine of the oily bacon and the fat glob of butter on my toast turned my stomach.

I was amazed that the other guests had an appetite at all, much less were in the mood to socialize. It seemed like I was the only one who remembered Beau's body being removed from the house in a stretcher, zipped up tight in a rubbery black bag that reflected frenetic blue and red lights.

"That's too bad. My bed was amazing. I need to ask Beatrice what brand the mattress is." She put a sausage link in her mouth, scraping the fork on her teeth in the process.

"So, Kass, did the party inspire any ideas for your wedding?" Mary Margaret asked.

I held back a guffaw, thinking she'd suddenly sprouted a sense of gallows humor. My uncomfortable smile faded when I saw she was being earnest. *These people are truly bizarre,* I thought.

"Um, I still haven't really put much thought into it," I said, partially lying. Out of the corner of my eye, I saw Cindy roll her eyes.

My dream wedding had come up in my mind many times, but the dream was always changing. I'd pictured Murray and me running off to city hall, him in his suit and scuffed Converse All-Stars and me in a white dress and combat boots. Maybe a little contrived, but it would be more "us" than some big, formal party. I'd imagined us and our family renting a home in the mountains, sitting around the campfire exchanging silly stories instead of vows while the family dogs played in the background. And there would be beer. Lots of beer. Maybe Zoey could paint the kegs.

But the honest truth was that I'd never once dreamed of a traditional wedding. It was clear what the Sedgemonts considered to be the norm: the expensive dress and a minimum of one hundred guests dressed in their finest formal attire. Those weddings were a blast to attend, but I couldn't picture myself as the *host* of one. Especially now that I'd seen how a Sedgemont party ended.

"The cops have already interviewed most of the guests, so they only have a few of us left," Cindy interjected, clearly not wanting to talk about our wedding. "They tried to talk to me before I'd had my coffee. You should have seen my face." Her face was, in fact, perfectly put together. Her skin was flawless, and her appearance didn't give away any clues about her lifestyle. Her plate had only a small pile of fruit, a black coffee, and a cup of dark green sludge. It was ironic, I thought, how some people were so strict about the food they put in their body, only to snort up whatever chemicals they were offered at a party. I'd been guilty of that too, I thought shamefully.

"So, who are they interviewing now?" I asked.

"Some guy," Cindy said. "Apparently he was at the party, but I never met him. He's kinda cute, though. Silver fox."

It wasn't surprising that she was emotionally oblivious to the trauma we'd all experienced last night. But *nobody* had brought up Beau. A flash of his body sprawled across the office floor invaded my mind, and I took a shaky sip of coffee. What was wrong with these people?

"He'll be staying at the house with all of us now," Beatrice's voice boomed from the doorway, and we all jumped. "When he's done with his interview, I want you all to welcome him."

I kept eating my toast. I felt like I'd been chewing the same bite for ages now, and the bread sat like cement in my mouth. Nobody at the table spoke, so the sound of chewing was amplified. I itched to get up and leave.

"Where is Murray?" I asked Beatrice, who had approached the table with a cup of coffee in her hand. I caught a whiff of liquor as she moved, but it was quickly overpowered by her rich, floral perfume. She glanced at me, her eyes scanning over my dress before she frowned and looked away.

"He was speaking with his father, trying to come up with a plan of action for the business. He's always been very involved, but it's time for him to step up into a role of leadership. The whole company has been upturned by Beau's death. Phillip is distraught. He won't leave the bedroom." Her tone was cold and dismissive of Phillip's pain. She was actively avoiding making eye contact with me. It was such a stark difference from the first two days of our visit here, where it felt like she had her eyes trained on me. Studying me.

Since when had Murray been involved in the company? He'd never mentioned his family's company, much less anything about his family *at all*. My mind was spinning. It was a relief, though, that someone had finally mentioned Beau. I glanced around the room, looking for a reaction to his name, but everyone continued eating, their faces completely placid.

Gloria cleared her throat, from the doorway, and we all looked up. "Miss Eve," she said, "the detective would like to speak to you in the Blue Room."

Eve set her espresso down and muttered under her breath, "Thank God. I can't wait to get the hell out of here." She exited the room, leaving behind a tense silence.

Beatrice began making conversation with each guest, positioning herself next to their chair, yet somehow always in the most flattering stream of sunlight. I wasn't very fond of Beatrice, but I couldn't deny the sting I felt at her sudden loss of interest in me. I'd clearly done something to hurt her feelings, and I wondered if I should try to speak to her about it. Maybe when I was less on the verge of throwing up.

I took a long drink of ice water that William had set next to my plate. *Maybe I didn't hurt Beatrice's feelings,* I thought. Maybe I just didn't perform well enough for her at the party. It was becoming obvious that I was a minor character in her story—just a pawn on a chessboard that she had her finger on, ready to put into action. But now she was moving around the room, eyeing up the other guests, measuring their usefulness to her. Who was which piece? What worth had she assigned to each of us?

As she glided through the dining room, each gesture and word perfect and elegant, it was clear that Beatrice was undoubtedly the queen.

*   *   *

When I finally found Murray, he was in the lounge, a stack of papers in front of him. He wore khaki pants and a blue and white checkered button-down. I'd never seen him tuck in a shirt until this weekend. He sat on an enormous leather sectional that took up half the room. It was oriented toward perhaps one of the largest televisions I'd ever seen, which was integrated into the wall so discreetly that I'd nearly missed it. Below it was a sweeping fireplace with built-in stone seating, a stack of logs and fire tools on one side.

As I rounded the corner, someone else came into view. It was Cindy. She was bright-eyed and seemingly oblivious to the nervous energy wafting through the house. And she had her sights set on Murray.

I stepped back and positioned myself where Cindy couldn't see me. She was standing a few feet away from him, her perfect body leaning toward Murray like an invitation. She swayed her hips back and forth as she talked to him about her life—her friends, her expensive vacations. I wished I could see his face, his reaction. He wasn't saying anything back, just letting her drone on and on, and I silently cheered him on.

She paused and pouted, "You okay?" She leaned over and gently rested her hand on his shoulder. Her tight dress was cut low at the neckline, showing her cleavage.

Murray raised his chin to meet Cindy's gaze. He rested his hand on hers, and my stomach lurched. Then he pulled her hand off his shoulder and mumbled something under his breath. Whatever it was made her flush bright red and turn on her heel, disappearing through the door to the kitchen.

I counted to ten, trying my best not to look like I'd been watching, and knocked on the doorway. Murray had dark circles under his eyes, and his lips were too tired to pull his face into a smile.

"Hey, sweetie," he said. He sounded exhausted. "Oh, nice. You found your dress. Told you it was still in your room."

I resisted the urge to correct him. There was no way it was in the closet the entire time, but there were more important things to talk about. "Yeah, it just turned up, I guess. I've been looking for you everywhere. What have you been doing?"

"I had to talk to the detective first thing, and then all this mess came up." Murray gestured at the coffee table full of papers, and I saw the business header: Sedgemont & Co. Yellow tabs dotted the edges, indicating where he needed to sign. Had he really agreed to take over the family company now that Beau couldn't? I would have hoped he'd talk to me about it first. There was no way he could run the company from Brooklyn. Acid rose in my throat at the possibility that we might have to move here. Would we live here in this house, with his parents?

While planning this conversation in my head, I'd realized that I might get caught in a lie and have to reveal that I'd been in his father's office. But the other option was to keep my mouth shut and possibly marry a man who was sneaky with money behind my back. I had to take the risk.

"Can I talk to you about something?" I asked him as I sat down next to him on the sofa. I tried to keep my tone light and casual, but the edge in it was unmistakable. Despite the plushness of the sofa, I was incredibly uncomfortable. My body was telling me to flee from the impending confrontation, but I knew I had to talk to him about what I'd found.

"Sure, what's up?"

"There were some papers lying around," I started to lie. "They were our bills. Your half of the bills."

"Lying around?" Murray asked suspiciously. "Lying around where?"

I gulped, trying to keep my panic from showing on my face. I had to lie. "In the Blue Room."

Murray's eyes sharpened. He was fully focused now. I studied the downward angle of his eyes, seeing how much he resembled the ancestral portraits that lined the walls of the home. He stared at me, his mouth slightly open. His tongue darted around in his mouth, back and forth across his teeth. He knew I was lying.

"Why didn't you tell me your parents were paying your half of the bills?" I asked, frustration doubling in the ensuing silence.

Murray kept staring, unblinking. It was like I'd short-circuited his brain with the question, and I was tempted to wave my hand in front of his face.

"Murray?" I asked instead, trying to keep frustration out of my voice.

"I was embarrassed."

"Embarrassed by what?"

He sat there, and I wondered if he was genuinely trying to think of a way to express his embarrassment or if he was trying to think of the most convincing lie.

"That I needed help," he said in a hushed voice. It was almost inaudible.

I nodded slowly. I'd had to ask my parents for help before, so I understood the shame that came from asking for a handout. But the difference was that when I asked my parents for money, I was taking from them what they barely even had. When Murray did it, his parents hardly noticed the money leave their bank account.

"How long have they been helping you?"

Murray was flipping his phone back and forth in his hand, and the glass screen caught the light from above and then went dark, again and again.

I reached out to stop him from fidgeting.

"Since college," he mumbled. He hadn't met my eyes this whole time. "But not for free. I've been helping with the company, and that's how they pay me."

He'd never mentioned helping with the company, and I'd never seen any sign of it. He was so absorbed in his work at the gallery that I wasn't sure how he had the time to do anything else. Maybe all the extra meetings he'd been going to weren't actually for the gallery, I realized. I exhaled loudly, and the noise of it surprised both of us. Murray flinched and finally looked at me. Tears were bristling on the edge of his lower lashes.

He was only giving me half the truth. Yes, his parents had been helping him, and it was a lie of omission not to tell me. I could live with that if it were the only lie. But my frustration was mounting as it became clear he wasn't going to tell the full truth—the truth about where all the money *he* earned was going. Either he hadn't realized I'd seen the glaring issue, or he thought I was too stupid to make the connection.

I hadn't even brought up the paintings. How long had they been buying out the gallery so that Murray could look successful? The sad thing was that he was actually amazing at his job. I was confident that if his parents hadn't bought out the gallery every time Murray was in charge of a show, that some rich art lover would have come along and done it. They hadn't even given him a chance to succeed on his own.

It was about control, I realized. His parents didn't fully believe in him, so although they knew he might succeed on his own, it was better if he made it on their terms and on their time. Money brought them instant gratification. Everything at the tip of your fingers—and if you couldn't reach it, you could sure as hell hire someone to push it toward you.

"I'm not going to keep asking you questions. If there's more you'd like to tell me—and I'm sure there is—you can tell me right now," I said, leaning back on the sofa. I crossed my arms out of reflex and uncrossed them, placing my hands on my knees. I wanted to look open to this conversation despite the irritation boiling in my blood.

Murray's eyes darted across my face, as though he were trying to determine how much I knew.

The silence was overbearing, and I wanted to shout, *"Just say it, already!"* Instead, I clamped my lips together, waiting for his next words.

"Everything I make goes to us," he said.

"What does that mean?"

"It means," he said, faltering, "everything I earn goes to our future."

"Murray, that's not telling me anything. You're not actually saying anything."

He sat there silent, the corners of his mouth twitching as if, inside, his tongue was twisting, stitching up some elaborate lie. "My salary goes into my savings account," he finally said, "where we can use it in the future. To buy a house or something. Or for our kid's college fund." His voice cracked as he fought off tears, and a wave of guilt swept over me. I loved this man, and up until now I'd trusted him with every cell in my body. But now I had no idea if he was telling the truth. On the surface, the thought of it was sweet and thoughtful, but why wouldn't he tell me about it if it was for both of us? Did I even believe him?

"And the paintings?" I asked, my voice shaking. I was trying to keep my composure because I knew Murray shut down at the first sign of a raised voice or tear. I was on the verge of failing.

He sighed, sounding exasperated and confused—a little frustrated with me, even. "What paintings?"

"Your parents have some of Lucas Goedert's paintings around the house." I gulped. I might have just given away where I'd been last night.

"They do?"

I searched his face, looking for truth. His eyebrows were stitched together, the muscles in his forehead rippling his usually smooth skin into deep crevices.

I nodded slowly, realizing he was genuinely confused.

He shook his head. "No, I read the invoices from the buyer—some rich guy from Calabasas. He bought out the whole gallery." His voice cracked, and his chin puckered and twitched.

"But I saw them. Here. In this house."

He leaned forward, closing the space between us. "That's my job, Kass. I think I would know who bought the goddamn paintings," he snapped, immediately recoiling at his own venom. My entire body tensed at his anger.

"You cannot speak to me like that, Murray," I huffed out in shock.

"I'm sorry," he spat out, tears coming to his eyes again. His tears were like weapons, twisting my feelings behind my back and pushing me in whatever direction he wanted. I stood up, unwilling to subject myself to this conversation any longer.

"Kass, please. I'm sorry. I thought I had finally done something on my own. This is so overwhelming. This house, my family. Please just stay with me." He sandwiched my hand between his, desperation making his fingers stiff and clammy.

"We'll talk later when you've had time to calm down," I said on my way out.

"Please, I need you," he begged quietly.

And I needed him too. But not this version of him—this version that could snap and curse at me when I was asking important questions. Not the version that would hide important things from me.

I walked through the entrance hall and opened the front doors, letting the humid summer heat pummel me.

20

As I squinted my eyes against the sun, I was shocked to make out trucks and cars outside the perimeter of the gate. There was a sea of people as well, their shapes gradually becoming tangible as my eyes adjusted. They were forming their own gate of flesh and bone, trapping us in.

I stepped off the front porch and into the full blast of the sun. The heat was dizzying and rippled off the gravel driveway, distorting everything in front of me in flickering waves.

The people outside the gate were unloading things from the beds of their trucks, as if they'd just gotten here. The fountain in the middle of the driveway provided the only shade inside the gate, and I crossed the driveway to sit on its edge, basking in the cool ripples of air that flowed over the water. I could already feel sweat soaking through my clothes.

In the shade of the fountain, I could make out faces now. The majority were men, dressed in T-shirts or short-sleeved polos with worn jeans. Their boots twisted on the gravel outside the gate as they unloaded their trucks.

What were they holding? I squinted my eyes to see. They looked like cardboard boxes.

I dipped my hand into the water and reveled in the chill. The people were lining up now, pressing their bodies into the iron bars of the gate. I could see now that they were holding signs.

"Murderers!" One sign read, the letters etched out in thick black marker. "Job thieves," read another. "Traitors to America!"

They were protesters, I realized, with the occasional reporter mixed into the crowd with a microphone poised for a sound bite. The heat had slowed my thinking, and I was embarrassed at how I must look, lounging by a fountain in my dress, watching the townsfolk protest against my future family.

"Hey, you!" someone yelled from behind the gate. I cupped my hand over my eyes, trying to peer through the sunlight to find the source of the voice.

I stood and wiped my wet hand on my dress. I was going to ignore them and go back into the house, but being inside seemed worse than cooking in the heat with a bunch of angry strangers.

"Ma'am! Excuse me, I have a couple of questions for you," a man called out from behind the gate. Another man stood behind him with a camera pointed directly at me.

I made eye contact with the reporter and froze. *Shit.* I pictured myself on people's TV screens, scurrying away like somebody who had something to hide.

I ambled forward toward the man with the microphone. I was only a foot or two away from the small crowd of people behind the gate. What was I supposed to say?

"Hi," I said dumbly, my face scanning the angry faces in the crowd.

"What is your name?" the man asked. He wore a blue polo that said WLOS News.

"I'm Kass. I'm just visiting," I said, not explaining my relationship to the Sedgemonts. It was a lie of omission, but it felt like the right move.

A woman stepped forward, jostling the reporter's shoulders to stand directly across from me, the bars still separating us. Who was the prisoner, me or them? "Were you there? Did you see it?" She had brassy blonde hair pulled into a ponytail topped by a black Appalachian State baseball cap. I couldn't tell how old she was, but her face was carved with deep laugh lines. She spoke with a thick Southern accent made raspy by years of North Carolina tobacco.

"See what?"

"The murder."

"No." I paused, both shocked that the news had already gotten out and not surprised at all. "Just the body." I clenched my jaw. I wished I could take it back, stuff the words into my mouth and swallow. Why had I said that?

Maybe it was because I hadn't had a chance to talk to anyone about it yet. Murray had asked me how I was, but it was the automated kind of question that a barista or a waiter might ask. It hadn't even felt like he'd listened to my answer: *"No, I'm not okay."*

Everyone in the house was distracted, so I couldn't be mad. But that didn't mean I didn't want to talk about it.

The crowd exploded in questions, and I stepped backward, aware of the sound of urgent footsteps behind me.

"I'm sorry—I shouldn't have said that. I don't know anything else."

"This isn't the first time a body has been found around this family," the woman said.

"What?" I rasped, just as a hand gripped my shoulder. I flinched, turning to see William's face, wrinkled with concern and something else. Anger maybe.

"Come on now, love," William said gently. He had sweat trickling down his temple, his black suit absorbing the heat of the sun.

"Are they ever gonna let you free, Bill?" an older man shouted. Others nodded, backing him up. "Not that we'd want you back."

I stood firm, more from confusion than resoluteness, and William pressed his hand more forcefully into my back, guiding me toward the house. His chin quivered, the words of the protester nicking an artery of emotion. Although he'd spooked me in the dark of the hallway last night, in the light of day he looked pitiful, withered by years of the Sedgemonts' rule.

Despite the heat and the crowd, I didn't want to go back inside. The house towered over us, the reflection of the sun in the windows offering concealment for those inside to stand and watch the spectacle.

My body shivered, already preparing for the discomfort of the cold, drafty house. I surrendered, letting William walk me back inside.

* * *

When William and I stepped into the entrance hall, he closed the door behind me, and I heard the click of the deadbolt and the rustle of fabric as he dropped a key in his jacket's interior pocket.

Was he locking them out? Or us in?

"Kassandra Baptiste," a man's deep voice echoed through the entrance hall, reverberating not as a greeting, but as an accusation. He was wearing gray slacks and a light blue shirt. His tie had been pulled loose at the neck.

I cleared my throat, trying to shake the tremor in my voice. "That's me."

"I'm Detective Campbell. We're conducting interviews today. You're up next. Come join us, please." The detective turned on his heels without another word and walked through the hallway to the Blue Room.

"Good luck," William whispered in a soft, low voice, and I had the sudden pang of missing my father.

I followed in the detective's tracks, turning left into the Blue Room. When I entered the room, the detective stood at a table near the bar cart. I eyed the bottles, still queasy from my hangover but wishing for a drink to take the edge off. A uniformed officer sat with a notebook spread open in front of her.

The detective motioned for me to sit down in a chair that had already been pulled out from the table. He wanted me to hit my mark, move directly into the stage light, and deliver my lines.

The seat of the chair was comfortable, but the carved wooden back jutted into my spine, so I leaned forward. I hoped it didn't make me look like I was on edge.

"This is Officer Garrett," Detective Campbell said.

I nodded at them both, unsure if I should introduce myself. They already knew who I was.

"You must not remember me from the party," the detective said in exaggerated disappointment, as if I'd hurt his feelings.

My brain stuttered, rewinding the night to try to place his face in my memory. I didn't want to find him there; I wanted to prove him wrong.

But there he was, standing slightly behind Janice, another woman nestled between them, her pregnant belly putting space between her and the others. I could picture Campbell's navy-blue suit with the dash of dark cranberry red of his tie. It had brought out the rosiness in his dark skin, which had been aglow with drink or dancing, maybe both.

"You looked pretty unsettled when Janice asked you if you'd ever been in trouble with the law. We all knew she was joking—she tends to do that—but that seemed to have gone over your head." He reached for a stack of papers in front of him and held them vertically, cracking the stack against the table to tidy the already neatly aligned papers.

He continued. "I thought it was strange, so I looked into you. I thought, maybe she does have a record. Maybe this nice girl has a not-so-nice past."

I bristled at the use of the word *girl*, as if I were a child, but I kept my face still. Underneath, my heart rate accelerated with each second that passed. His eyes stayed locked on me, scrutinizing me for any flicker of a reaction.

"I read a lot about you, Ms. Baptiste. About your time at school—or more so the time you weren't actually there. The university seemed very concerned about you."

"Everyone has rough patches."

"That's fair." He took the pitcher from the table and filled his glass, then my own and Officer Garrett's. I wanted him to hurry up and speak. He was toying with me. "It's just that most people's rough patches don't put them on the wrong end of a police investigation."

My jaw clenched, locking my voice away.

Detective Campbell matched my silence. He looked at me inquisitively, his face relaxed and even a bit friendly. I took a sip of water.

He broke eye contact to extract a photograph from his stack of papers. My throat clenched. I already knew what it was going to be as soon as I saw the flash of platinum, the wispy curls.

He spun the photo around on the table with a flourish and pushed it toward me.

Reflexively, I reached out and grabbed it, pulling it toward me and holding it with both hands like a precious jewel. Something to be protected.

"Jacqueline Russo," he said.

The pain of repressed tears building in my throat made it hard to breathe.

"I've already been through this so many times. Please," I whispered. "Please don't make me do it again."

Campbell took a moment, and I could practically see the cogs of his brain spinning, trying to decide how he was going to play me.

"Death is traumatic," he said. The gentle tone of his voice surprised me. "So tell me, Kassandra, how does a young woman your age find herself in the midst of not one, but two suspicious deaths in her short life?"

My cheeks and underarms were burning hot despite the chill in the house. "I had nothing to do with Beau's death last night, or with Jacqueline's death. You should know. You have all the records."

"Yes, I do have all the records." He thumbed through the papers and pulled out a small stack, stapled together in the right corner instead of the left. For some reason, that bothered me. "And according to these *records*"—his tone was derisive now—"you're completely right. Nothing to do with it."

My muscles eased a bit, then constricted even more as he pulled out another stack.

"Except . . ." He paused, tapping the paper. He didn't flip it around so I could see; I couldn't make out a word from this angle. "Except for the tiny issue of one of Jacqueline's family members telling us the opposite."

I froze, unable to bring myself to blink, afraid that he was going to pull another trick out of his stack of papers, and my eyes burned. I knew exactly which family member he was talking about. Jacqueline's brother. He despised me. Maybe he was right to.

"This person claims you're responsible. And that you dragged your friend down into a spiral. That you were responsible for her death and got lucky that the security cameras were at just the wrong angle so that you couldn't be seen. And call me crazy, but doesn't it strike you as one hell of a coincidence that you have a record of being accused of murder, and here you are again, only a few years later. Accused again."

My stomach churned with the threat of vomit. Someone had accused me of murdering Beau? That couldn't be right. I had been at the party, in the stupid dress, being paraded around to everyone, getting gawked at like a zoo animal. "Who did it?"

"Sorry?"

"Who accused me of killing Beau?" Could it have been Cindy? She was enough of a snake to do something like that and had been bold enough to imply it at breakfast.

Campbell ignored my question. "I'm not at liberty to say. But, Kassandra, it's undeniable that it would benefit you greatly as a future member of the Sedgemont clan to keep the business in the bloodline. With Beau out of the way, the eldest Sedgemont son can take over: your future husband. And I heard just a few minutes ago that he will be assuming control. Congratulations, by the way, on the engagement."

Hot pain pulsed in my mouth as I bit down harder on my tongue. I tasted iron. I crossed my arms in front of me and blinked back tears of rage. He was right. I would be benefitting from Beau's death financially, even though I didn't want to be associated with the Sedgemont business, and I absolutely did not want to live in this goddamn house with Murray's family. *My future family,* I corrected.

Officer Garrett looked at my crossed arms and wrote something down. I tucked my arms back into my lap and began picking at my cuticles. "We know you were absent from the party from 9:00 to approximately 9:20 PM. Can you tell us where you were?" Garrett asked.

Silence. The taste of iron in my mouth was overwhelming.

"How did you get those scratches on your arm, Kassandra?" Campbell asked.

"Should I have a lawyer for this?" I asked with a snarl in my voice. Officer Garrett wrote something down.

"Wants lawyer. Definitely guilty" was what I supposed she'd noted.

"I thought you might ask that. You're well versed in these types of things aren't you?" Campbell said. He leaned back in his chair, and the fabric of his shirt stretched against his muscular frame.

"We're just trying to get to know you and a few of the other guests," Officer Garrett said. "But if you're formally requesting representation, we can make arrangements."

"If you're asking a group of us not to leave the house and are questioning us, it seems a bit more serious than just 'getting to know us.' We're basically under house arrest."

"No, we *encouraged* everyone to stay at the house. You can leave at any time," he said.

"And how would that make me look?"

"I think you already know the answer to that."

Anger pulsed red, clouding my rationale. It was spilling over, filling my mouth with venom. "Wait, if you were at the party *and* drinking, isn't that some kind of conflict of interest?" I glared at Detective Campbell, whose eyebrow flickered into an arch before settling. He smiled, his teeth white and shining, a stark contrast to his deep skin. Officer Garrett shifted uncomfortably in her seat.

"A man is allowed to have a glass of champagne and a dance with his wife." I could hear the smile in his voice as I picked at my fingernails. When I looked up, the smile was nowhere to be found.

"Were you there? When we found the body?"

"No. We left early. My wife says pregnancy and high heels don't mix." His voice softened at the mention of his wife. His Bad Cop routine was clearly over.

I remained silent.

Campbell rose from his chair, and Officer Garrett followed suit. I stayed seated, feeling woozy.

"Thank you for speaking with us. We'll be talking to the other guests throughout the day and may need to speak with you again. Don't go anywhere."

"I thought you said I could leave at any time."

He gave a breathy laugh and pulled a business card out of his pocket. "Whenever you feel ready to talk." They left the room, bickering about where they'd eat lunch and commenting on the wall of protesters blocking the gate. I stayed seated. The business card lay heavy in the palm of my hand, and I gripped it hard, feeling its edges bite into my palm.

I had nowhere to go. Maybe I would be stuck in this house forever.

21

I FINALLY ROSE FROM the table when a commotion erupted in the dining room. Many voices were speaking excitedly all at once. I was ashamed to even hear the sound of happiness—it felt inappropriate to just be near it. Aside from the detective speaking to me, the Sedgemonts and their guests had somehow made it appear like nothing had happened, that we were just a group of people recovering from a late-night party instead of a murder.

Janice, Cindy, and Lyle were all standing around the dining room table, oblivious to Gloria trying to snake through them to clear empty glasses and plates of half-eaten food. They were drinking mimosas now. Beatrice stood next to an unfamiliar man, his posture hunched yet somehow cool and collected, like he was too tired to bother. Beatrice waved a hand at Gloria as the housekeeper reached for Beatrice's coffee mug, and Gloria promptly left the room.

"In case you didn't meet him at the party, I would like to introduce you all to Lawrence Holcroft, our lovely financial advisor. He traveled all the way from New York just to celebrate with us. Although the night didn't end the way we wanted it to, it was lovely to be able to spend time with him."

Lawrence stood next to Beatrice, in khakis and a button-down shirt. He had a bony frame, and his thinness sharpened his cheekbones into a whetted blade. When he smiled at us, his eyes wrinkled, making the deep purple circles under them disappear. For a moment he looked fresh and awake, but then his smile faded, exhaustion returning.

"Sorry I wasn't able to join you for breakfast this morning. I had to make a few phone calls and speak with Murray," said Lawrence.

I assumed Lawrence was discussing the company's finances with Murray, gearing him up to take over for Beau. The thought of it filled my chest with heavy lead. According to Detective Campbell, Murray was now the head of the company. He'd turned in the papers without ever discussing it with me. It was a done deal.

"It was a such a shame you couldn't join us for dinner the other night. But alas, busy man, busy schedule. Too busy to eat it seems," Beatrice chirped, and the guests laughed.

So, *this* man was the mysterious missing guest our first night here—the financial wiz who had left an empty seat at the table.

Cindy flicked her hair behind her shoulders and batted her eyelashes as she introduced herself. I imagined her getting ready early this morning, hoping that a handsome rich bachelor would become enamored with her. *Maybe she'll leave Murray alone now,* I thought bitterly.

He spoke to her warmly, mirroring her flirtation. I couldn't help but notice that occasionally his eyes drifted to me, lighting up in recognition. But why? I'd never met him. I stared down at the coffee William brought me, trying to connect his face to the memory that was stirring in my hungover brain. Then I remembered.

The glow of my borrowed cigarette, his vintage lighter glinting off the spark as I inhaled. I blushed as I thought of my rude exit, cutting him off from conversation with a curt "thank you" as I'd already begun to walk away. I was even more embarrassed by my paranoia afterward, convinced that the slightest noise nearby meant he was trailing behind me in the dark, when the whole time it had been Mary Margaret, in the greenhouse with her secret lover. Last night I'd mistaken him to be only a bit older than me, but in the morning light, I could see he was easily twenty years my senior, if not more.

Cindy was not so subtly interviewing him. He lived in Manhattan and knew the Sedgemonts through some sort of convoluted financial advisory role. I swore I'd met at least five men at the party who assisted the family with their finances. Maybe it wasn't so strange, and that's what it was like to have so much money that you needed a full-fledged army to wrangle it all and force it to mutate into an even bigger monster.

Lawrence peeked over at me for the third time, and Cindy followed his gaze. Her perfect face clouded with jealousy before she regained control, a polite smile wiping her envious look away. She turned back to him, and they continued speaking as I left the room.

I meandered aimlessly around the house, not feeling particularly welcome anywhere without Murray by my side, and too restless to sit in my room, when I heard a whimpering coming from the Blue Room bathroom. I stood silently by the door, listening. There was a woman inside, sputtering and sniffling in between tears, occasionally blowing her nose.

Instinct kicked in—I pitied whoever it was—and I knocked on the door lightly. "Are you okay?" I asked.

There was a rustling inside before the door opened, and Mary Margaret appeared in the doorway. Her formerly unblemished, smooth skin was mottled with hives, and mascara ran down her face in inky streams. Nevertheless, "I'm fine," was the first thing she said, her voice cracking and rising at the end.

I stared dumbly at her for a second before reaching out and putting a hand on her shoulder. Mary Margaret wasn't someone I particularly liked, especially after hearing her and Cindy gossiping about me, but I hated to see anyone cry. I expected her to flinch and pull away from me, but instead, she leaned her full body weight into my hand, and I had to raise my other hand to keep her from toppling us both over. Once I was sure she wasn't going to fall, I released my hands, and she wrapped her arms around me.

"Oh, Kass. It's too much," she bellowed into my hair. I rubbed my hand along her back, in a stupor at her sudden show of emotion. I could feel the knobs of her spine through her dress, the bones of her thin arms pressing into me so much that it hurt.

"What's too much? Talk to me," I said softly. She was crying harder now. I suspected that, like me, she was shaken by the thought of someone lying dead upstairs while we drank and celebrated. But now that I was feeling how truly thin she was, I thought perhaps she was confiding in me about something else. She hadn't eaten this morning and had stared at us all while we shoved greasy bacon and scrambled eggs into our mouths.

"I made a terrible mistake," she wailed, her body heaving with sobs.

Was she talking about cheating on Lyle? Or did she have something to do with Beau's death? I stiffened as I thought of her glaring jealously at Beau flirting with a beautiful young woman at the party. Maybe the two were related.

Footsteps approached and Murray appeared, his face twisted with concern. He mouthed to me, asking what was going on. I pushed Mary Margaret's hair out of my face and mouthed, "I don't know," as I stiffly patted her back.

Murray began to walk away, but a floorboard beneath him creaked and Mary Margaret's cries came to a sudden halt. She pulled away from me, unwinding her spindly limbs from mine. As she turned her head to look, I saw that her face was flat and completely devoid of emotion. It could have been that she was embarrassed by her extreme show of guilt.

But as she straightened herself and walked out of the room, I couldn't help but wonder if it had all been an act.

* * *

After disentangling myself from Mary Margaret, I stood awkwardly with Murray in the Blue Room. We no longer felt at ease alone together, and the silence that used to be comfortable and easy was charged now.

"What was her deal?" Murray said with a scoff. The judgment in his voice set my teeth on edge.

"She's scared, Murray. Just like me," I said sharply, reminding him that he hadn't let me stay with him. Reminding him that he'd picked his mother over me.

"Kass, I'm sorry." He paused and his apology filled me with hope, but it immediately dissipated when he continued, "but you have to let that go. This is her house, her rules."

"Why is nobody taking this seriously? Somebody was *murdered*, Mur. Mary Margaret and I have every right to be—"

"Murray!" Beatrice called from the kitchen. How was it that every time I tried to talk to him, we were interrupted by someone? William walked by the doorway, and I wondered if he had been listening. Had he signaled to Beatrice that I was trying to talk to him? The thought of someone always lurking outside a doorway sent a chill down my spine.

"One second," Murray said, already walking away.

"Are you serious?" I huffed, but he was already too far to hear me.

I wandered purposelessly around the house, trying to warm my limbs. My limbs were stiff and shivering from the air-conditioning. It had been chilly when we'd first arrived, but each day it had grown colder, as if the house were declaring that I was not welcome. To add insult to injury, there was also a damp, rotting smell coming from the vents, pushing into each room with the air-conditioning.

I didn't know where I was supposed to go now, what I was supposed to do. I didn't feel welcome in any room but my own, and even that wasn't comforting. I wanted to bury myself in Murray's warmth—to bring back the sheer, addicting comfort of being held by someone I trust. I tried to picture myself walking up to him now, burrowing my face into the crook of his neck. Would I feel that comfort? Was there any trust left?

Maybe I could go outside again, let the sun warm my skin, welcome the heat of it. The only problem was that the protesters were still in full swing, blocking the gate with their thick sea of bodies and signs. I could hear them from the entrance hall, shouting, some of them laughing. I wondered what they thought of me. If they hated me.

My phone buzzed in my pocket, and my steps faltered. Every time my phone vibrated, a wave of nausea rushed through me. The past few texts had been mundane, Zoey checking on me, or a coworker ignoring my paid-time-off status with an urgent email. I took my phone out and prayed that it was Zoey. But it was another anonymous DM.

You're next.

My phone slipped from my hand and landed with a dull thud on the floor. I stared at it, lying there with its glowing face blazing up at me. The gray icon of the anonymous person stared back at me, demanding attention. I bent over to pick it up, and stomach acid filled my mouth, burning the back of my tongue. I nearly retched.

I marched to the front door. I felt trapped, like each dark corner of the house hid the shadow of the person who was texting me. Each message had arrived at just the worst moment, and that had to mean it had been the perfect moment for my tormentor—for whoever it was that was feeding off my life, watching it like a performance.

The realization pummeled me—an unwanted epiphany. Until now, I'd only thought they were watching me through social media. But I'd stopped posting any digital crumbs of my life. If they weren't finding them online, could they be watching me here at the estate?

I gripped the knobs on the front door with both hands, ready to fling them open, when I remembered William had locked the door. I shook the door furiously, not caring how much noise it made as the looming wood and iron doors rattled in their frames. He hadn't locked anyone out; he'd locked us in.

I gnawed on a fingernail, trying to think of a way out. I looked up over the banisters to the second and third floor, eyes running along the detailed wood paneling of the walls.

Gloria's staircase.

"Kass," Murray called to me from the entrance hall.

"What?" I said, spinning around. I wasn't in the right headspace for a heart-to-heart, or whatever the hell it is he wanted. The threat of an anxiety attack was building in my body, my fingertips and toes going numb and tingling.

"We need to talk about everything. We have a lot of big decisions to make."

"Please don't act like I have any say in those decisions. You already signed the papers. And there are more important things to think about right now."

"Like what?"

"You've got to be kidding me. The dead body that was just removed from the house, for one. And I think they're coming after me now."

He stared at me, his eyebrows knitted together in confusion. "Who? What are you talking about?"

"I've been getting messages since we got engaged. I don't know who they're from, but the last one said, 'You're next.'"

"Show me."

I pulled up the most recent message on my phone. *You're next.* My hands were shaking now, panic still building in my chest.

Murray let out a belittling chuckle. He might as well have slapped me in the face. "It's probably just some troll. You know how people are."

He was talking to me like I was a hysterical child. I stared at him, unable to respond.

"Or maybe they mean you're next to get married. You know, because you posted about our engagement. I wouldn't make a big deal over nothing," he half-heartedly assured me. His tone was dismissive, and he wasn't looking me in the eye.

"I'm not making a big deal over nothing, Murray. This is a threat."

"Calm down, Kass. There's nothing to worry about."

"I can't do this right now," I said, practically panting. I was having trouble controlling my breathing. I needed to get out.

I hurried toward the back of the house, pushing on panels in the hallway as I went. I could hear Murray's footsteps behind me for a moment, but they quickly stopped. I could practically feel his stare burning the back of my neck. To Murray it probably looked like I was drunk, bracing myself against the wall. It didn't matter though, because he didn't call after me or even follow me.

Menacing gray clouds peeked in through the French doors at the end of the hallway, threatening violence if I stepped outside. I ambled toward them anyway, still pressing against the wall looking for the concealed doorway. As I got closer to the end of the hallway, the wall gave way with a click under my palm.

With a deep breath, I stepped in and closed the door behind me. I stood frozen for a moment in the unfamiliar darkness before I came to my senses and used the flashlight on my phone to find the light switch. I flicked it on, and the bare bulbs came to life.

I could only assume that going down the passage would lead to Gloria's basement apartment, and I said a hasty, selfish prayer that she wouldn't be there so I could slip out without a trace. I began down the thin, steep stairs, cautious of where my feet were at all times. When I got to the bottom and pushed open the panel, I tried to pull myself together in case Gloria was there. I inhaled and stepped through.

It took a few seconds for my eyes to adjust to the dark room, the afterimage of the glaring lights fluttering and drifting in front of my eyes each time I blinked.

The laundry room was dark, and it seemed nobody was down here. I tried to picture where Gloria could be in the house. Maybe she had been in the passageway as well, right behind me. I shuddered at the thought.

I snaked my way through her living space and slipped out the door to her patio. There was an ashtray filled to the brim with cigarette butts, colored in the same rich berry shade of lipstick that Gloria always wore.

The sky overhead was darkening, making it look like it was early evening rather than lunchtime. I knew it probably wasn't safe to be outside with the oncoming storm and the protesters, but I kept going, walking straight for a copse of trees. It was better than being inside. I didn't have proof that my harasser was nearby, but every time I received a message, the hairs on the back of my neck rose, and my skin prickled, as if they were behind me, their hate burrowing under my skin.

I reached a patch of trees that offered some privacy from the protesters, but their anger was still audible. Slumped against the trunk of an old, gnarled tree, I reveled in the coolness of the earth through the thin fabric of my dress. My back stuck to the rough tree bark, but I didn't care.

I felt so helpless and so alone. I needed to talk to someone.

I unlocked my phone and dialed Zoey's number. Even though she was an aloof, eccentric artist, she was the most logical and brutally honest person I knew. She would tell me how to fix everything. She could calm me down.

Thunder rumbled in the distance. The temperature had drastically dropped, and the sun was losing its battle against the clouds, casting everything in a sickly green-gray shadow. As I listened to the phone ring, squirrels and birds rustled overhead, finding shelter in the treetops and hedges. Maybe I should find shelter too.

A robotic voice on the other line told me that I'd reached Zoey's voicemail, and I ended the call before it could finish.

I opened my photos app and scrolled all the way back to 2017. The screen was filled with a display of platinum blonde, our obsessive friendship narrated in a tidy grid.

I thought it had begun to rain, but they were tears smacking against the screen.

Tilting my head back, I stared up into the canopy of leaves above me and let myself think of Jacqueline.

22

IT WAS SPRING of 2018, the end of our sophomore year at NYU. We had been drinking a lot, getting more than our money's worth from our fake IDs. We hadn't gone to classes all week and instead were studying the art of bingeing. Days one through eight were alcohol. Then on day nine we'd met some rich banker type at a bar, who'd given us bags of coke like he was passing out candy. Jacqueline had stared at the powder in disgust at first.

"Why not?" I'd said. "A little won't hurt, right?" The men had egged us on, and my heart raced, thrilled by being on the precipice of something dangerous, something so unlike us. When we both finally gave in, Jacqueline's eyes had a glint in them I'd never seen before.

We'd hung around the men for a week or so, and they'd thrown cash at bartenders and waiters, dazzling us with a lifestyle we'd never seen. At first, we were just arm candy—but one of them had grown attached to Jacqueline, despite being old enough to be her father.

He paid no attention to me, and I returned the favor. He'd kept calling me Kacey, but Jacqueline . . . he remembered her name. He'd become a bit obsessed with her, the two of them sneaking around without me, staying up until the early hours of the morning at fancy bars, drinking twenty-dollar cocktails like water. I couldn't even remember what he looked like, aside from his jet-black hair and portly frame. In my memories of those weeks, all the men looked the same. A crisp suit, gelled hair, and a five o'clock shadow. It wasn't accurate, but they didn't matter enough to be remembered in any greater detail.

We'd continued on like this, past our failed sophomore exams, our grades just barely good enough to keep us from having to repeat the entire semester. Weeks went by and our parents had been texting more and more, asking when we would be coming home for summer break.

Admittedly, we both knew, even in the moment, that we should stop, that we should remove ourselves from that man and his friends. We'd become reckless, rail thin and pale, but the sparkle in our eyes was feverish and determined, like it was our fate to run ourselves into the ground for the sake of a little fun.

One night—I believe it was the fourth month of our binge—we'd been out. Not with that man and his friends—we'd picked a bar where we'd never seen the man she'd been hanging out with. Jacqueline had said she needed a break from him, that he'd become a little overbearing, that his gifts had become bribes. Every time I remember her telling me this, I'm flooded with the shame of knowing that I saw the vine of finger-shaped bruises flowering up her wrist and had done nothing. Said nothing. But neither had she. Neither of us wanted to risk losing the new lifestyle we'd become dependent on.

The lights had been low and glowing gold against the black marble bar. Everyone around us looked like New York City royalty, wearing chic, expensive outfits; an air about them as they walked into the room that they were meant to be here—meant to be anywhere in the city because they owned it like gods.

That night, our usual trick of picking out the richest and most amenable person in the bar to buy us the cocktails we couldn't afford had worked. I was sipping the most expensive gin I'd ever had at the behest of a short, animated man who'd claimed he'd had a five-thousand-dollar cocktail at the Baccarat Hotel not once, but *twice*. After asking if he could take me to the hotel for a night cap in order to try it, I'd denied him, so he'd settled on making me taste just one of the liquors in the drink. I played along, settling on Nolet's Reserve Gin.

"It's only a hundred bucks. That's nothing to me, babe," he'd said, and I'd smiled.

Two hours later Jacqueline and I had accrued a crowd around us. We'd become quite talented at schmoozing like we belonged. You just had to tell people what they wanted to hear. We weren't taking advantage of them, really. Well, maybe at first, but they seemed to like it. They had joy in their eyes as they flaunted their money for two pretty young women who stroked their egos. It wasn't just men; it was women too. Greed and pride don't distinguish between genders.

Neither of us had yet realized that it was the last night of our binge. Our last night to make the city our playground and throw away hours chasing highs.

At some point in the night, a man in a sleek navy-blue suit had wedged himself between our bar stools, hands outstretched behind us and gripping the backs of our chairs. After introducing himself, he'd opened his hand to show us two capsules in his palm, a cloudy white powder inside.

We'd eyed him suspiciously at first, and he'd stared back playfully, his pupils swallowing the blue of his irises. We'd only had a few drinks, and nothing else that night, and we were eagerly seeking out our next high.

"Open your mouths," he'd said, his voice gruff and alluring. And we did.

He'd slid the capsules between our lips, one at a time, the ritual of it intimate, the danger of it enticing.

The rest of the night was a blur as we moved from bars to nightclub booths, lights flashing, sweat dripping down the backs of our tight dresses. None of the faces or names mattered, but we loved each and every one of them like they were family.

That is, until he walked in. The man who had grown enamored with Jacqueline, so hungry for her company that he'd visited each of our usual haunts every night until he'd finally found us.

The sun was beginning to rise, and the rolling waves of euphoria had become limp with sweat. The moment she saw that man, her face had become stiff and unmoving. She'd untangled our sweaty limbs from those of our temporary friends, and I'd fought back, not wanting the night to end just yet.

"He's here," she whispered, her hands gripped hard around my wrists.

"Who?" I tittered, mistaking her intensity for excitement.

She didn't answer, and instead stooped low, weaving us through the crowd. She still gripped my arm like a leash, and in the dim light, I saw that the bruises around her wrists crept up toward her shoulders, some fresh bluish-purple ones and others yellowed with time. In that moment, I understood, and I crept low behind her until we ran out into the night.

When we arrived at the subway, we'd sat hunched on a bench, waiting for the train. Not a single person was nearby, and the silence around us shivered with violence. The night had taken such a swift turn, and something unspoken was broiling between us.

I worked up the courage to say what we both knew would eventually come, what we'd both been dreading. I kept my eyes on the dirty ground as I spoke, my voice cowardly and soft.

"We need to stop."

Jacqueline didn't speak for minutes that dragged on and on, but I could feel her staring at me, her gaze angry and sharp. I was too weak to meet her eyes.

"That's rich coming from you."

Finally, I looked at her, and the set of her face made tears sting in my eyes. Her jaw was tense, the muscles beneath her skin pulsing in anger. Her eyes were red and ringed with dark makeup. I was suddenly glad nobody was here to see us. As the beginnings of sobriety crept in, I could see we looked as terrible as we felt. We probably had for quite some time now; we just hadn't been able to see it under the low lighting and constant onslaught of manufactured dopamine.

I said nothing. My dry tongue rolled around my mouth, tasting the stale alcohol. I wanted to brush my teeth and get in bed, sleep for days. I wanted to take back the mess I'd dragged us into, erase the bruises from her arms.

Jacqueline stood and paced in front of me, closer to the edge of the platform.

I rose unsteadily, my arms wrapped tight around my chest. It was a warm summer night, but I was shivering, my body fighting against the months of toxins I'd inflicted on it.

"We can still go out," I said, trying to bargain to keep our friendship afloat. "We just need to cut back."

"Don't fucking tell me what I can and cannot do, Kassie." She spun around and her face was close to mine, her shoulders pulled back, wide and threatening. She was the only one who called me Kassie. It had always been special, but now it sounded profane.

"I'm not—"

She poked a finger into my sternum, and the force of it was sharp and startling. "You're the one who started all this. Don't act like you're perfect. What was it you said? *"A little won't hurt?"* Well it did fucking hurt, Kassie." She held her arms out, the bruises a trail of accusations along her skin. "And you didn't do shit to help. All of this is your fault."

Anger fired in my brain, and my vision blurred with it. I was drunk with it, eager to feel something now that my system was bereft of every chemical I'd been using to keep myself afloat.

"It's not my fault you can't control yourself," I bit back, defiant despite my hypocrisy.

Her open palm came hard and fast, too quickly for me to move aside. I felt the sting of it across my face and ran my tongue along my gums, tasting the iron tang of blood.

Anger and guilt swelled inside me, and I pushed her. She stumbled backward onto the thick stripe of yellow paint that lined the edges of the platform.

I gasped as she lost her balance, but she regained control and barreled back toward me, pushing me as hard as she could. The back of my head cracked against the thick concrete pillar and she pressed my shoulders into it. My feverish heartbeat echoed the thrum of the oncoming train.

Her breath was rancid as she roared over the train, "Don't ever speak to me again!"

She turned to walk away and stumbled as I gripped the long metal chain of her purse that she'd strung across one shoulder. She turned to rip her purse from my hands, but I let go before she began to pull, too tired to fight back. My ears buzzed with pain, and I just wanted to give up. The train rumbled closer now, all the sounds in my head and around me too much.

She must have miscalculated the strength of her pull, thinking I would fight back. Her ankle wobbled in her tall heels, and I watched in horror as she lost her balance one final time.

The sound of the train was deafening, but I could still hear her scream as she fell.

23

RAIN BEGAN TO fall steadily over the property—soft, slow patters on the crown of leaves above, then fast and angry. I stood quickly, blood rushing to my head and knocking me off balance for a moment. Reflexively, I started toward the front door and then remembered it was locked. My clothes were already nearly soaked through, and I raced toward Gloria's apartment.

Through the door I rushed, eager to get out of the rain, not even pausing to wonder if Gloria would be in her apartment.

"Jesus Christ." Gloria's voice startled me. She stood in the laundry room, frozen behind a tower of crisp white bath towels. I'd clearly frightened her too, as she'd knocked over a portion of her hard work onto the floor.

She scowled at me. "You can't come in that way. This is a private area."

"I'm so sorry. I got caught in the rain. William locked the front door . . ." I trailed off.

She approached me with a towel in hand, the gesture soft, but her face still hard with irritation.

"I didn't mean to scare you. Or invade your space. I'm sorry."

She nodded but stayed silent. In that moment she reminded me of my mother, who was skilled in wielding disappointment deftly like an axe—a much deadlier weapon than anger.

"Have the police spoken to you?" I asked.

"Yes."

Her reticence to speak to me cut deeply, and I could tell the rumors of my involvement in Beau's murder had reached her. She picked up a wide laundry basket and began filling it with folded towels.

"Gloria, if you know anything about Beau's death, please tell me. Or tell the detective."

The laundry basket was full now, and she propped it against her hip, ready to leave and continue her work. "I can't help you," she said. "Now if you'll please excuse me, I'm very busy."

I positioned myself in front of her, blocking her from moving through the doorway. "Please, you have to help me. The police think I did this. You haven't known me long, but you have to know I didn't hurt Beau." My voice cracked as I said his name.

"I don't know anything about the party."

"*The party,*" she said, as if she couldn't bear to say Beau's name. Her resolve was crumbling, her face relaxing as she studied my face. "But I know those boys are trouble."

"Which boys? The twins? Murray?" I spat out quickly.

"The twins," she said with her eyes downcast. She was chewing on her lip as if she were trying to keep the words in her mouth.

"Why are they trouble? Gloria, you have to tell me." I restrained myself from grabbing her shoulders. If I did grab her, I didn't know whether I would shake her or wrap her in a hug. I needed comfort. I needed assurance. But she didn't owe me anything. And I knew that.

"Come with me." She set the basket down and took my hand, dragging me out of the laundry room and into her apartment. Despite the glass French doors opening out onto a back patio, it felt like we were both trapped in here. How could she live here? With these people—these monsters?

If I didn't do anything and Murray became the head of the company, I would have to live here too.

She locked the French doors and inched close to me, whispering. "About five years ago, the twins were brought back from boarding school. Nobody ever told me what happened—nobody ever *tells* me anything; I just overheard it—but there were detectives swarming the house for weeks. They came all the way from New Hampshire."

"What were they investigating?" I asked with a trembling voice. I desperately wished for a cigarette. Or a drink. Something to take the edge off.

"They were questioning the twins in the Blue Room. It's directly above this room, and with the vents I can hear nearly every word." Gloria took a deep breath and shook her head. "From what I could understand, a girl died—another student at the boarding school. She was in the same grade as the twins."

"How did she die?"

"She had pills in her hand when a faculty member found her. Some kind of sedative." Gloria's voice cracked, and she paused to grab a glass of water off the table. As she took a sip, the water in the glass trembled, sloshing a single drop down her chin. She wiped it away.

"So why were they interviewing the twins?" I asked.

"When the toxicology report came back, there were no pills in the girl's system. It sounded as though she was choked. They were interviewing her closest friends, including the twins."

Both of us stood in silence, as if paying our respects to the young girl.

"So, what happened? With the detectives?" I asked after a moment.

"They just stopped coming back. I don't know anything else," she said with a shrug.

"Gloria"—I paused, trying to think of how to express myself—"were the twins always . . . were they always the way they are now?" I thought of Emmett's drinking, Kennedy's skeletal face and the way they pushed away everyone around them.

"No," she said. "They changed when they went to school."

"How so?"

"Kennedy used to be a happy boy. Healthy. Emmett was . . ." She faltered. "Emmett was a strange boy. Somehow along the way, they've switched lives."

24

LATER, GLORIA LED me up the hidden staircase and into the first-floor hallway, checking first that nobody was around. According to her, I wasn't supposed to know about the staff staircase, and if Beatrice saw us come out, Gloria would be in an enormous amount of trouble.

My phone buzzed in my pocket, and while I didn't even want to look at it for fear of another threatening message, my fingers itched. I caved, unlocking my phone. It was a text from Zoey.

Sorry I missed your call. What's up?

I began texting her back, when there was a loud knock on the front door. William appeared seconds later and unlocked the door, letting in Detective Campbell and Officer Garrett.

They spilled into the entrance hall, their energy abrasive against the smothered, stifled air in the house. Officer Garrett held a bottle of Diet Coke, and the sight of it struck me as odd until I realized that it was because nothing in this house had labels or tags. Not the food, not the towels, or anyone's clothing. It was as if this house was a world of its own, and everything that entered the house was bespoke just for the Sedgemonts.

All I wanted was to prove to them that there was someone in the house who had ill will for me, enough to accuse me of murdering Beau and maybe to hurt me as well. If I could just show them the messages I'd been getting on social media, maybe they could help me.

Adrenaline pulsed through me at the possibility of having someone on my side. A bit of it was fear—I hadn't shown anyone these messages yet, and a part of me felt that if I showed someone, it would make it real. I wouldn't be able to ignore it anymore. I opened the Instagram app and fumbled through the messages menu, ready to show the detective everything.

"Excuse me," I said as I approached them. "Detective, Officer, can I talk to you?"

The detective looked me up and down, eyeing my wet clothes. "Sure, but you need to make it quick," Campbell said. "We've got a lot more people to talk to by five."

I pulled out my phone and held the messages out in front of me like an offering. "I should have mentioned it earlier, but I need to show you these messages I've been getting. At first, I thought it was just a troll or an ex or something, but they're more threatening now. It could be related." I cleared my throat, trying to sound more confident. "I think it's related."

Their eyes danced across the screen. I expected their faces to light up at the prospect of a lead, but instead their eyebrows furrowed, and they were looking at me now.

"How do we know you didn't just send these to yourself?" Campbell asked.

"How would I even do that?" I said, incredulous.

"You can do anything with phones these days. Desperate measures."

"They've been messaging me since Murray and I got engaged a few days ago—before I even met Beau. This is the fourth one."

"Well, if it started days before the murder, it doesn't sound like it's related. Excuse me." He motioned to William, already completely removed from our conversation, and then looked down at his notebook. "Could you bring me Kennedy, please?"

William nodded and ascended the stairs, coming back moments later with Kennedy in tow. He was wearing jeans that were too loose for his frame and a plaid button-down shirt. He looked worse as the days progressed—the circles under his eyes a deep purple bruise surrounded by ashen skin, and with dry, chapped lips.

As he passed me, I waited for the smell of stale alcohol, but there was none. Instead, he smelled like Old Spice and fresh laundry. He raked his fingers through his hair with trembling hands. I wondered how long it had been since he'd had a drink.

Detective Campbell walked him into the Blue Room, and Officer Garrett closed the door behind them.

There was a rustling above me. It was Emmett, his eyes sharp and focused on me. A smile spread across his face, perfectly friendly, but I'd seen how he was looking at me in the moment before the smile. Everyone was sizing me up, trying to decide if I was capable of murder.

He sauntered down the stairs and stood next to me, in the middle of the entrance hall.

"Some party, huh?" he said. His hands were in his pockets, and he bounced on his heels. I could feel the energy radiating off him, the excitement too much for his body to contain. "You take a shower in your clothes?"

I said nothing. I'd been so determined to show Detective Campbell the messages that I'd briefly forgotten my clothes were completely soaked through. The corner of my lip twitched.

"How did your interview go?" he asked.

"Not great."

He waited for me to say more, but I stood in a daze, staring at the door to the Blue Room.

"Not surprising."

I ignored the jab and stumbled away from him, weak with dehydration and panic. Uniformed officers were ushering in a team of crime scene investigators, their white forensic suits looking foreign against the backdrop of the traditional decor. More police officers trailed behind them.

Maybe fifteen minutes later, Kennedy emerged from the Blue Room and instantly began trailing behind Emmett like a shadow. Campbell and Officer Garrett stood in the Blue Room doorway, whispering something to one another.

Emmett nodded toward the crew of crime scene investigators. "Why are they here again? I thought they already came?" Emmett asked Campbell.

"The crime scene has been tampered with," he answered, frustrated by the interruption.

My heart stuttered, and saliva evaporated in my mouth, my tongue desiccated with panic. I thought of the mess I'd made in the office last night. After the team was done collecting evidence, I had overheard an officer tell Beatrice that they would have a crew arrive the next day to clean up, but otherwise they were finished investigating the crime scene. I would have never gone in there if I thought they would be back. I felt sick at my naivety and dug my fingernail into the palm of my hand, trying to regain control over my body.

"Tampered with?" Emmett asked.

"Yes, that's what I said," Campbell said, and walked away.

The twins' eyes were wide in shock at Campbell's tone, a dumbfounded expression on their faces. It didn't appear they were used to not being catered to and that Campbell's brusque manner was a first for them.

"What a dick," Kennedy mumbled as he took a bite of a sandwich and retreated into the kitchen. Emmett stared up to the second floor for a moment, watching Campbell and his team of investigators make their way to the crime scene.

I waited, frozen in panic. I thought of my blood-stained hands touching the drawers and the papers, my crimson knees dotting the floor like ellipses. How could I have been so stupid? My alcohol-soaked brain had been certain they were done investigating the crime scene. They'd spent only an hour taking swabs and pictures, and dusting surfaces for fingerprints, before hauling the body away.

A low groan of trepidation began in my throat. I gulped it away. I crept up the stairs to my bedroom. I moved with intention, picturing myself as an actor on one of the stages I designed, moving with easy confidence and purpose. But inside, every cell was convulsing with terror. I had made an error that was about to ruin me.

As I passed the team of investigators on the second floor, I glanced at the open office doors and saw a hint of the disarray inside. Detective Campbell was looking at his phone but glanced up as he saw me out of the corner of his eye. I could feel him studying me as I walked up the last flight to the third floor. When I got there, instead of going into my bedroom, I stood on the third-floor landing and pulled out my phone, pretending to be checking my email, in case someone walked by.

There was a din of professionals below, cameras clicking, and terminology being dictated into handheld recorders, where it would be immortalized, the evidence of my foolishness on display for anyone who was suspicious enough to come after me.

"Hand impressions along the rug, approximately five inches wide," a woman said. Someone responded, too soft to make out their words.

"Two drawers have been opened. All drawers are empty except for one containing a silver necklace," the crime scene technician continued.

I hadn't taken anything with me, which in hindsight was incredibly stupid, considering my bloody fingerprints were dotted over Phillip's papers, including the bills he'd paid for with Murray's name on them. I was also one hundred percent certain that there wasn't a necklace. Whose was it?

"Kassie," a coy voice whispered behind me. The nickname made the hairs on the back of my neck dance. I shivered in my damp clothes.

I spun around to face Cindy, perfectly coiffed and smirking, her arms wrapped in front of her chest, one hip cocked.

"Cindy," I said back.

"There's a rumor going around that you were missing at the party. Funny how people are saying the same about Beau." She pointed at my scratched arm. "Is that a kink or something?"

"If you're trying to play Nancy Drew to get in Detective Campbell's pants, he has a wife. Not that it would matter to someone like you."

She snickered. "You should really get yourself together. You look like a wet rat."

"Thanks, Cindy. Always a pleasure," I said. I was hardly listening. Instead, I was watching as an investigator walked down the stairs with a clear bag. Inside was the necklace that the crime scene tech had said was in the office. Its silver shone against the lights, the metal dotted with clear, glistening gems. It was the necklace Beatrice had lent me, the one she made me change back into for the party. I hadn't even been wearing it when I went in the office. Why would the papers with my bloody fingerprints be missing, but my borrowed necklace be there? My head spun with confusion.

"I had a great talk with Murray this morning. I don't mean to pry, but are you actually ready to help Murray lead the family business? Like, did you even go to college?"

I rolled my eyes so hard spots of black crowded the edges of my vision. "Yes, I graduated from NYU. Ever heard of it?" She made a dismissive sound and opened her mouth to speak, but I cut her off. "And if you're talking about your 'conversation' this morning in the living room, he didn't look particularly friendly when he swatted your hand away."

She blushed. "Figures you were eavesdropping. Someone always is in this stupid house." She looked down the hallway as though checking for a shadow moving in the distance. "Anyway, you should probably change," Cindy said, eyeing my wet, limp dress. "Or you might catch your death."

Her words looped in my head as I hurried to my room. Depending on who said it, the phrase could be harmless. But from her, it seemed anything but.

*   *   *

Once I got to my bedroom, I slid my wet dress off and shivered violently as the icy air bit into my skin. I wanted to dip beneath my blankets and pull them over my head. Instead, I pulled on a pair of dark jeans and a creamy wool V-neck sweater.

The shivers waned as I glanced at my shape in the mirror. The scratches on my arms—something I'd clearly forgotten about before speaking to Detective Campbell—were covered now. I couldn't believe how stupid I was, showing up with an arm covered with fresh wounds. I knew what they were thinking: fingernails scraping down my arm in the middle of a confrontation right before I landed the fatal blow. I would never do that to someone. Not on purpose.

I picked my wet dress up and put it to my nose, thinking I could smell the distinct tang of mildew, but as I inhaled deeply, it wasn't in my clothes. It was something else, the smell of it thick in the air. Either way, I still needed to take them down to the laundry room. I might as well take my ruined pajamas down and make one last-ditch effort to get rid of the stains. *The bloodstains,* I thought, my stomach curdling.

When I went to grab them from the open drawer I'd hung them over, they weren't there. The drawer was closed. I opened it and shuffled back, nearly tripping. My pajamas were neatly folded.

I picked up the flannel pants and held them up to the light. There were no stains in sight. They looked perfectly new.

A piece of paper fluttered to the floor, and I bent to pick it up.

Your secret is safe with me.

That was all the note said, its declaration scrawled in a messy, scratchy hand. It had the hasty carelessness of a man's hand, and I thought of William, standing in the shadows with a peaceful grin on his face.

Had he been smiling because he thought I'd killed Beau? Had he been proud—on my side? I couldn't think of any other reason he'd wash Beau's blood from my clothes, why he would keep his mouth shut about seeing me creep out of the office the night of the party.

If he was on my side, though, who put the necklace in the office? There was no way I could have missed it, not even in the dark.

I put my pajamas back in the dresser, along with the note, and closed the door. I picked up my wet clothes, cringing at the drip of cold rainwater down my wrists.

I snaked my way through the estate, feeling like I was trapped in some sort of infinite time loop in this damn house. Between each floor of the staff staircase, I stood on the tiny landing and noticed I could make out whispers of conversations flowing through the vents at the top of the wall. While they looked old, the vents were intricate in design, and I thought it odd that they would put such expensive vent covers in a staff passageway.

As I moved further down into the house, the voices changed with each vent. It sounded as though the house was whispering to me, but each room held a different person captive, a new secret to be whispered.

When I reached the bottom floor, I was startled by the deep, mournful tones of cello music seeping out of the Blue Room. I clicked the panel closed and peeked out into the first-floor hallway. It was five o'clock and the police had left, leaving us isolated in the house. As if on cue, Beatrice moved into the Blue Room doorway, just barely catching me exiting the staff staircase.

She looked me up and down, taking in my outfit change. "Much better."

"Thanks," I muttered, and turned away.

"A storm is coming," she called after me. I turned halfway to face her.

"There's already one here," I said.

"It can always get worse," she replied, but I kept walking away as I listened to her croaking voice hum along to the sweeping cellos.

Beatrice was right. A more turbulent storm was brewing in the distance, and the air had an increased heaviness to it. The sky was threatening beyond the trees, dark clouds morphing into menacing shapes and creeping, inch by inch, closer to the house.

25

WHEN I REACHED the laundry room, I tossed my clothes in the washer, added detergent, and turned it on. The machine was elaborate, with nearly two dozen settings, and it took me a moment to figure out which buttons to push.

I sat at the table that Gloria used to fold laundry and pulled out my phone, scrolling through social media without taking any of it in. Photoshopped bodies and smooth faces in ads, friend's selfies, hometown pyramid schemes. None of it mattered.

I looked up from my phone at the sound of a hushed voice. It was as though it was right behind me, whispering softly onto my skin, and I shivered at the thought of the walls reaching out to cup a hand to my ear.

The washing machine whirred, and I fumbled with the buttons, trying to stop the machine so that I could hear better. I stood stock-still and held my breath. It was Murray's voice drifting through the ceiling vent, and it sounded like he was talking to Beatrice. I could understand every other word.

I slid the chair out from the table and climbed onto it. It wobbled beneath my weight. I stood taller now, trying to get as close to the vent as possible. The air that was coming out of the vent was ice cold, but I braced myself against it, determined to listen.

". . . found the papers. They're gone," Murray said.

Beatrice said something I couldn't make out, but it sounded dismissive.

"You're not listening, Mother."

There was silence, and then they began speaking at the same time, their voices heated and garbled.

"So what, Murray?" she interrupted. "So she knows we help you out now. It's a bump in your relationship. Welcome to marriage."

"Just because she's not your ideal daughter-in-law doesn't mean you can treat her like trash."

"How dare you not be more grateful. I told you to find a suitable wife, and *that* is who you drag in? When I told you it was time to settle down and get married, I meant with someone like Cindy, for Christ's sake. Someone who could be behind the wheel of the company with you. Do you really think Kassandra is capable of that?"

"I proposed to her because I *don't* want to be behind the wheel of the company. I don't want any of this."

Beatrice continued berating Murray. "Since you've made up your mind about this girl, you either marry her and get your portrait on the wall, or you remain a failure and you'll be forgotten. You either train her to be who we need her to be, or you get rid of her. What will it be?"

A moment passed, thick with silence.

"She's digging. I can tell," Murray hissed.

"And what exactly are you worried she'll find?"

Murray paused. "You know."

There was a light thump, and I imagined Beatrice setting down her cocktail and rising to meet him.

"You've cost this family enough. It's time for you to fix your own mess for once."

Murray's voice was unsteady now, likely from the scalding. "Someone's going to talk."

Beatrice spoke after a moment of silence. "Then stop them."

* * *

All the guests had congregated in various rooms on the first floor, as though we were sinking deep into the damp earth, along with the house. I was sitting on a sofa in the lounge, my feet curled up beneath me, with a book on my lap that I'd pulled at random from the shelves. I wasn't absorbing a single word of it. I was using it more as a shield. Murray sat on the other side of the room, doing his best to seem absorbed in whatever he was reading on his phone. By the intent, unmoving muscles of his face, I could tell he was trying not to look at me.

How had we fallen apart so quickly? The first night we'd spent together, talking in that dingy bar, I'd had the immediate sense that I'd known him forever. Perhaps I should have known that a relationship like that—the *whirlwind* as my mom had called it—would fall apart with the same momentum.

I could hardly look at him now as I replayed his and Beatrice's conversation. *"She's digging,"* he'd said. There were so many unknowns, so many questions I was trying to unearth. Which scared Murray the most?

Then stop her.

"I think I'm going to book a flight for tomorrow morning," I said. My voice was flat with defeat. I could hardly afford the fee to change my flight, but it was better than being here.

Murray studied me for a moment. It was as if he'd never seen me before. "I don't think that will look good. The detective still hasn't said we can leave."

Someone cleared their throat behind us, and Murray and I turned to see William standing in the doorway. "Mrs. Beatrice has asked that all guests join her in the Blue Room for drinks at six o'clock."

"Thank you," said Murray.

I sighed. It was bizarre to be having a cocktail party when not even twenty-four hours ago a man had been lying dead one floor above us. I wondered if this was Beatrice's version of a wake. Or maybe it was a celebration, I thought darkly. A celebration of getting Beau out of the way and having her eldest son take over. Was that the plan all along?

The storm outside was approaching, and rain beat down on windows like fingernails tapping against glass, impatient and wanting in. We had twenty minutes until we had to meet for drinks. There was a floor lamp across the room, its light battling pitifully against the oncoming darkness. I reached over to turn on another lamp by my side, telling myself to be still.

But I sat there fidgeting, my restless mind wandering through the walls of the house like a ghost, floating over the papers I'd found in Phillip's office, the conversations I'd heard. It landed, unexpectedly in my bedroom, on the little baggie in my clutch—the one I'd found in the bathroom at the party.

The part of myself that I thought I'd moved past, that I'd worked so hard to get rid of, began to speak to me, drowning out the safe voice that I'd curated for myself. I was amazed by how quickly it took over and had me walking up the stairs, pulled forward like there was an unstoppable magnetic force. Murray didn't even look up as I left the room.

I shut my bedroom door behind me and pressed my back against the door as I stared at the clutch on the vanity. *This will make the cocktail party more special, more fun. Wouldn't everyone want me to have more fun? We can all pretend that nothing bad is happening.*

I gnawed at my nails, arguing against the voice. I'd been my own little version of sober for years—at least from the vices that had caused me and Jacqueline so many problems. Only Murray and Zoey knew I was sober. Zoey had looked at me confused when I told her, staring at the wine in my hand.

"Oh, so you're *California sober*," she'd said with an approving nod. "Got it, cool." We'd laughed about it, but it was accurate. A casual sobriety. I would never actually tell anyone else that I was sober, with the wine and weed and all. But maybe, I realized, I never told anyone I was sober so that one day, maybe someone might offer me a little bump at a party, or a bit of molly, as if it were all harmless to me. And I would accept without their judgment.

It's just one tiny bag. A little won't hurt. This will be it—you won't buy any more.

I winced as a raw hangnail stung against my saliva. I put one foot in front of me and then put it back, pushing my spine into the door.

You deserve this.

Maybe I did deserve it. Yes, I did deserve a little break after all the bullshit. Someone had been murdered in the next room, for Christ's sake. And on top of that, someone had been texting me, threatening me, and my relationship was ripping apart at the seams, and goddammit, yes, I deserved a break. I stepped forward once, then again, my body moving of its own accord.

I sat down at the vanity and let muscle memory take over. I felt relief at my decision to finally give up and give in. I emptied half the baggie and stashed the rest in my purse. I bent over the vanity with a rolled-up bill, when my bedroom door jerked open, smacking into the dresser.

"What are you doing?" Murray asked suspiciously.

"Nothing," I said. I was pathetic. "Doing my makeup." I pulled out my face powder and makeup brushes, covering up the white powder on the vanity.

"I just wanted to see if you were okay. If you wanted to talk." He closed the bedroom door behind him, but it didn't latch and creaked open about an inch.

"Sure. Fine," I said tersely, thinking only of the powder behind me. I couldn't let him see it. I fully turned and pressed my back into the vanity, blocking his view.

"I know I haven't been completely honest. But you have to believe me when I say everything I've done, I've done for our future." He began to pace the room, and my muscles tightened as he gained a new vantage point on my almost relapse. I shifted with each of his steps, trying to look casual.

"Are you okay? You're acting weird," he said.

I cleared my throat. "How could you sign those documents to take over the family business without talking to me first? I can't live here—"

I was interrupted by the bedroom door swinging open again. Why did everyone feel entitled to barge in here? "Miss Kassandra?" William entered the room halfway. "Oh, hello, Murray. Are you both ready for cocktails?"

"Yes, thank you, William. We'll be down in a minute." Murray sounded relieved, like he didn't want to have this conversation, even though he was the one who started it.

"I'm going downstairs," he said. His eyes briefly landed on the unfurled bill on the vanity. A brief expression of doubt formed on his face, then faded away, almost as if he was beginning to understand what I was doing but had decided he couldn't be bothered to care about it. "Are you coming?"

I stood from the vanity, hesitation pulling me back to my little secret under my makeup. Murray was watching me closely, and I gave in and followed him out the door. He walked in front of me wordlessly, and I stared at his back, thinking of how our conversation would have gone if we hadn't been interrupted.

No conversation in this house went unobserved. Every attempt to reconnect with Murray ended with a summoning to another part of the house, and I was sick of it.

I thought of the vents in the staff staircase and the conversations floating through the house. It was becoming clearer that these interruptions weren't an accident. I clamped my mouth shut and resolved that I would be more careful with my words. You never knew who was listening.

26

I T WAS JUST after six o'clock, and we all stood in the Blue Room, each of us with a drink in hand as we pretended we weren't studying one another. I took sips often, unable to resist the urge to obliterate my worries with alcohol.

I felt a bit twitchy, and I slightly regretted the coffee I'd had so late in the afternoon. I tended to drink coffee when I was anxious, despite knowing caffeine will make anxiety worse and that I should just have herbal tea instead. It was like some part of my brain wanted to make it worse because the further I pushed myself into anxiety or depression, the more likely I was to collapse into old habits. A self-fulfilling prophecy.

I took a gulp of my wine, trying to balance out one poison with another. Life was full of ups and downs, and I apparently liked to experience the highest and lowest points all at once.

Janice and the newest guest, Lawrence, were standing near the bar cart, talking animatedly. They were chatting about the city, and although I didn't want to speak with anyone, I felt a pang of loneliness at being left out of the conversation about my home. I glanced over at Murray, who was pouring a drink next to them and then naturally joined into the conversation. Were they all pretending Beau had never died? Did they not realize his murderer could be among us?

Cindy meandered over to me as she worked the room. Her voice was low, a little sultry. "You look like you're already having fun," she said as she eyed my nearly empty wineglass.

"Not as much as you," I spat out. She'd been twitchy since the moment she'd walked over, grinding her teeth together as she faked a smile. It was clear she was using more than just wine to get through the night.

She looked at Murray, who was speaking to Janice and Lawrence, telling them about the city as if it were Terabithia. Cindy's face shifted, the amused light in her eye snuffed out. I followed her gaze. Murray had suddenly left the conversation and was now speaking closely with Mary Margaret, both of them smiling comfortably. Mary Margaret brushed a quick hand against Murray's collarbone, pulling away a hair or piece of lint.

Cindy was studying me now, waiting for a reaction. And she was right to look for it, because it was there, crawling its way up to my face from my burning chest. But I forced it down.

"What a gold digger," Cindy whispered. She gestured to Lyle, who was also watching Murray and Mary Margaret, a scowl on his face. "I think jealousy is her foreplay. Funny, since she's the territorial one."

The look on Mary Margaret's face as she watched Beau flirt with women at the party flashed into my mind. They had both just reentered the room, and while I had never seen the man's face in the greenhouse, I was almost certain it was Beau. Now that he was dead, had she moved on to another target—another rich man without a wedding band?

A few more sips of wine—it was medicinal, I reminded myself—and I left Cindy without a word. I wanted to march over to Mary Margaret and Murray—their names even sounded like a those of a sweet old couple in a children's book, what a treat—but I nestled myself against the bar cart and made expectant eye contact with Janice and Lawrence. I didn't really want to talk to Lawrence—he sent shivers up my spine for some reason—but there were no other people in the room that felt like a good option for distraction. I smiled at Janice, waiting for her to loop me into the conversation. I blinked, realizing I'd been staring at them wide-eyed. My head was spinning, my muscles so clenched that they were beginning to spasm, but I needed to at least appear relaxed.

"We were just talking about how nice it is to celebrate a young couple in love," Janice said, finally roping me into the conversation. I highly doubted that's what they'd been talking about before I joined them.

It's funny, I mused to myself, how miserable Murray and I actually were, and how our relationship had taken a complete nosedive since we'd arrived at this house. Instead, I lied, "We're so happy to be here with everyone."

"It's just a shame that a dark cloud has to hang over the memory," Lawrence said. He exhaled through his nose in a huff, a facsimile of a chuckle, and pointed out the window, "Literally and figuratively."

The sky was a sickly greenish-gray, and it looked to have soaked into his skin and graying hair, leaving him pallid. Still, he was handsome and dressed richly like all the other guests.

Murray was standing alone now, grazing the snacks that William had set out, and the urge to confront him about the conversation I'd overheard with his mother was overwhelming. I approached like I myself was a storm, my heart pumping hard.

"We really need to finish talking, Murray," I whispered. My words were rushed, and I knew I sounded out of control.

"Not right now, Kass."

"It'll just take a second. Please."

He studied my eyes, the pink, flushed skin of my cheeks. "Not now. You're drunk. Already."

I stared at him. The venom in his voice was shocking, and I could see I disgusted him. We had fallen apart so quickly. I didn't know if our relationship was salvageable, but I had to at least try. "I've had one glass of wine, Murray. I'm not drunk."

He eyed me in disbelief, almost like he felt sorry for me. "Maybe we'll talk later. When you've sobered up." He walked away.

I froze with shame—shame in how much I'd disappointed myself, and shame in how fucked up my relationship with Murray had become. I'd let myself get so swept up in our relationship and had spent so much time convincing my friends and family that we were perfect for each other that I'd convinced myself too, but this whole time I hadn't known him at all.

The guests moved throughout the room, shuffling conversations and drifting to others like an uneasy tide. I found myself talking more but saying less. I told people what they wanted to hear, agreed with whatever opinions they spewed out. Their voices were placid and content while they pretended nothing bad had ever happened and that we weren't trapped in this house. Regardless of everyone's fake smiles, I could feel the suspicion in their gaze as they studied me. I knew what they were wondering: *Are the rumors true? Is Kass capable of murder?*

At some moments I could hear myself speaking, playing my role as the happy guest in this delusional cocktail
party. Meanwhile, my mind was somewhere else, completely removed from the conversation—from the house,
even. If I imagined hard enough that I was somewhere else,
maybe I would blink and find myself there. Transported by
wishful thinking and an unwillingness to accept reality.

*   *   *

It was half past six and we were growing restless waiting
for Beatrice. From what I gathered, it was unlike her to be
late, and it was setting everyone on edge. We were arranged
in a haphazard circle, some standing and staring at the
drinks in our hands, others seated and looking around the
room as though they could strike up a conversation with it.
It did feel like that at times—that if you got close enough
to the walls and uttered the right words, they might speak
back. I was too afraid to know what they would say.

The house had grown increasingly dark now that the
storm was directly overhead, and William made his way
around the room turning on lamps, adjusting the dimmers
to the most flattering brightness.

Beatrice wasn't here yet, which I found particularly
annoying, and Phillip sat in his chair by the window with
a listless expression on his face. He always seemed so helpless without her, but when they were together, he looked
miserable. He'd mostly been holed up in his bedroom
since Beau's death, but when he did come out, his eyes
were swollen and ringed with red.

I thought of my future with Murray—if there even
was one. If we could salvage the mess of our relationship,
would we still end up like his parents? I'd always seen
myself in a happy, playful marriage like my parents', but

now I felt doomed, stuck forever in this gigantic house with a husband who was secretive and dishonest with me. Was that worse than being alone?

Kennedy stood at the wide window, staring out at the storm clouds churning above us. Emmett, on the other hand, sat in a plush armchair like a king, eager to host this little gathering in Beatrice's place.

William had found what seemed to be the perfect lighting, and on cue, Beatrice entered. Thunder rumbled, roaring like applause. She sat in her favorite armchair across from Phillip, and William immediately arrived with a martini. All of us watched her, waiting.

Cindy broke the silence. "Mrs. Sedgemont, thank you again for giving us a place to stay during this troubling time."

She sounded as though she'd practiced that very line in her head. I stared out the window, too annoyed to even look at her.

"It's the least I can do," Beatrice said over a clap of thunder. It was ridiculous that they were speaking about it like this was a friendly gathering rather than a lockdown ordered by the police.

"Can you believe these losers?" Lyle said as he looked out the window. "It's pissing rain, and they're just standing there in their plastic Walmart ponchos, thinking they're making a difference."

The crowd outside had thinned a bit, but their protest was still going strong. It was difficult to make out their chants over the steady rain, but they were there, distant and furious. Many of them held umbrellas above their signs, unwilling to relent in spite of the rain. Nevertheless, the wind whipped the rain in every direction, and many of the signs were slowly degrading.

"Repent!" one commanded in red marker that had bled and dripped down the poster board.

Beatrice's order to Murray replayed in my mind. *You either train her to be who we need her to be, or you get rid of her.* I took a sip of wine, trying to chase the memory away.

As William topped off our drinks, I found myself easing into this new role I'd written for myself. Or had Beatrice written it for me? I had no choice either way. Mary Margaret sat next to Lyle in an armchair that William had pulled in from the corner of the room. She was sulking, pushing her overfilled lips out, fluttering her long lashes. She shifted dramatically in her chair and sighed, desperate for someone to offer her an ounce of pity. I couldn't help myself and had to deliver my lines.

"So, Mary Margaret. How are you doing? After everything?" I asked, my voice saccharine, but she lapped up the attention. She dipped her chin and peered down at her hands, which were clenched together in front of her. Beatrice looked on approvingly. I wondered if her thinness had a purpose—a manufactured frailty that lured in rich men before the fatal strike.

"I think I'm okay. It was such a shock," she dabbed at the corner of her eye as if to wipe away a tear, but her eyes didn't gleam in the dim lights at all.

Lyle examined his wife, taking in her childlike suffering. This was clearly how she got her way. "It's outrageous that the police can force us to stay here," he lamented. "Can't they schedule appointments for us to go to the station or something?"

"Yeah, as if this is the worst place in the world to be stuck, Lyle," Emmett said snarkily. His posture was crumpled, and for a moment I mistook him for Kennedy.

"Oh, I'm sorry that I'm not comfortable with being investigated. Unlike you." Lyle's face was red, and his lips were set in a tight snarl.

"Enough," said Beatrice. Her voice had been quiet, but the cold anger behind it silenced the room.

Emmett ran his hand over his stomach, as if wiping away wrinkles or crumbs. He was now sitting up straight, and the smile had returned to his face. "It's nice to have the house full of people again," he said. "Despite the circumstances," he added as an afterthought. His cheeks were flushed, and his whiskey sloshed in his glass as he gestured.

"Is it, though?" Kennedy mumbled. He was slunk down in his chair, his chin nearly touching his chest.

The lights flickered once, and a murmur of worry rippled through the room.

Beatrice glared at Phillip, and on cue, he struck up a conversation, like a dog performing a trick. Everyone joined in half-heartedly. I watched as people's eyes drifted around the room mid-conversation, a whisper of worry in their eyes, or perhaps suspicion.

I took a sip of my wine. It had a full-bodied, earthy tang, like it had been aging in a barrel deep beneath the house for years. Murray was sitting next to me, but he turned away from me as he spoke to Lyle. It seemed every cell in his body was pulling him away from me, and I wondered what the final straw would be. My unwillingness to move to North Carolina to run the company? Or his lie about the bills? I couldn't even tell if he was embarrassed. *He should be,* I thought bitterly.

Cindy got up to use the restroom, and I watched Murray's eyes follow her for a moment. Jealousy boiled the wine in my gut. I wasn't usually a jealous person, but when I was, it formed a toxic sludge in my body. I felt ill.

I missed the New York City Murray who offered me undivided attention, who would pause anything he was doing when I walked into the room. North Carolina had an infantilizing effect on him, and I no longer even knew the man next to me—this stranger who sat by me in starched khaki pants and a crisp button-down.

Bile crept up my throat, and I washed it down with more wine. I was starting to feel a bit woozy, as I hadn't eaten since breakfast. My body was revolting against the careless treatment I was subjecting it to.

"I need to use the restroom. Excuse me," I said. I could feel everyone's eyes on me, burning into my back, but I kept walking.

Someone grabbed my arm, and I yanked it away, turning around to see Emmett, a concerned expression on his face.

"Everything okay, Kass?"

"Just an upset stomach."

"You know, my parents mean well. I know they can be a little overbearing."

"A little?" I huffed.

He steered me away from the Blue Room, and as I glanced back, I saw everyone was staring at us.

"Father makes the money, but Mother is the one who keeps everything running smoothly. The protector. She can hide even the biggest mistakes with enough money."

I grimaced at the word *mother*.

That poor boarding school girl, I thought. That had to be what he was talking about. How could he say that so casually? "In all honesty though, Kass, it's great that Murray found someone just like him. You'll fit into the family perfectly." On the surface, his words were kind, but there was venom in his delivery. His jaw jutted out, the tips of his teeth showing.

The lights trembled once more, sending shadows flickering across the walls and Emmett's face. Thinking about what Gloria had told me about the boarding school investigation, I gulped down remnants of acidic wine that rose in my throat. She had said it was just the twins who'd been investigated. Why was Emmett making it sound like it was actually Murray?

"W-what?" I stuttered. "What do you mean, I'm just like him?" My head was reeling, and I felt sick to my stomach.

Emmett studied me, and his expression shifted. His jaw relaxed and his eyes widened, an epiphany flittering across his face. What was going through his head?

"Kass," he said, his voice gentle now, almost apologetic, "do you not know?"

Lightning lit up the room, and the lights in the house flickered once before something popped, shuttering us into complete darkness. The storm must be right above us, as thunder immediately boomed, vibrating the glass in the windowpanes. It was so loud I could feel it in my bones.

Emmett grabbed my arm, and the heat of his hand was startling against my cold skin. I ripped myself away, putting space between us.

"Don't!" was all I could muster.

"I'm sorry," he said. "I didn't mean to. It's so dark." He sounded terrified. I could only make out the outline of his tall frame in the darkness. "Do you have your phone? Can you turn your flashlight on, please?" The questions were frantic, and his voice rose an octave.

I did have my phone. But I didn't turn on the flashlight. I walked away, using the barest hint of light from the glass ceiling to stumble my way further into the depths of the house, leaving him stranded in the shadows.

Despite not wanting to spend another second with the rest of the guests, being in a group felt like the safest place to be. But there was something I had to do first. Before I made my way back to the Blue Room, I pushed open the panel in the first-floor wall and stepped into the hidden staircase. The lights were still out, and I used my phone to illuminate the thin passageway.

I sat on the bottom staircase and texted Zoey:

This family is fucking PSYCHO.

She texted back quickly, always the reliable shit-talking friend that everyone needed: *What'd they do? Want me to come kick their asses?* She added a little fist emoji at the end. I wished I could blink and be back in her apartment, watching her make her bizarre paintings.

Someone DIED at the party. Police are all over the house investigating. We're stuck here.

WTF?? What happened? Are you okay?

I began to text her back, but Emmett's words earlier made it hard to focus. More accurately, it was what he hadn't said that sent my mind reeling. What had he meant when he asked me if I knew? Did he mean the boarding school death?

I swiped out of Zoey's text mid-sentence and opened the internet browser. I couldn't remember which Northeastern state Gloria had said the boarding school was in.

Connecticut boarding school death, I typed in, but all the results were for a preschool.

I tried again, with New Hampshire this time. My screen immediately flooded with hits. The first result read, *"Girl, 15, found dead in Exavius Academy dorm."*

The article was short, just a brief piece by a local news station.

> *Police are investigating the death of a 15-year-old student at Exavius Academy. The female student was found dead Monday night, October 2, 2013, by faculty member Ms. Holly Brigands. Brigands immediately notified the police, who are conducting an ongoing investigation. A memorial service will be held for the Exavius community on October 10, at 8:00 p.m.*

I scrolled down, looking for comments. There were only two. The first was *"Sounds fishy. The town knows what the students are like."*

The final comment simply read, *"Murder."*

My heart was beating faster now, and confusion made my head spin. I was grateful that I was already sitting down; otherwise, I was sure my trembling legs wouldn't support me.

I deleted my search terms and now entered just *Exavius Academy death.* The first article to appear was from December 2013, only a few months after the girl's memorial service. It was titled *"Exavius Academy receives $100 million donation."* I clicked into the article and skimmed it, learning that an unnamed benefactor had made a large donation, and the school intended it to go to financial aid and enhancing facilities. There was no information about the donor, but I had a strong feeling that I knew exactly who it was.

I opened the school's website and found a campus map. The Sedgemonts loved attention and recognition, and I hoped that to thank them for their donation, the school had named a building or athletic field after them. But as I stared unblinking at the screen, my eyes burned. There was nothing there. All the breadcrumbs had dried up, and I'd been left with no insight or proof that the Sedgemonts were involved.

There has to be more about this boarding school, I thought, but as I clicked through the rest of the articles, it became clear that this was the only information available. It was like someone had washed the internet clean. Not even the name of the student who had died was revealed, likely because she was a minor, but it was still suspicious.

I couldn't bear the thought of Murray being involved in that girl's death. I hoped that I had read too much into what Emmett had said. My mind was spinning to come up with explanations—something that would make these strings of disjointed information line up and make sense.

According to Gloria, the twins had been at the center of the investigation. She had made no mention of Murray at all. Could Emmett have been toying with me? What would he gain from that, though?

Yet, my brain argued, Emmett had seemed so sincere when he asked me if I knew. It was like he thought I was some kind of monster, someone who'd be fine with marrying a murder.

Could it be true? Could I have fallen in love with a murderer?

And the way Emmett grabbed me, my brain interjected, the thought unwelcome. I couldn't help but think of it, the way he latched onto me like he was searching for comfort and protection. It was as though he'd been afraid to let go, terrified that the darkness swallowing the house would eat him alive too.

Pushing myself up from the stairs, I followed the beam of my flashlight to the Blue Room.

* * *

William was in the process of lighting every candle the Sedgemonts owned, and the room glowed a beautiful gold that danced as the air shifted. Gloria set out more snacks despite the majority on the table remaining untouched. Meanwhile, Lawrence played bartender and was taking drink orders from all the guests.

"Good thing you were well prepared." Lyle motioned toward the candelabras set up around the room. The two on the fireplace mantle were enormous, dripping with wax from thick white candles that gave off the most light in the room. The candlelight was dizzying as shadow and light reflected off the golden-framed mirror above the mantle.

"The power goes out often during summer storms," Emmett said behind me. His voice startled me, but I didn't turn around to meet his eye. He must have followed me in the dark. I wondered if had seen me open the panel to the staircase.

I did, however, meet Murray's stare. His eyes trailed back and forth between us, suspicion all over his face. Emmett must have entered the room right after me. I blushed, knowing how it must look.

I sat down and put my phone facedown on the arm of my chair. After reading the articles about the boarding school death, I didn't even want it touching me. The other guests continued their conversations, but glanced at me covertly as if they would be safer with me in their line of sight.

Lawrence brought me a glass of wine without asking, but I turned it away. I'd done enough to muddle my mind. Now I needed it to be clear.

My blood rushed through my body, and my heartbeat pulsed in my fingertips. The words were bubbling up, the need to understand too much to resist. I knew I shouldn't. "So, Lawrence, what sort of advisory role do you play for the family?" I asked with a polite smile.

He turned away from Janice. "I help the family with investments, both personally and for their business. And the occasional philanthropic contributions."

I nodded. "That's nice. What sort of organizations do you support?" I directed the question both at Lawrence and my future in-laws.

I expected Beatrice or Phillip to step in, but Lawrence was enjoying talking about himself. "Usually the arts or protecting historic homes, like this one. And there are a few academic endowments."

"How generous. About how much? One hundred million?"

Everyone in the room gawked at me, and I gulped, astonished at my own pointed words. A gust of wind outside whipped into the chimney, and the fire spat and crackled.

"I'm not sure off the top of my head, but yes, there have been some hefty donations made to the community."

"Not just this community, right? Also in other states? Up north?" My heartbeat was throbbing in my neck, and as soon as I finished speaking, my teeth clamped together, frantically grinding. I couldn't believe what I was saying. A part of me regretted it, but a fragment of me was thrilled by the chaos.

"Not really sure," Lawrence said dismissively. "Emmett, Kennedy, more wine?" The twins waved him off, their eyes on me and shining with delight. I was astounded that they'd denied a drink. Instead, they were choosing to get high on the turmoil I was causing.

Phillip stood from his chair, poorly concealed panic playing across his face. He began to speak, when suddenly the sound of glass shattering sliced through the room. Cindy and I screamed as the other guests stumbled backward, deeper into the room and away from the noise.

The floor-to-ceiling window gaped open, and a strong wind whipped through the room, splattering us and most of the furniture with cold, hard drops of rain. Very quickly I felt a dampness all over my skin and clothes from the humidity and the fog that swarmed the room.

Phillip shouted for William and Gloria, who stood in shock for a moment before racing out to search for something to cover the window.

I shot up to my feet, my phone crashing to the floor with the force of it. What broke the window? The shattered glass on the floor shimmered in the candlelight, and I was startled by the sick beauty of it. Among the glass lay a thick red brick. It was wrapped in plastic wrap, and there was something secured beneath it.

I bent down to pick it up. It was heavy in my hand, and water beaded on the plastic wrap stretched around it. I began to pick at it, my heart racing, when Kennedy grabbed it from my hands. "Don't touch that," he said. He sounded angry, but underneath I swore I heard concern. He sat it on the end table next to Beatrice, and we all stared at it, none of us sure of what to do.

"I'll call the police," Lawrence announced, already dialing. He left the room, his voice drowned out by the din of panicked murmurs.

William and Gloria entered, carrying large black tarps. Both of them had sopping wet hair, and their usually picture-perfect appearance was disheveled. They must have had to go to the greenhouse.

They immediately began attempting to secure the tarps over the window while Beatrice argued with them over what to use to secure it to the walls without damaging the wood. William held a staple gun and duct tape, but Beatrice tossed the staple gun aside after waving it angrily in William's face. William rushed out again to get a ladder and came back even more drenched.

Kennedy gripped the brick in his hand, picking apart the plastic wrap to get to the note beneath. I joined the other guests as we watched him rip his way closer to the paper. I was biting my nails to the quick, and Murray roughly pulled my hand away from my mouth to stop me. That habit had always annoyed him. My nail beds were red and swollen, the cuticle on my pointer finger bleeding in a crimson crescent around the nail.

"What does it say?" Emmett asked in a deep, commanding voice that contradicted his cowering body language. Duct tape ripped with a screech as William and Gloria worked to secure the tarp to the window. It was only half covered, but the room was even darker now without the view to the outside. I was growing claustrophobic without being able to see the storm and crowd outside—if

I could just keep an eye on the danger, maybe I would feel a bit safer.

But maybe the danger is inside the house, I thought, my fingers returning to my mouth. Murray scowled at me but didn't bother to tell me to stop.

Janice had her back pressed into the wall, her entire body rattling with fear. Lawrence had returned from calling the police and stood slightly in front of her, protective, and I wondered for a moment if there was something going on between them.

Kennedy tore the last of the plastic wrap away from the brick, exposing the note below. *"Traitors"* was scrawled in thick, messy black marker. The same word that had been painted on the family's disused factories. Phillip rushed over and ripped the note from Kennedy's hand. "Give me that," he said as he balled it up angrily and tossed it in the fireplace.

"No!" Janice shouted. "You should have kept that for the police!"

"How did they get close enough to throw a brick through the window?" I asked, looking out the remaining front windows. Protesters paced behind the distant gate, slick with rain. Their numbers were dwindling as the storm worsened. Only the angriest remained.

The silence in the room was charged as we all came to the same realization.

"Someone must have broken through the gate," Kennedy said, his voice full of fear. "One of them is on the property."

28

"Nobody panic," Beatrice commanded to the room. "All the doors and windows are locked. They can't get in the house."

"Yeah, except for the giant gaping hole in the wall," Kennedy shouted, his voice cracking.

"Could it be the same person who set off the alarm at dinner?" Mary Margaret asked.

"What?" Janice wailed in panic.

A rumbling thump came from deep within the house, sending us all jumping. I thought of the staff corridors behind the walls and shivered at the possibility of a stranger lurking behind them, listening to every word we said.

"Clearly they can just break more windows if they want to get around the locks," Lyle pushed back, his voice slurring. "And it's not as if the alarm system will work during a power outage." He motioned to the discrete panel on the wall that I hadn't noticed before. It was well hidden, but now that I saw it, it had three distinct buttons for different emergencies; medical, fire, and police.

This must have happened before for them to have installed a panic button. I'd had no idea I was on the verge of marrying into a family so hated by the surrounding town that they would be regularly attacked. It was no wonder that Murray would move so far away, disassociating from his family in every way he could. *Except for the money that kept him tethered,* I thought bitterly.

Beatrice raised her hands, and in the glow of the candlelight, she looked saintly. "Might I recommend we all go to our rooms to catch our breath and freshen up a bit? Each of you take a candle. William," she snapped her fingers at William, who was already lighting candlesticks. The old-fashioned silver handles gleamed in the golden light.

William handed a candle to each guest. The flames danced along the ceiling wildly as guests trailed out of the Blue Room and up to their rooms. Mary Margaret lost her footing on the first stair, and Lyle helped her up, despite being unbalanced himself. The adrenaline mixed with alcohol was making everyone far more intoxicated than I'd thought. I was glad I'd turned down Lawrence's drink earlier. I needed to be ready. For what, I didn't know.

Soon, the house grew quiet, and all I could hear were the unsteady footsteps of the guests drifting to their safe spaces, interrupted only by the booming thunder that shook the very foundation of the house.

*　　*　　*

I stood in the entrance hall, watching the guests wander off with their candles, eager for a safe place to rest. I knew I needed to speak to Murray, but he'd slipped away too quickly, and I couldn't find him anywhere. I wondered if he knew I was looking for him and was finding solace in the dark, hidden away from me.

The darkness that swallowed the house made my imagination kick into overdrive. I concentrated on ignoring the shadows surrounding my candlestick's pitiful circle of light. The flicker of candlelight made it look like the sad eyes of the Sedgemonts were following me as I passed their portraits.

When I found Murray, he was staring out the window in the living room, swaying slightly back and forth.

"Murray?" I called out, and he turned around, his eyes taking longer than normal to focus on me. I wondered how many drinks he'd had. He wasn't that different from his brothers after all.

"I need to talk to you," I said. I swore I saw his eyes roll as he faced me.

"What is it now?"

"What are you worried I'll find, Murray?" I was startled by how strong my voice was, while inside I was cowering.

"What?" was all he said, his lip curling with bored skepticism.

"I figured you would know how much you can hear in this house. That you'd be more careful when you talk about your suspicions of me."

I couldn't tell if he rolled his eyes again or if he was just that drunk. "Okay," he dragged out the vowels impatiently. "Care to elaborate?"

The affected timbre of his voice set me off. "Oh my God, you even talk differently now."

He threw his hands up. "How do you want me to talk?"

"I just want you to tell me what the hell it is you and your mom think I'm digging up. I heard you through the vents."

"Well, that wasn't me talking. Maybe it was one of my brothers. Or maybe it was your imagination."

My eyebrow rose in defiance, warning him not to continue, but he just stared back at me with blank eyes. He tried to rest a hand against the windowsill but missed and stumbled. His cheeks flushed with embarrassment, and he pressed his back into the wall for balance.

"You should really get a glass of water or something," I said.

"That's rich coming from you." His face was flushed now, splotches of red high on his cheeks.

That phrase shook me. I'd heard it before, and it echoed in my head every day. Jacqueline had spat that in my face in the subway and now here I was, standing before my fiancé, who hated me just as much as she did. I stood there, challenging him to go on.

Murray sighed, and for a moment I thought he was backing down. "I don't know why I ever thought this could work."

Tears stung my eyes. The ring on my left hand felt like an anchor. I could barely stand against the weight of it.

"Mother kept telling me over and over that I needed to settle down. She wanted me with someone like Cindy, so I picked you instead—the exact opposite. You were so different that I thought it might trick my brain into forgetting the life my parents want me to live. It did at first. No nest eggs, no boarding schools and buildings with your name on it." He sighed. "But we were never going to work."

"You know what, Murray? Fuck you. You've spent our whole relationship pretending to have nothing to do with your family because you're such an outsider. This trip has done nothing except prove that you're just like them and that maybe I like the fantasy version of you more than whatever this is." I waved my hand out in front of me.

"You think I used you to be a different person, but what about you, huh? Miss half-assed sobriety, yeah, fuckin' right. You used me to forget just as much," his words were slurring together, but each still slapped me in the face. "You talk to her in your sleep. *'I'm sorry, Jacqueline, I'm so sorry.'* It's your fault she's dead—you said so yourself. You're just as bad as me."

Tears streamed down my face. He knew. He'd known the full truth this whole time but hadn't said a word. "What do you mean I'm just as bad as you?" I asked quietly. I took one step back, suddenly frightened by his confirmation of my suspicion.

His eyes widened at the realization of what he'd said. His cheeks were a deep crimson and covered in a sheen of sweat. I expected him to spit something hateful back, or even yell. His hands flinched, balling into fists before he released them stick-straight, as though he were fighting against the instinct to lash out. He shocked me by turning on his heels and staggering out of the room without another word. His gait was quick but graceless as he struggled out the door.

Tears of every emotion poured down my face. My heart ached as I watched him stumble away, but at the same time I was furious. It was clear that our relationship wasn't going to survive, and all I cared about now was leaving this place with a clear conscience and a clean record.

My mouth was dry and the stale taste of wine made me want to gag. I needed a glass of water. As I stood at the kitchen counter, taking slow, pained sips, I could still hear the other guests moving through the house, stumbling around. Someone was in the living room, snoring, oblivious to the events around them. They all sounded as drunk as Murray had, but the clamor was fading. It was only seven o'clock, but the quiet and dark that hung over the house made it feel like midnight.

By the time I'd finished drinking, there was barely any noise at all.

29

With the house silent, my head began to swarm with emotions I'd been trying to push away. My boiling anger with Murray was reducing to a simmer, and now all I felt was a deep sense of despair. Our lives had become completely intertwined in the short time we'd been together. Every night we fell asleep together, and every morning we woke up, already knowing what the other would be doing for the rest of the day, already expecting our own days to be affected by the other's in some way.

How would I wake up knowing that he wouldn't be in my life anymore? How could I fall asleep without his body heat comforting me?

Hot tears fell down my face, grazing my lips with salt. The house had been so loud for days, and I hadn't realized that although it was anxiety provoking, it provided enough distraction that I didn't have to think about how much my relationship with Murray had failed so easily. And had it ever been that strong if one visit to his family home could destroy it? Could I really pride myself on having once had a healthy relationship if I was simply acting as a conduit— a person he could stand near so he could become a different person and rebel against his parents? Could I ever look back fondly on the love we'd had if the whole time he was just fulfilling his mom's orders to find a wife? I'd probably been an easy target. Desperate for love.

I wondered if every time I stepped away from him, he reverted to who he was, a man who lies, a man who was possibly involved in the death of that boarding school student, or at least complicit in its cover-up.

The silence in the house allowed me to hear the chorus of nighttime activity outside—frogs calling to one another somewhere in the woods, the occasional sad coo of an owl stalking them from the trees.

It hadn't struck me as odd when the house began to quiet down. After the trauma of the brick blasting through the window of the Blue Room, it was normal that each of us found some quiet corner of the house to recompose ourselves. Or to hide. But as I listened to the wildlife outside, realizing how silent the house was, uneasiness crept in. Lawrence had said he was calling the cops after the brick was thrown through the window. Shouldn't they be here by now?

I wiped away the traces of tears—my eyes had now grown dry at the realization that something was wrong. There should at least be a murmur or a footstep. But the only audible thing was the beating of my heart acting as percussion to the wildlife outside.

Maybe I should go speak to Murray—talk to him about what we needed to do. My initial thought was what we could do to save our relationship, but that quickly faded. *What we need to do to make our split as easy as possible,* I corrected. There was no salvaging us. Not after all this.

My body resisted moving from my perch behind the kitchen island, both from wanting to avoid further confrontation with Murray and from something primal in my brain telling me that this level of silence was abnormal. I should be hearing something—William and Gloria cleaning up the Blue Room, maybe Beatrice and Phillip bickering.

I walked into the entrance hall and peered into the open doorways of the living room and the Blue Room. There were candles lit in each room, but only one solitary candle in the entrance hall, perched atop the table in the middle of the room, casting a meager circle of light around it. There was no one in the Blue Room, which was unusual as there were half-empty drinks still strewn about, barely visible in the candlelight, but I could see the tops of two heads sitting on the living room sofa. Must be napping or on their phones, I thought.

Still, the hairs on my forearms raised as my skin reacted to movement rippling through the air. Someone was moving through the house, but I couldn't hear a thing. All I could sense was a disturbance—like an animal who becomes aware of prey lurking in the dark woods before they even hear a noise.

A shape appeared in the hall. There were no candles lit in the hallways, and it was too dark to tell who it was. They were moving closer now, and the candle next to me rippled in response. On instinct, I stepped backward out of the circle of light. If I couldn't see them, then they damn well shouldn't be able to see me.

Slow, steady footsteps approached, and the candlelight rippled faster now, casting the room in an undulating glow of twitching shapes and shadows that made my head spin.

When the figure finally moved into the light, I jumped, startled by the sight of another person after so long. It was Lawrence.

I stood as still as I could in the shadows, hoping he couldn't see me. My breath hitched in my chest as he looked around the room. He was moving through the house like a predator, like the stealthy bobcats that Murray had told me live in the North Carolina mountains. He was looking for someone, something. He was hunting.

A flash of lightning cut through the night sky, closely followed by a low rumble of thunder. The lightning illuminated the room, only for a second, but it was enough to bleach the room with light and give away my position.

The room was swallowed by darkness once more, but it was clear he was looking right at me.

"Ah," he said. "There you are."

30

Lawrence inched closer, approaching the candlelit table in the middle of the entrance hall. I took a step back, nearing the front door, every fiber under my skin prepared to bolt.

"Where have you been?" he asked calmly. The juxtaposition of his gentle question and the threatening stance of his body made my heart stutter, unsure whether to calm itself or beat faster.

I wasn't sure how to answer. What did he want to hear? "I was in the kitchen," I said, my voice cracking. "Getting a glass of water." The mention of water made me realize how dry my mouth was. I smacked my lips together, and when they parted, the skin clung together like Velcro.

"Where is everyone else?" he asked. It was such a normal thing to ask, but something about his face was off. I studied him as he waited for me to answer. One corner of his lip was slightly raised, and his eyes shone wild in the candlelight, almost as if he were about to cry. Or laugh.

Had he done something to them and was seeing if I knew yet? My heartbeat thrummed under my skin. My body was telling me something was wrong, but my brain couldn't piece together what exactly that was.

He stepped closer to me, unhurried but with intention. The flickering candle on the table was behind him now, and I could no longer see his face. He was just the dark outline of a man, continuing to move toward me.

I stumbled backward, the two of us in a dangerous dance, with only the storm as music. "What are you doing?" My voice was shrill. Childlike.

He raised his hands casually to the side as if to say, *"What do you mean?"* But he was still creeping forward.

"You're scaring me. Back up," I commanded. My voice had none of the power I was hoping for, and it had no effect on him.

Lightning flashed again, illuminating the room for just a moment. Long enough to see Lawrence's face. As he kept coming toward me, faster now, he was shrouded in darkness, but when he got close enough, all I could see was the sinister grin spread wide across his face.

CHAPTER

31

Lawrence was close enough now that I could feel body heat radiating from him, the warmth almost pulsing from him with his heart beat. I wanted to push him away from me, to step aside and put space between us. But he'd backed me into the front door's alcove, and there was no space.

My breath quickened, but I tried to slow it, not wanting any part of me to touch him, not even my breath. I reached behind myself slowly, grasping at the cool wood of the door against my back. I found the doorknob and began to twist when he grabbed my arms by the elbow, pulling them out from behind me.

"Don't touch me," I exclaimed.

Surprisingly, he let go, but that didn't stop him from creeping even closer to me.

"She was *mine*," he grumbled, spittle spraying against my face.

"What are you talking about? Who?"

"Don't play dumb with me."

I stayed silent, too afraid to speak. I felt that any moment, he might grip my arms again or strike me. My body was coiled with fear, my muscles gripped and ready for pain.

"I've watched you for years. It's amazing how many people will accept a follow request if you put a boring white woman's name and a pretty picture."

My brows knitted together in confusion as I studied him.

He continued. "The first time I messaged you wasn't really planned. I was already drunk, pissed off, thinking too much. Then your announcement came up on my Instagram feed. You were engaged. You looked so different. Healthy, put together, happy. It was a slap in the face. So I did it, I finally messaged you after all those years."

A shiver ran up my spine at the thought of him swiping through my photos. Studying my life.

"How long have you been watching me?" I asked, my voice pitiful, almost like I was about to retch.

He ignored my question. I don't think he even heard it. "I was going to get her help. I knew she had a problem—that both of you had a problem. The second I realized you two were avoiding me, I knew you were ruining her. She refused to get help, even though I offered to pay for it all. All because of *you*. She couldn't leave *you*." His face was twisted in anger, his lips pressed together in a sour grimace.

Jacqueline. I heard her name in my ear as I realized who he was talking about, almost as though she stood behind me, whispering it to me, making sure I'd never forget. I didn't recognize his face or his name. My head spun with confusion, and I closed my eyes to think, to slow my mind. This infuriated him even more.

"Do you not remember me? We met in 2018. Jacqueline and I got engaged shortly after."

Engaged? No, there was no way Jacqueline would get engaged without telling me. She hadn't even told me she was dating anyone. Of course, we'd both been going club to club, talking plenty of men and women into buying us drinks and dinners, giving us drugs.

"I'll admit, I look much better now. Years of not being able to force down food has made me handsome, according to women. That's all you all care about, anyway. Looks and money, nice clothes and expensive clubs. Well, and drugs for you. How lucky that you weaseled your way into the Sedgemonts' lives. Congratulations on finding someone with a past just as fucked up as yours."

Confusion was giving way to rage in my chest, hot and tingling through my whole body now. Jacqueline's bruised arms, dragging me through the crowded club, away from the man that followed her every move. It was him. "There's no way Jacqueline would marry you. She said you were a fucking creep." I spat in his face, but he didn't even flinch.

"Maybe you told her everything, but she clearly kept a lot from you. It hurts, doesn't it?" He finally wiped his face. His pupils had swallowed any color in his irises. There was nothing but rage behind them now. He was a wild animal.

"How did you even know I would be here?" I asked.

He laughed. "I didn't know you would be here. I'm a lucky man. Sometimes things just fall into your lap."

He got closer to me, and his eyes drifted down my chest. I closed my eyes, too terrified to even wonder what he was thinking. The air stirred as he approached and his finger grazed against my collarbone, then slowly down my sternum. He smelled of stale cologne and the sharp, musky scent of adrenaline-tinged sweat. Bile rose in my throat, and I clenched every muscle as if it would protect me from whatever he was about to do. His touch disappeared, and then there was a tug around my neck. I opened my eyes wide, in shock.

I stared at him, but his gaze was no longer burning into my skin. Instead, he focused on my necklace in his hand. Jacqueline's necklace.

"This is her ring. I gave her this." With the fist that clutched the necklace, he swung into my face. Something cracked in my mouth—was it my jaw or my teeth?—and I tasted blood. The sickest part was that I felt the necklace chain graze against my skin as he struck me. It was quick, but the sensation lingered on my skin. Like Jacqueline was lashing out at me one last time. Blaming me for what happened.

"No, it was her necklace. She wore it all the time. She said she'd had her grandma's jewelry melted down after she died." As the words left my mouth, I realized they were a lie—that most of what Jacqueline had told me in the last months of our friendship was a lie.

His mouth contorted into a snarl and he threw the necklace to the ground. The metallic ping of it hitting the floor reverberated painfully in my head. It was the last thing I had of her, and he'd just ripped it away from me.

As if he could tell what I was thinking, he said, "You wore that necklace like a trophy. Like a goddamn buck head on your wall." His body was coiled, and I knew if I didn't do anything, he would hit me again. And this time, I wasn't sure if I would still be standing afterward.

I pushed him away from me with every last ounce of strength I had. He stumbled back, tripping over the rug behind him. All my muscles clenched as I watched him lose his balance, falling backward. His head gave a sickening crunch as it slammed into the side of the table. The table teetered over before falling, sending its contents and the lit candle crashing to the ground.

My breath stuttered out. I stood there, unsure of what to do. I took one step closer to him. His chest wasn't moving. I rubbed my eyes hard, trying to think of what to do. I needed to call the police, but my cell phone wasn't in my pocket. Where the hell was it?

Just then, he gave a heaving breath and a groan, and I flinched backward, hands in front of my face, ready for him to lurch at me, but he stayed there, lying on the floor with his neck oddly contorted against the table. But now, his chest was moving slowly, as if he were in a comfortable sleep. I shuffled backward, slowly at first, then ran on my tiptoes up the stairs and to the hidden staircase.

Once I found my cell phone, I could call Detective Campbell and end this. I could make this right.

32

THE HOUSE WAS eerily quiet, other than the sound of steady rain and thunder. Moving through the unfamiliar dark made my efforts more difficult as I bumped into walls and furniture, tripping over rugs just like Lawrence had. Where were the others? I hoped they'd heard Lawrence and me fighting and had called Detective Campbell, and that help was on the way. But the complete lack of noise filled me with doubt.

Once I was on the second floor, I pushed open the staff staircase and felt around for my phone where I'd been sitting earlier, trying to find information about the Sedgemonts' boarding school, but my cell phone was nowhere to be found.

An angry puff of breath escaped me as my frustration built, making every cell in my body vibrate. I stumbled up the staircase, feeling along every step in the darkness as I tried not to trip my way up, but my phone was nowhere to be found.

Keen to check my room, I made my way up the stairs. The house was still silent, and adrenaline pulsed in my blood, intoxicating yet sickening. On the third-floor landing, I pushed the wall and opened the door slowly, emerging out into the hallway.

As I crept down the dark hallway, I passed the closed doors of guest bedrooms and listened intently for anyone inside. I had no idea where the guests were—it would make sense if they were hiding behind a locked door, maybe packing their things so they could leave as quickly as possible. There were no sounds inside the rooms. No rustling of fabric being folded and placed into a suitcase, no panicked breathing, or furtive cell phone conversations. It felt like I was completely alone in the house.

Could I have possibly killed Lawrence? I'd seen him breathing, but what if that was only temporary?

It was either me or him, I assured myself.

I twisted the handle of my door and slinked in, pulling open the curtains in the hope that the staccato flash of lightning would illuminate my room and allow me to find my phone. I turned over my suitcase, threw back my bed covers, and slid the items on my vanity into my toiletry bag, but found nothing. I opened my clutch from the party, my mind knowing there would be no reason for it to be there. There was the half-empty baggy of powder, and I felt sick at the sight. I threw the purse back down on the floor. Even when terrified, I was drawn back to it, tempted by just a look.

A noise behind me startled me. My brain had barely registered it, it was so quiet. I stumbled forward into the vanity while I watched in the mirror as someone approached my half-open bedroom door, only a murky shadow visible in the dark. I braced, expecting someone to come barreling toward me. Instead, the door slammed shut, and a key rattled. I must have only stunned Lawrence instead of seriously injuring him, and now he was coming after me. He was locking me in.

CHAPTER

33

I RAN AT THE door, trying to twist the knob and wrench it open before I was locked in. My body smacked against the door, my hand going to the knob and wrenching it back and forth. It was fruitless. He'd locked me in, and I still couldn't find my phone. Lawrence must have taken it. He was too calm and collected to be working alone. Were the twins helping him?

There was a strange, faint smell and I sneezed as I walked to the window. All the protesters had gone home. I wished there were just one person out there—maybe whoever threw the brick through the window was still there. I could open the window and scream for help. But would they even help me?

That drew an idea—maybe there was some sort of ledge I could crawl out on. It would leave me vulnerable to the storm, but what choice did I have aside from sitting here, waiting for the inevitable? I unlatched the lock and tried to push open the window. It was stuck, so I threw my weight into it, wrenching it upward, but it didn't move at all. Sweat was building on my skin, and I swore I could smell panic radiating off me—a sharp, animal smell.

There was only one more window, and I stumbled over to it and tried again, but to no avail. I crouched down to examine the window ledge and tears came to my eyes. The windows had been painted shut.

The last option was to break the glass. I ripped the sheet from the bed and wrapped it around my fist, all the way up to my elbow. Bracing myself for the impact, I put all the force I could muster behind it and slammed my fist into the glass.

It didn't even crack. I repeated it with my elbow, swinging it backward, but it didn't make a difference.

"Shit," I hissed, pain building in my arm and discouragement welling up, too intense to control. I unraveled the sheet from my arm, stepped back, and kicked the window, desperate to hear the glass splinter. But the glass was too thick, and I was too weak.

Energy drained from my body, bringing me to my knees. There was no way for me to get out.

Tears ran hot down my cheeks. I stared listlessly at the floor, which I could only see in detail with each flash of lightning. Thunder clapped, and I winced like a scolded child recoiling from the shouts of an angry parent. At home, the sound of a storm was soothing, but as the house vibrated with the wrath of the thunder, I was battered, like a ship at sea, unable to point out the shore and left alone to battle the elements.

Lightning illuminated the room again and I noticed a warped baseboard that ran under the window. It was lifted slightly from the wall. Although I was certain it was probably just from humidity, it gave me an idea. Older houses often had small doorways for crawlspace or attic access. Maybe there was one in my room.

I dragged my fingers along the wood paneling, searching for a divot, a crack, anything to indicate there was a hidden doorway. The wood was smooth beneath my fingers, but as I got closer to the dark shadows in the corner, it changed. It was growing cooler now, clammy to the touch. I pulled my hands away and touched my fingertips together. There was definitely moisture.

I returned my hand to the wall and felt again, pushing harder this time. I recoiled as my fingers sank easily into the disintegrating wood, as if I were digging in freshly turned soil.

This house was not as perfect as it seemed. It was rotting from the inside, from secrets and betrayals. Just like this family. Just like me.

34

I RUBBED MY FINGERS together, disgusted by the bits of wet wood that clung to my fingertips.

Someone was approaching from the staircase, heavy feet on wood. "Emmett? Kennedy?" I called out. My hackles raised at the silence.

I stood, looking around the room for something else to block the door. My eyes landed on the chest of drawers next to the door and I threw my body weight into it, trying to slide it in front of the door for protection. It was a massive piece of furniture, and struggled to grip the glossed wood. The footsteps were coming faster now, spurred by the noise I was making.

I threw myself into the side of the dresser, my collarbone giving a sickening pop and a rush of agony as I met the wood with my shoulder. Just as the dresser reached the door, the knob began twisting, the metal creaking and scraping against the back of the wood dresser. My eyes were wide with panic as I stood frozen in the middle of the room, waiting for them to burst through.

To my surprise, the noise completely stopped, and the only thing I could hear was rain pounding against the windows, interrupted by the occasional clap of thunder. The room was dark without any electricity, and I couldn't see much more than the shapes of the furniture.

Lightning bleached the room with light and thunder shook the floor beneath me. In the few seconds of blinding light, I saw something on the wall where the dresser used to be.

Cautiously, I approached, not wanting whoever was outside to hear me moving around. I reached the wall and placed my palms against the wallpaper.

As I groped and scratched at the wall, I realized it was some sort of door that had been completely hidden by the dresser. The thought of me asleep in the quiet, comfortable darkness while someone had access to my room made me shiver with disgust. I felt violated. Ironically, the very thing that someone may have been using to gain access to my room these past few days could be the thing to save me now.

Another pulse of lightning illuminated the room, and I stared at the squat door. If I stood, it would only come up to mid-thigh—I would barely fit. I hated tight spaces but had no other choice. I just needed to get it open. There was no handle or button anywhere and I scratched at the wall in frustration, wincing as one of my fingernails split from the pressure. I brought my hand to my mouth to soothe the sting, and then I thought of the staff's staircases on each floor.

Something clicked as I pushed both hands against the right side, releasing the door from its latch. A breeze from inside the passageway blew the door open and dust wafted into my face, tickling my lungs. The smell inside was rank, somehow both damp with moisture and dusty. I held back a cough. If the person outside knew about this doorway, they might go to the other end and catch me there and I would be trapped inside like a rat in a maze.

I lowered my head and peeked in. It was a tight space, but just spacious enough for a full-grown man to crawl through. The entire passage was made of rough, unfinished subfloor and my hands and knees stung as splinters penetrated my skin. With each movement, I felt them go deeper and I bit my lip, trying not to cry.

I can do this, I told myself. *Just keep going.*

As I moved through the small space, streams of murky light bled through. I could see now that the damp smell came from a mural of black mold that was feeding off the unfinished wood, poisoning the house from deep inside the walls.

When I reached one of the illuminated portions of the passage, I realized there were vents leading into the room beyond. I crawled toward the decorative vent plate; although I could see into the room, I could only glimpse a portion of it. The bed was between the vent and the door, blocking most of the view. I peered in. It seemed like no one was there. The floor was covered in clothes and heaps of towels. A crumpled suit lay close to the vent, and I recognized it as Lyle's. This must be Lyle and Mary Margaret's room.

Was there also a hidden doorway into their room? I fumbled along the wall next to the vent, and my fingers touched the familiar lines of a small doorway. I prodded at the door with my bloodied hands until the mechanism popped, but I couldn't get it open.

Why would the Sedgemonts have hidden entryways into each guest room? The possibilities ranged from nosey to sickening.

I was about to try to push my way through when a door creaked open—the door to Lyle and Mary Margaret's bedroom. I held my breath and shifted slightly so I could see through the vent. I held my body taut, my muscles clenched as the bedroom door opened wider.

Two large feet cautiously entered the room. They were men's shoes, expensive-looking loafers. I couldn't see above the person's knees, so there was no way to tell who it was.

Nobody can find me inside the walls, I told myself. I just had to keep quiet, and I could make it out. I sat there, stock-still, until the man walked out, leaving the door open behind him.

Still trying to stay quiet, I moved more feverishly now. Although the unfinished wood was harsh against my skin, it was sturdy, and I didn't think anyone could hear me as I snaked my way behind the guest bedrooms. My only problem was that I had no idea where this passage would take me.

Another vent was ahead of me, and I moved toward it, ignoring the pain. This vent cast more light than the others, and when I reached it, I realized it was because it was connected to the hallway. A candle had been lit in the hallway, but it was failing its battle against the shadows.

I paused, looking around to see if anyone was there. Suddenly, the still flame began to dance. I held back a gasp.

"What was that?" a man whispered. Again, I couldn't tell who it was. The same two feet from earlier passed by the vent. Outside of the reach of the candle's flame, the hallway beyond was so dark that I couldn't tell if the man had gone down the stairs or further down the hallway to the other guest bedrooms.

Continuing along until I reached another vent, I waited a moment to ensure that no one was there. Right next to the vent, there was another small doorway built into the wall. I attempted to press it open, but again, I couldn't get through. Heat flushed my skin as I panicked, desperate to get out of the small space.

I gave it another push, and it didn't even move an inch. My body was beginning to fail me, too tired from the pain. I threw myself back in frustration. Could there be a dresser in front of this doorway as well?

My breathing was erratic and I closed my eyes, trying to slow it. I let out a puff of pent-up frustration, and then someone whispered, "I can see you."

35

AN EYE PRESSED against the vent, staring back at me. I held back a scream. It was too dark to make out any more details, but I was certain there was the same smug glint in the iris that I'd seen earlier in Lawrence's eyes.

I scrambled backward, smashing the back of my head into the wall behind me. He moved his face away from the vent, and the floor creaked as he rushed out of the room. He was coming for me. I had to get out of here. If he met me at the end of the passageway, I'd be trapped. I had no idea where it would take me—did he?

Ignoring the stabbing pain of splinters burrowing into my palms and knees, I kept moving, passing more vents. I disregarded them now, terrified that if I looked out, I would see Lawrence's eye pressed into it again, watching me.

There were no cobwebs, which made me sure that someone regularly crept behind the walls. I shuddered at the thought.

Eventually, the passageway came to an end in front of me. There were no more vents to let the light in, and I froze at the prospect of moving blindly into the pitch-black darkness. My choices were to fumble in the dark for another doorway, or I could turn around. I thought of Lawrence's sinister whisper through the vents and shuddered.

"I can see you."

I couldn't risk passing by the vents again—I had to see if there was another way out. I began fumbling around in the dark, searching for a doorway. My fingers found the familiar shape, and I pushed, trying to be as quiet as possible.

The door creaked open, and I paused, listening for any sounds beyond the impenetrable darkness. What room would I be in when I entered through the door? I tried to picture the layout of the home, myself snaking behind the walls, but I couldn't place where I might be.

There was that smell again—overwhelming and chemical—making my nose twinge. It was gasoline, I realized, my breath coming faster. It was so thick in the air that I could practically taste it on my tongue.

I stepped through, trying to orient myself just through touch. I was on the landing of a staircase now—it must be the staff's staircase. I thought of the little doorway that Gloria had claimed was storage during the party—that must be the same doorway I'd just stepped through. Hope bloomed in my chest—I could find my way out now.

Painstakingly, I made my way down the stairs, feeling carefully with my feet before I took each step down. I paused halfway down, my body aching from skulking on all fours through the walls, when I heard someone behind me.

My throat closed, and I was gripped in panic. Lawrence must have predicted where I'd go, because the footsteps were coming faster now, banging down the steps and barreling toward me. My feet moved quickly, muscle memory taking over. As I approached the door leading out to the second floor, they were so close behind me that I could feel the air shifting, sending shivers up the nape of my neck.

Struggling with the door, I nearly let out a scream of frustration, or a cry for someone to help, when I got it open and spilled out into the hallway. Someone grabbed me, startling me. A yelp escaped my mouth as a large hand gripped my face from behind, silencing me. Then Emmett appeared in front of me.

"Be quiet," he ordered.

I struggled against the person behind me and sunk my teeth into his fingers. He hissed in pain but kept his grip tight.

Emmett appeared in front of me and I sucked in a breath, shocked to see him working with Lawrence. Why would he be helping him?

"Let her go," Emmett whispered.

I nearly stumbled forward when I was released.

"Jesus Christ," I heard from behind me. A moment later Kennedy appeared by Emmett's side. It wasn't Lawrence after all. My head spun with confusion.

Kennedy shook his hand, waving away the pain. There was a distinctive ring of teeth marks on the flesh between his thumb and forefinger.

"Stay the fuck away from me." I pointed one shaking finger at them. I gritted my teeth, trying to keep them from chattering.

"We're trying to help you," Emmett said.

"Why should I believe you? Your family is sick. I know all about that girl's death. The one at your school."

I backed away, expecting them to lurch at me. Instead, Kennedy's eyes filled with tears.

"That wasn't us—" Kennedy began to explain.

"Don't," I interrupted.

"Kass, it wasn't us. It was Murray," Kennedy pushed back.

I listened as Kennedy stumbled over his words. "Murray met his girlfriend during his junior year at our boarding school, and a few months later he got expelled for bullying. She was our year—eighth grade—so we became close while she and Murray dated long-distance while he went to a private school here in North Carolina."

I recoiled at the thought of my fiancé forming a relationship with a girl who hadn't even been in high school yet—it made me sick to my stomach.

Kennedy continued, speaking so quickly that I nearly couldn't keep up. I glanced around, looking for signs of Lawrence. I tried to focus on Kennedy, but I knew we were only moments away from Lawrence ambushing us. "Mother, Father, and Murray visited for family weekend in 2013, and Murray was pissed that we'd become so close with her. We were all drinking in our dorm room when Murray flipped out. Just because our fingers touched when I handed her a bottle of liquor. He attacked her. We tried to pull him off her. We even broke his nose, but not even that stopped him."

Emmett jumped in, describing how they fought to pull Murray off her, fists smashing into noses, clothes ripping in gripped hands, but he'd been so much bigger and filled with a blind, alcohol-soaked rage. "By the time he realized what he'd done, it was too late. He called our parents, and they took care of it."

I remembered the article announcing the donation to Exavius Academy. Beatrice and Phillip had covered up Murray's violence with lies and money. They couldn't have their family name tarnished.

I thought of Gloria saying how changed Kennedy was, how he used to be outgoing and talkative. He must harbor guilt that just the accidental touch of his hand sent Murray into such a rage. I wondered if this was the reason why Beatrice babied the twins so much—because her eldest son had not only murdered their friend in front of the twins but had also made them accomplices to the cover-up.

Beatrice had been trying to wipe Murray's past clean. If he could have a nice, normal marriage with a good career, and kids one day, then it would cleanse him of his dark past, and he would earn his place on the Sedgemonts' wall of portraits. But what if that darkness had followed him? What if one day, that jealousy piqued again, and I accidentally woke that side of him? I stared down at the gleaming solitaire stone on my ring. The weight of it made it topple to one side of my finger.

"We couldn't protect her from Murray," Kennedy said, tears welling in his eyes at the thought of his friend, "but we can try to protect you."

The words spilled out, and relief filled Kennedy's face. He had been holding this information in his body like a toxin that had made him sicker and sicker as the days passed. Now the only thing he could do was try to keep me from harm, something they'd failed to do for their friend at school.

"If you're trying to help me, why didn't you tell me sooner? Why were you such assholes this whole time?" I hissed at them.

"We thought you knew— I mean, Cindy knew, so why wouldn't he tell you? We thought he'd told you and that you were okay with it," Kennedy confessed. "We thought you were just like them." Kennedy motioned to the wall of portraits, their judging eyes hardly visible in the shadows.

The floorboards above us creaked, and our heads snapped up, looking at the ceiling.

"He's right above us. Come on," Emmett commanded as he motioned for both of us to follow him. We made our way to the staircase and froze at a scraping noise behind the wall that set my teeth on edge. The twins studied the walls. I could tell what they were thinking—Lawrence didn't know the house like they did. We had the advantage.

"Hurry," I said, and we dashed down the stairs, Kennedy and Emmett moving two steps at a time, but my weak legs only allowing me to step cautiously down, one at a time. A deep, throbbing ache pulsed through my body as the anesthetic of adrenaline subsided. Splinters from crawling behind the walls were still embedded in my knees and hands, and with every step the splinters embedded themselves further into my skin. I held back a whimper with each step.

We reached the bottom floor, and the realization hit me. "Where is Murray? Where is everyone else?"

Kennedy's eyes filled with tears, and my stomach dropped, unprepared for what they were about to tell me. But instead of speaking, they ushered me into the Blue Room.

Wind lashed against the tarp on the window as we approached, the storm still brutally angry outside. The duct tape around the sides of the tarp had been ripped away from the wall by the force of the win, and rain whipped in, soaking the rug.

And something else. A body. I ran toward it to see Phillip's face, his eyes closed and unmoving against the steady beat of raindrops.

My hand covered my mouth, holding in a scream.

"They're not dead," Kennedy soothed, "but I think they've been drugged."

"They?" I asked, dumbfounded.

It was then that the twins walked me through the rooms of the lower floors, showing me the crumpled bodies of the Sedgemonts and their guests.

36

I SPRINTED TO MURRAY, putting my ear to his nose and mouth to listen for breath. Relief swelled in my ribs at the soft puff of his breath. He was still breathing, albeit shallowly. Out of habit, I brought my hand to his face, gently cupping it, before I pulled away. I was relieved that he was alive, but now that I knew what he had done, I didn't know if he deserved to be. The thought made me queasy.

"Find a phone," I ordered, keeping my voice low. Lawrence was still somewhere in the house, hunting us. "Call the cops. Detective Campbell."

"I don't have my phone," the twins mumbled, nearly in unison.

"Then go get one," I barked, louder this time.

They stood there, overcome by panic as they stared at their family's crumpled forms, and I wanted to scream at them in frustration.

Beatrice was in the same state as Phillip and Murray as she lay motionless in front of her favorite chair. She was elegant even in her chemical twilight sleep. Her makeup was still in place, but a piece of hair had fallen across her forehead. It was the only time I'd ever seen her show a slight imperfection.

Lawrence must have slipped something in everyone's drinks. Right after the brick had come through the window, he'd charmed us all into a false calm, pouring extra drinks to keep everyone's mind busy. I remembered feeling ill from anxiety and the alcohol already coursing through me, so I'd turned him down. The twins and I were the only ones who had refused his drinks.

Emmett's nose twitched at the chemical smell drifting through the air. "What is that smell?" he asked.

A sound above made us all jump—the thump of someone dropping something heavy.

"It smells like gas," Kennedy said. "We need to get out."

"What the fuck is he doing?" Emmett's voice cracked with fear.

"He's coming for us. He knows we know," Kennedy said, his face even more pale than it usually was.

"What are you talking about?" I spat out. They had no idea about my past. Should I tell them? No, I should keep my mouth shut. If I died here and they survived, I didn't want that story to continue. I wanted it to die with me. Die with Lawrence.

Emmett spoke this time. "He and Beau were embezzling. We hadn't told Father yet, but we were using it as leverage against Beau so he wouldn't try to take leadership of the company. Lawrence must have talked him into the scheme in the first place, because Beau crumbled under pressure and wanted to confess everything to Father. We think he and Lawrence got into an argument the night of the party. Lawrence had to shut him up. Now he has to shut us up too."

"Jesus," I muttered. So Lawrence had been telling the truth—meeting me here had just been by chance, and he'd been working the family's pocketbook like a puppet master for years without ever knowing I would soon be a part of the family.

That wasn't true any longer, though. When I got out of here, I was going to tear away every thread tying Murray and me together. I would go back to *my* family—to parents who loved their children instead of trying to control them, who cared more about showing each other affection than showing off their money. I wouldn't miss the luxury of this house, and I longed to curl up on my parents' cramped but comfortable living room sofa with a mug of cheap, powdered hot chocolate in my hand. I had to get back there.

The twins were frozen in panic, and I needed to do something. I cleared the tight, grasping fear from my throat and barked orders. If they weren't going to get us out of here, I was.

"We haven't found everyone. Where are the other guests? William and Gloria?" I spoke quickly, adrenaline coursing through me like pure electricity. "You two, get them out of the house." I motioned to Murray's, Beatrice's, and Phillip's limp bodies.

They both glanced out the window and into the looming storm clouds, the lightning still actively piercing the sky above us. But they moved without hesitation, the two of them lifting Beatrice's body first.

If she were awake, I knew she would complain about how inelegant this all was, how overdramatic. Emmett had his hands under both her armpits, her arms slumping downward and swaying with each of her sons' steps. Kennedy gripped her under her folded knees. One of her loafers fell off, but they continued.

I ran to the living room, skirting around the sofa to see Mary Margaret, Lyle, and Janice passed out in various degrees of disarray. All of them were breathing shallowly, and Lyle was still holding a drink in his hand, the amber liquid inside threatening to spill out of the tilting glass. As I shook him by the shoulders, trying to wake him, his eyes fluttered open, only to roll around in his head before his pale, clammy eyelids closed once more.

I didn't have time to waste trying to be polite. I fumbled around in Lyle's pants pocket, searching for his cell phone. His pockets were empty except for a half-used sleeve of nicotine gum. The entire time we'd been trapped in the house, every single one of us had kept our phones on us at all times. It was ridiculous that the twins and I didn't have our phones now, until I realized Lawrence must have swiped them during the panic of the brick shattering the Blue Room window. I'd knocked my phone over after the brick smashed through the window. He must have taken mine during all the chaos.

Staggering over to Janice, I rolled her limp body over and gasped with relief when I pulled her phone out of her back pocket. The screen was locked, and I tried using facial recognition to open it, but her closed eyes must have prevented it.

"Janice," I bellowed, tapping on her face. "Wake up." Her eyes began to flutter but then closed again. I tried pulling her eyelids open, but without someone's help, I couldn't open both of her eyes and hold the phone at the same time. I pulled my hand back and gave her cheek a light slap. Her eyelids wavered open, and I held the phone in front of her face, seconds ticking by as I waited without breathing. Janice mumbled in protest as her phone unlocked. Whatever drug was in her system was too strong to overcome, and she fell back into a deep sleep.

There was a loud noise in the entrance hall. I stumbled out to see the twins tugging on the knobs of the enormous front doors. Kennedy began yanking wildly on the knob, and the giant doors creaked and rattled against the long row of deadbolts that ran all the way to the top of the door, nearly out of reach.

"Stop!" I growled at them breathlessly, knowing the noise would lure Lawrence here any second. Wind whipped against the tarp in the Blue Room, and it billowed in with the rain, occasionally getting caught on shards of glass, ripping the tarp into pieces. "Do you think you can get them through the window?"

"I don't know." Kennedy rubbed at his sweat-slicked brow. "We can try."

"Good. I'll go find William and Gloria."

Detective Campbell's card was crumpled in my back pocket from earlier, and I pulled it out as I made my way to Gloria's apartment, dialing his cell phone number with trembling fingers. He answered on the third ring, and I immediately began to speak, telling him that Lawrence had tried to drug us all and was on the loose and dangerous. I was describing one of the protesters throwing the brick through the window when he interrupted me. The tone of his voice stopped me in my tracks on the stairs down to Gloria's apartment. My knees began to shake.

"It's interesting that you're calling, Kassandra, when I just received a call five minutes ago."

"I didn't call you five minutes ago." My voice cracked. I was so confused. "Please, just get here. We need help."

"No, you didn't call. Lawrence did. He told me the same exact story. Except in his version, you're the dangerous one."

37

"No, that's not right," I heard myself say, distant and distraught.

The realization of what Lawrence was doing struck me with full force, and I stumbled back onto the base of the stairs, gripping the handrail with my right hand as my left hand clutched the cell phone. He was setting me up. He must have been the one to accuse me of Beau's murder—the one who spread the rumor through the house.

Detective Campbell was speaking on the other end, his voice stern and judging.

Jacqueline's death hadn't been on purpose. But it had been my fault, in the end. But I'd never been found guilty of anything, despite the long investigation. Lawrence wanted justice, and if he couldn't get it for Jacqueline's death, he would frame me for this.

But how could someone do that? Sacrifice so many lives just to make a point?

"We're on our way, and when we arrive, I suggest you cooperate," Campbell said. The line went dead.

Sobs racked my body, and the tears were beyond my control now. But I needed to find Gloria, so I kept moving.

The smell of the gas was stronger now, the vapors seeping through the vents and floorboards.

When I entered the laundry room, everything was dark except for the gray light of the storm coming in through Gloria's open patio door. The curtains were pulled back but drenched from the rain. A pack of cigarettes and a lighter sat on the porch table, the tobacco soggy and spilling out like damp soil. The door must have not been fully closed and was blown open with a gust of wind—another way out. My chest swelled with hope.

A muffled cry came from behind a door that I'd never entered. I swung the door open. Gloria was sitting against the foot of her bed, her makeup smeared with tears. Her deep berry lipstick made a red ring around the fabric that someone had secured between her teeth. Her arms were tied, and she squirmed against the restraints. Whoever had done it had done a hasty job, and when I went to untie her, she was only moments away from escaping herself.

With shaking hands, I freed her, both of us crying. We were both weak, but I managed to pull her up to her feet, where she stood for a moment, woozy from shock. Her tears were coming harder now.

"Go out the door and run as far as you can," I ordered. She didn't hesitate and sprinted out into the rain.

I raced back up the stairs to the entrance hall, preparing to see the twins heaving limp bodies through the Blue Room window.

There was no one there.

Beatrice still lay disheveled in the entrance hall—she'd only been moved a few feet since I'd left. There was a low-level hum coming from upstairs, but I ignored it, unable to think about anything other than getting everyone out. I moved into the Blue Room where the Sedgemonts still lay crumpled on the floor. They looked shockingly peaceful despite their haphazard positions.

Where the hell were the twins? Maybe they'd gone to look for William—to find someone else to help get everyone out the window. Fear crept in at the image of Gloria tied up at the foot of her bed—Lawrence might have done the same to William.

When we'd first arrived, Murray had told me about his attic apartment, and I began running up the stairs two at a time, silently begging that I'd find him there. My lungs were burning in my chest, but I kept moving upward through the house, which was illuminated by the flashes of lightning and moonlight seeping in through the domed glass ceiling.

Once I got into the hallways, however, it was nearly pitch-black. I kept my hand on the wall, dragging it as I stumbled through the dark, fumbling for the impression in the wall to open the staircase.

I remembered seeing William there as I peeked out of the office that night, standing sentinel like a ghost. A shudder passed through me, but I kept moving.

When I found it, I slipped into the dark staff staircase, making my way slowly up to the third floor. I'd never been any higher than this, so I moved carefully as I found my footing.

I yelped in surprise as the door panel leading to his room flew open, hitting me in the face and shoulder. I was falling backward, my body tipping and my stomach lurching at the sensation of gravity pulling me downward.

There was no handrail to reach for, but my hands reached out anyway. My fingernails touched the wall just for a moment, and there was the sick sound of them screeching down the walls before it was too late.

My shoulder broke my fall and I landed in a heap at the foot of the stairs. A groan escaped my mouth but was lost in the sound of the twins shouting.

"We need to get out," they were yelling, nearly in unison, some primally linked part of their brains joining together in fear.

My skull and side throbbed with a red-hot pain, and I nearly collapsed back on the floor. Kennedy yanked me up by my injured arm, and I howled as my vision skittered, blackening around the edges.

Finally on my feet, I was supported by Kennedy, who was practically dragging me down the stairs, with Emmett on our heels, muttering, "Go, go, faster!"

That was when I smelled the smoke.

38

"HE POURED GAS everywhere. The candles. Oh shit." Emmett was breathless, panic rising in his chest, muffling his words as he muttered a new curse word with each exhale.

"Where's William?" My voice cracked as I inhaled smoke. It was only a whisper now, but it was growing stronger by the second. I coughed, the noise booming in the tight stairway.

"We couldn't find him."

The stairway was filling with smoke pouring in from the vents that connected to the attic apartment. Kennedy pushed open the panel to the second floor, and we spilled out, taking frantic, desperate gulps of air. Smoke swirled around us, thick and menacing, like a supernatural beast, forcing coughs from our lungs.

There was a low, thrumming roar as the fire gained traction in the attic, feeding off the wood beams and insulation. Somewhere beneath it, though, there was another noise. Barely audible, but it filled me with hope.

Sirens.

Kennedy readjusted his grip on me, hoisting me up as my strength continued to waver. My body begged me to give up and lie down on the floor—to give in to the exhaustion—while my brain screamed in alarm. The sirens were getting closer as we moved down the stairs, the bodies of the Sedgemonts coming into sight in the entrance hall.

The Blue Room came into view, and William stood, back hunched and teeth grinding as he tried to lift Phillip up and out the window.

"William!" I yelled. He lowered Phillip to the floor and turned. The left side of his face was shimmering with thick scarlet and crimson. My mouth hung open, incapable of forming words as I stared at the bloody wound in alarm.

The smoke grew thicker, more threatening, and I realized with terror that if we didn't get out now, we would go up in flames in an instant.

"Are you okay?" I cried out as we ran to him. His legs gave way, and he fell to one knee.

"We need to get him out," Emmett bellowed, draping William's arm over his shoulders and heaving him up. William's hand dug into Emmett's shoulder, the thin skin of his hands splattered with age spots and deep purple veins. "Kennedy, get Mother!"

Emmett and William climbed over the lip of the window, glass crunching under their feet. Emmett winced as a shard of glass ripped through his pants, leaving a gash of red on his thigh.

They were out of the house, and Kennedy was struggling to drag his mother closer to the window.

A floorboard creaked and I screamed as Lawrence came up behind him, wrestling him to the ground. He drew his arm back and slammed his fist into Kennedy's face, crashing into his nose with a sick crunch. Kennedy lay there, unmoving. Was he dead? My mouth filled with saliva, and I turned my head away, sure I would vomit.

Terror gripped me, all my muscles clenching so tight that I couldn't even take a breath. Smoke billowed around the domed glass window above the entrance hall. I imagined the flames creeping down from the attic to devour the wood and rugs, all the fine things that the Sedgemonts had collected over the years, feeding the fire like fuel. It was only a matter of time before the grasping, desperate inferno found its way downstairs and devoured the entire house.

Three loud pounds rang out as fists pounded into the front door. "Detective Campbell. Open up!"

"Help!" Lawrence screamed. I stared at him in utter confusion. The terror that filled his voice was so convincing that for a moment I believed he was afraid for his life. But that went away the moment he bared his teeth at me, a full smile spreading across his face.

Lawrence reached behind him and pulled something out of his waistband. Many of the candles had burned out, and it was too dark to see at first, but a flash of lightning made it clear what it was.

My stomach clenched, and I stepped backward from the gun. The metal flashed bright silver, and I recognized it as the ornate revolver from Beatrice's closet.

I put my hands out to the side, slowly raising them, my palms open to him, begging.

He held the gun by his side, standing still before taking a breath.

"You never paid for what you did," he said mournfully.

"What will this do to change that?" I yelled over the roar of the incoming sirens. The smoke was thicker now, and I struggled not to cough. The chemical smell of the burning attic insulation made me gag, and I was growing dizzy with the fumes.

The pounding on the front door was louder now, the sound of fists moving on to something bigger, heavier.

"You were lucky then, but not this time." He raised the gun and I closed my eyes, resigned to my fate.

I'd spent many of my nights thinking of Jacqueline. I could still hear the roar of the oncoming train, accompanied by the shrill pitch of her scream. I never meant for it to happen, but I lived with the guilt every day. Now I'd lost Murray, our relationship ruined by his family and his own terrible past. How could he live with something like that—something he did on purpose and without suffering, while I was plagued with guilt every night when I tried to sleep? I realized that I'd never really known him at all.

If I closed my eyes and just let this happen, maybe I would finally find peace.

The gun shot made my eardrums spasm in pain, the sound of it ricocheting against the domed ceiling, a striking cord against the percussion of sirens outside.

But I felt no pain.

I opened my eyes and looked down, waiting for the shock to wear off and allow the pain to wash over me. But as I scanned myself with my eyes and hands, there was nothing.

Lawrence was bent over, fingers digging into his side, the gun still clutched in his right hand.

He'd shot himself. My head was spinning, my breath picking up as my mind formed questions that I couldn't keep up with.

Lawrence took three steps forward, closing the gap between us as he winced. Blood was seeping through his shirt now. The bloody wound was swallowing up the fabric of his shirt, making his body show the pain that he'd felt inside for so long.

He pulled his sleeve over his hand and wiped down the gun. He grimaced but made no noise as he made eye contact one last time before dropping the gun at my feet and collapsing.

The front door caved in with one loud *bang* as police officers spilled in. I stared at Lawrence, and he smiled back at me before closing his eyes and letting out a pained howl.

THE MOMENTS THAT followed were stretched out, each second becoming a full minute, each heartbeat and clap of thunder rattling my entire body.

There was so much noise that it was painful. Police yelling, Lawrence screaming for help. Emmett had crawled back through the window at the sound of the gunshot.

"What have you done?" he was screaming, hunched over his brother. The cops jostled me, not knowing he was screaming the question at Lawrence, not me. They all thought I'd done this. The only one standing. The woman with a gun at her feet. A smattering of victims dotting the floor.

"Step away from the gun," Detective Campbell ordered, his deep, velvety voice booming over everything else. "Call the fire department," he shouted to the officers.

I tried to take a step back, but my feet dragged and my legs shook with fear, making me stumble. Campbell grabbed my arm, not out of compassion or for safety, but with anger. I swore I could feel the heat of it searing into my skin, pulsing from his fingertips like hot fire pokers.

He dragged me away from Lawrence and out the front door. He paused, jerking me out of the way as three paramedics stormed into the entrance hall with stretchers, concern and determination smeared across their faces.

They'd all been fooled.

Two other police officers escorted Emmett out behind me, pushing us out into the dark of the night with the frenetic heartbeat of red and blue lights. A fire truck barreled down the driveway.

Dizziness and dismay made me weak. I shut my eyes against the pouring rain and claps of lightning. Behind my eyelids, the lights danced. I was transported, my mind somewhere else entirely. The low lights of the club, elaborate lights dancing across the faces of the people inside. I could see Jacqueline's face. She was smiling back at me, her pupils wide despite the flashes of light that practically blinded us, distorting our senses, along with the loud music.

Her hands were on my shoulders, her favorite place to put them while we danced, the chemicals rushing in. We'd felt so safe. How could we have been so naive?

"I love you," I heard Jacqueline whisper one final time.

Tears rolled down my face, and I was back in my body. I didn't want to be here. The smoke choked me, and the sound of the firefighters trying to snuff out the flames was deafening. The police pulled Emmett and me further away, jostling us toward the cop cars.

My eyes remained closed against the noise and the pain in my shoulders as Detective Campbell gripped my arms and cuffed my wrists. I opened my eyes. Just like the night of the party, I stood outside and stared in wonder at the estate's windows lit up with a golden glow. Only now, it was the glow of a fire that was building in the attic, traveling down the hollow walls of the estate.

I closed my eyes again and tried to go back to that addicting memory, the lights on Jacqueline's face, the sense of complete freedom.

I tried to imagine my best friend saying the only thing I wanted to hear, but the one thing that I never would.

I forgive you.

40

TWO DAYS HAD passed, days of flickering fluorescent bulbs, bare mattresses, and burnt coffee on an empty stomach.

The twins and I were being held on suspicion of attempted murder and arson, among many other things I was sure. It had been hard to keep track, with little to no sleep.

When Phillip and Beatrice woke in the hospital, the first thing they did was call their family attorney for all three of us. That was when things really began to shift, when the food became organic takeout instead of cold turkey and rubbery vegetables, when the detectives became a bit gentler. I thought of all the people who couldn't afford a good lawyer, who were left here to rot at the hands of the system.

I wasn't sure why Beatrice and Phillip had bothered to hire the attorney for me—to protect their reputation, I assumed. Perhaps it was guilt for what their son had done, for using me to move him further away from his dark past. Either way, I was grateful.

When we were first brought into custody, I had been in so much shock that I couldn't speak, could not even make a noise. In retrospect, that had probably made me look more suspicious, more mentally unstable than I was. But what was there to say? Lawrence had executed his plan perfectly. Well, almost perfectly.

The energy of the interrogation room had shifted when Detective Campbell walked in, dressed in dark jeans and a white button-up shirt with the sleeves rolled up. He looked exhausted, and his eyelid twitched as he sat down in front of me. They had taken off my handcuffs, and I rested my hands on the table between us, trying to signal peace.

"Miss Baptiste," he said, sighing as he sat down, "you're free to go."

I stared at him blankly. I'd imagined those words so many times, yet I didn't feel the relief I'd expected. I couldn't make sense of my emotions, but I could feel hope beginning to bud in my chest.

"Why?" was all I could muster. The Sedgemont lawyer had encouraged me to say as little as possible. The interviews prior to this had been tense and aggressive, with the police nearly certain I'd been responsible for the whole thing. They'd been convinced that I'd murdered Beau at the party, and that once the other guests realized the truth, I'd tried to kill them too.

"We have enough evidence to pin this on Lawrence, who is stable in the hospital now, by the way. He lost a kidney, but he'll lose more than that when all is said and done." He gave a weak but satisfied smile.

My entire body was buzzing with hope now. I pressed my clammy hands against the metal table, trying to absorb the icy chill of it. "Evidence?" I was still in the habit of one-word sentences.

Campbell began to explain, letting out one long sigh before the first word. His hands on the table mirrored mine: peace.

"Lawrence has confessed," Detective Campbell said. "He claimed to have a relationship with your friend Jacqueline. He said he needed justice for what happened to her."

The phrasing seemed purposeful and nearly knocked the breath out of me: *"what happened to her,"* not *"what you did to her."* It had been an accident. A terrible accident that I had played a part in, but that I'd never meant to happen.

I thought of the desperation Lawrence must have felt when he realized he couldn't prove his theory that I'd pushed her. The only solution he could find was to frame me for the murder of the Sedgemonts and their guests. I cringed at the thought that if the cops hadn't arrive in time, their unconscious bodies would have been consumed by flames. Would they have woken up? Or would it have been a painless death? My armpits prickled with sweat, and I blinked my eyes hard, reminding myself that they were all safe now. All the guests had been quickly removed from the house and transported to the hospital. They were all recovering from the effects of the high dose of the date rape drug gamma-hydroxybutyric acid, commonly known as GHB, that he'd slipped into everyone's drink during the storm.

"When did he plan all this? Did he know I'd been dating Murray?" I asked.

"He claims he didn't know you would be there, much less that you were dating him. His assistant never showed him the invitation and just added 'Sedgemont Party' to his calendar. You took him by surprise."

I thought of my engagement photo I'd posted that had begun Lawrence's series of anonymous messages. Murray's face had been obscured as he bent down on one knee, and my lack of regular posts on Instagram had kept Lawrence from realizing the connection we shared with the Sedgemonts. The party being on the anniversary of Jacqueline's death had just been a twist of fate, a coincidence that had made him see red the moment he'd laid eyes on me.

"The twins told me Lawrence and Beau were embezzling from the company. Is that true?" I asked.

"Yes. The night of the event, he and Beau got into an argument. They had been embezzling money from the company for years, but with the recent sale of the factories, they got sloppy. The twins started sniffing around when they realized Beau might be taking over after Phillip's retirement. When Beau realized the twins knew about the embezzling, he panicked, telling Lawrence that he wanted to come clean to Phillip. Things got heated and Lawrence attacked him. You know the rest."

The memory of Beau's body still nauseated me, his blank eyes staring up at the ceiling, his cold hand reaching for the letter opener in his gut.

Me being at the party had sent an already-violent Lawrence into a tailspin, and he'd made it his mission to ruin my life. He'd almost succeeded, drugging the remaining guests and planting the GHB in my toiletry bag. The fire had begun in the attic because of a toppled over candle, but he'd tried to use it to his advantage when he realized his plan was falling apart.

The only reason Campbell was sitting here telling me this was because the fire had never reached Gloria's apartment, where the estate's security system had been tucked away in a cellar closet, surrounded by concrete. I hadn't known there were security cameras dotted throughout each room in the house. The thought sent a shiver up my spine, but I was also grateful for them because they were the only reason I wasn't going to prison for the rest of my life.

In between the time it took the police to safely retrieve the security recordings and bring them in for viewing, the detectives had found easy targets with the twins and me, both of us with our pasts wrapped up in terrible accidents and police investigations—things we had to live with forever that weren't necessarily our fault.

Sitting there, listening to Campbell explain the details of Lawrence's plan, made my skin feel clean, as guilt sloughed off me. I was weightless now that I no longer wore Jacqueline's necklace.

I'd lived with that weight around my neck, defiled by shame for my past, every day for years. But in that time, I'd found love and lost it, and become a different person with a purpose in life other than to get high and shirk responsibility.

All the while, Lawrence had stewed in his anger, letting it consume him while he continued to feed off other people's lives and money.

I would be leaving this room and these handcuffs behind, along with my relationship with Murray, but when I returned home to my family, I would still be whole.

In the ashes of the Sedgemont house, I'd found absolution.

Once I'd been allowed to leave the interrogation room, I went to the restroom to rinse my face. The image that stared back at me in the mirror was startling. Pale skin, bloodshot eyes. The expanse of freckled skin across my breastbone was empty of ornamentation now, and I raised my hand to feel the place that used to be shielded by the warped metal of Jacqueline's pendant.

I looked in the mirror and said the words I'd wanted to hear for all these years. But now I knew it wasn't Jacqueline I needed to hear them from. It was me.

I forgive you.

ACKNOWLEDGMENTS

THANK YOU, READER, for spending time with my characters. You wouldn't be reading this without my amazing Crooked Lane team: Holly Ingraham, Rebecca Nelson, Madeline Rathle, Dulce Botello, Jill Pellarin, Heather Venhuizen, Matt Martz, and Thai Fantauzzi Perez. Holly, thanks for taking a chance on my book and helping me polish this story.

To my agent, Katie Shea Boutillier: Thank you for tolerating my chronic overthinking and for standing up for your writers. Your enthusiasm is contagious, and I'm lucky to have you on my side.

It's both an honor and bittersweet to thank you, Mom. It's unfair that you can't see your name here, but I'm grateful you got to see this book get an offer and read the first draft. I'll never forget giving you the first draft and telling you, "Do not ever speak to me about the sex scene." And of course, the first thing you say after reading is "So, how about that sex?" I wouldn't have my sense of humor without you, and certainly not my love of reading and writing. I love you.

To my husband, Tyler: You are an amazing husband, father, and friend. Years ago, one random Sunday, I woke up and decided I wanted to write a book. Without you, that thought would have ended there. You are my biggest supporter, and thank you for letting me lean on you. I love you. Ellie, you can't read yet, but I love you too. You are my best distraction and my biggest source of joy.

To the rest of my family, especially Dad and Keith: You gave me the privilege of a good education, and that ultimately led me here. I love you both. Thank you to the Trents, Deckers, Boyds, and everyone in between. To the Turners: You've accepted me as your own, and I'm forever grateful. Special thanks to April and Matt for being nothing like Beatrice and Phillip.

To all my friends who hyped me up since my first query letter and listened as I tried to describe the labyrinth of the publishing world; and to all my writing friends, especially Faith Pierce: Publishing is brutal, and you've been a constant source of knowledge and comfort throughout it all. Thanks to my betas and CPs, Faith Pierce, Elnora Gunter, Alix Kelinda, Allison Hubbard, Paula Gleeson, and Suja Sukumar. Thank you to my favorite teacher, Candace Owen-Williams. The books you assigned still haunt me in the best ways over a decade later. Finally, thank you to my writing groups, The Rockets and 2023 Debut, for providing a space for both commiseration and inspiration.